Never Again Once More

Also by Mary B. Morrison

SOUL MATES DISSIPATE

WHO'S MAKING LOVE

JUSTICE JUST US JUST ME

Never Again Once More

MARY B. MORRISON

DAFINA BOOKS
Kensington Publishing Corp.
http://www.kensingtonbooks.com

DAFINA BOOKS are published by

Kensington Publishing Corp.
850 Third Avenue
New York, NY 10022

All Kensington Titles, Imprints, and Distributed Lines are available at special quantity discounts for bulk purchases for sales promotions, premiums, fund-raising, and educational or institutional use. Special book excerpts or customized printings can also be created to fit specific needs. For details, write or phone the office of the Kensington special sales manager: Kensington Publishing Corp., 850 Third Avenue, New York, NY 10022, attn: Special Sales Department, Phone: 1-800-221-2647.

First Dafina hardcover printing: August 2002
First Dafina trade paperback printing: May 2003
First Dafina mass market printing: April 2004

10 9 8 7 6 5 4 3 2 1

Printed in the United States of America

This novel is dedicated to my soul mate Pernell Bursey, to everyone who does not know his or her biological parents, and to my niece Delisia Melvina Noel. Although another family adopted you, Delisia, we pray one day you'll know you have an entire family who loves you, especially your mother—my sister—Debra Noel. Your adoptive parents asked that we have no contact with you, and we've honored that request. Your birth given name was changed, and unfortunately we don't know your new name. Delisia, you have a wonderfully humorous brother Omar, four aunts, two uncles, fifteen first cousins, and, of course, your mother eagerly waiting to bond with you, my love.

Acknowledgments

I give thanks to God for blessing me with the courage to pursue my literary passion. Each time the road ahead darkens, the Lord sends my guardian angels to shine a redeeming light, reminding me my humanitarian purpose is forever greater than myself. I express gratitude for Reverend Dr. Elouise D. Oliver and my Oakland East Bay Church of Religious Science family for guidance and motivation.

Thanks to my wonderful son, Jesse Bernard Byrd, Jr., for his unconditional love and support. To the superwoman who catapulted my dream into a reality, I'm eternally grateful for my editor, Karen Thomas. I must thank my agent and backbone, Claudia Menza, for never being too busy. I immensely appreciate my Kensington family: Walter Zacharius, Steven Zacharius, Laurie Parkin, Joan Schulhafer, Jessica Ricketts, and Mary Pomponio, thanks a million.

A special love note is extended to one of the world's greatest writers, E. Lynn Harris. Thanks for your quote, but more importantly I value your unsolicited kindness and words of encouragement through my former self-publishing endeavor and present novelist career.

When all I had was my poetry book, *Justice Just Us Just Me,* God sent me a best friend and brilliant publicist, Felicia Polk. After *Soul Mates Dissipate* was released, He blessed me with Rodrick Smith, and no greater duo than Smith and Polk exists in public relations. I also thank L. Peggy Hicks of TriCom for organizing my tour, because she is the top diva of literary promotions. I thank my supporters: Patrik Henry Bass of *Essence* magazine, Glenn R. Townes of *Upscale* magazine, Dr. Jeff of WLIB, Cliff and Janine of KJLH, and a host of others.

I love each of my siblings with all my heart. Thanks for being my foundation: Wayne, Andrea, Derrick, and Regina Morrison, Margie Rickerson, and Debra Noel.

I'm blessed to have fantastic friends. Thanks to Bennie

Allen, Linda Gayle Brown, Michaela Burnett, Marilyn Edge, Kendra Hill, Vanessa Ibanitoru, Brenda Jackson, Naleighna Kai, Gloria Mallette, Marcus Major, Karen E. Quinones-Miller, Carmen Polk, Exavier B. Pope, E. C. Rhodes, Ronald Salaam, Joseph Smith, Simone Smith, Carl Weber, Kenneth Williams, and my mentor, Vyllorya A. Evans, for your unwavering support.

Last but sincerely not least, I thank the distributors, booksellers, book clubs, and you the reader because you are the wind beneath my words.

And so it is,
Mary Beatrice Morrison

E-mail: AskMaryBMorrison@aol.com
Web site: www.marymorrison.com

Prologue

What did love have to do with anything?

If Jada Diamond Tanner had the answer, she'd be richer. After parting from her soul mate, no relationship was quite the same, including her ten years of marriage to Lawrence Anderson. While her body moved forward pushing her life ahead, Jada's spirit remained with Wellington. Like a child insistent upon staying with his father after a divorce, her spirit said, "Naw, you go ahead. I'll wait right here for you." Although Jada loved Wellington, his infidelity rendered love insufficient to preserve their engagement.

Whosoever said, "If you love something, set it free. If it returns . . ." must have not known Wellington Jones. Not as Jada did. He tasted like a sweet caramel candy square slowly melting in her mouth, trickling down her throat into the depth of her intestines, flowing through her bloodstream into her receptor cells. He was her life-support system. Undeniably, his rib had become a permanent part of her anatomy. Each of her taste buds savored the richness of all his bodily fluids. Whenever their lips merged and their tongues danced to rapid heartbeats, Altoids' wintergreen freshness iced her insides like frozen sickles embracing a snow-covered roof. With magical touches, Wellington's mere presence sent chills up Jada's spine.

If you love something, set it free. Set it free echoed repeatedly. Day after day the words rebounded like a basketball bouncing off the edge of the rim. Less than an inch away from scoring, Jada had desperately wanted to reunite with her soul mate, but couldn't find the emotional fortitude. Year upon year *set it free* resounded.

The best sex they had shared came after their first relationship-threatening argument. The warmth of his nine-inch rod penetrating her moist womanhood was all of a sudden a memory. But near the end, Jada had to credit Wellington for trying to keep her when he asked, "Where do we go from here?"

She had already given their unresolved issues countless consideration. The most logical solution remained the same, so Jada stood firm on her final decision and replied, "I'm still in love with you, Wellington. You will always have a place in my heart. I don't know where we go from here. But I do know I've renewed my lease on life. I have a business to start and a plane to catch to Los Angeles. Maybe I'll call you. Maybe I won't." Watching Wellington walk out of her Oakland Hills penthouse for the last time was by far the hardest thing she'd ever done.

Jada was adamant, but when she boarded that plane the next day, she could have worn a white straight jacket instead of a black leather blazer. The more she told herself, "Don't call him. Be strong," the weaker she'd become. Both of her Myers-Briggs personality tests—taken five years apart—resulted in an ISTP (Introverted, Sensing, Thinking, Perceiving) rating. Jada was a terrific analyst and businesswoman, and great at following up on unresolved issues. Diva should have been highlighted as one of her qualitative traits. Even the "Brain Works" test rated Jada perfectly balanced. Maybe she was too balanced. Her left brain discounted the right, and her right conflicted with the left, which explained why she had such difficulty deciding whether or not to stay with Wellington. Professional decisions were much easier than personal choices.

Trying to bamboozle her way out of depression, Jada initiated conversation with the elderly man seated next to her in first class. The moment the aircraft landed and the captain turned off the fasten seat belt sign, she powered up her cellular phone. The left brain keyed in zero zero one to call Wellington so the right brain could tell him she'd be on the next plane back to Oakland to be with him forever, but she was obsessively thinking and couldn't convince herself to press the talk button. Jada's heart grew so heavy at times she could hardly breathe. Short, quick, and frequent intakes of oxygen accompanied mucus buildup in her nostrils that intensified tears, migraines, and nausea.

Had she ended their relationship to avoid looking foolish? Jada's best friend Candice had warned her Wellington couldn't be trusted. Jada masked a happy face because Candice was meeting her at the gate at LAX, and Candice harbored no sympathy for her breakup with Wellington. Would Candice have accepted the same advice about Terrell? No man had ever slam-dunked Jada, and she wasn't about to let Wellington set a precedent.

Before Jada could yell, "Time out!" the referee—Wellington's evil mother Cynthia Elaine Jones—called a foul on her when it should have been a charge because Melanie Marie Thompson knocked her down, ran her over, and literally scored with her man. And Broom Hilda had twitched her nose to cover up a lie because she wasn't Wellington's biological mother; the lying bitch was his aunt. Allen Iverson stripped his opponents over a hundred times in the playoffs, but this wasn't the frickin' NBA. Stealing was a crime. So why did Jada feel as if she was the one serving the life sentence?

By moving from Oakland to the Los Angeles area—over

five hundred miles away from the scene of the crime—hopefully her emotional wounds would mend. As she faced every challenge, Jada had grown secure knowing Wellington was only a phone call away. The distance that existed between them: one hour by plane, five and a half by car, one heartbeat by spirit. Close enough but yet far enough, too.

Jada ignored the voice inside her head that whispered, "Go back. Take that chance on love because life is one huge risk, and each day you screw up, if the Lord allows you to see another, you have at least one more opportunity to get it right. Your entire existence is an audition, and you are forever rehearsing until you take your final bow." A melody interjected, "Don't wanna be a fool never again." Luther Vandross's lyric was emotionally correct. No way was Jada going to bend her backbone and flop into Wellington's arms like a desperate woman afraid she'd never find another man to worship her inner beauty as though she were a true Nubian queen and make love to her sweeter than all the chocolate in Willy Wonka's factory.

Like liquid cement solidifying, Wellington's renewed loyalty gradually reinforced their foundation. Over time they became very best friends. Secrets that should have been shared only with God, Jada also confided in Wellington—except one thing.

Chapter 1

"Lord give me strength," Jada whispered as she dropped her cell phone into her purse. Inhaling through her nose, she removed her electronic notebook from the overhead compartment and sighed heavily. Never mentioning Wellington Jones by name, she had posed multiple relationship questions to the stranger seated next to her in row one, since he had been happily married to the same woman for over fifty years.

"Sir, thank you for lending an ear." Jada took one step back, allowing him to retrieve his belongings. His brown scuffed briefcase was torn at every corner, and the gold-plated latches had turned mostly silver. The black rubber beneath his walking cane was worn to the slanted wood.

The elderly man licked his dentures, scratched his receding hairline, and replied in his raspy voice, "That's why God gave us two. One so we can listen to how selfish we sound and the other for us to hear. Seems as though you've been listening, but you're so busy hearing yourself, you haven't heard what he's trying to tell you. I've managed to stay married because my wife, she respects my manhood and doesn't try to reduce me to being one of our twelve kids." Then he dug into his butt, relieving himself of a wedgee.

Respect was earned, not given because a man was anatomically correct. "But did I mention to you"—Jada moved closer so the person beside her wouldn't overhear—"he impregnated another woman?"

The old man wasn't as kind to speak low in return. "So did the Reverend Jesse Jackson, but you don't see his wife abandoning him. And if Hillary can forgive Bill, why can't you forgive . . ." This time he dug deeper into his butt and grunted, "What's his name?" His hand quivered, touching hers.

Frowning, Jada said, "Wellington," for the first time during their discussion.

"Yeah, that's it. Jandra, you're a pretty girl. I'll tell you like I've told all of my kids, 'Pride and love is like oil and water. They don't mix.' The sooner you realize that, the healthier your relationship will be."

He still hadn't pronounced her name correctly; but his wisdom surpassed her logic, so Jada moved ahead of him, impatiently waiting as the exit door opened.

The flight attendant smiled cheerfully. "Thank you for flying the friendly skies." Absent her smile, the attendant resembled one of the girls from Robert Palmer's rock video "Simply Irresistible": pale face, straight black hair slicked back, and red lipstick.

Jada's lips parted, but she didn't respond. Instead, she stretched her five-foot-nine frame until an arch formed in her lower vertebrae. When her black thigh-high boot crossed the threshold and landed on the walkway, a gust of cold air raced up the front split in her cashmere skirt and kissed her red lace thong. Briskly tracing another passenger's footsteps, Jada wished Candice would be late so she'd have an excuse to avoid reliving her best friend's wedding and honeymoon plans.

Not only was Candice timely, but she was the first person Jada noticed when the attendant opened the second exit door leading into the concourse.

"Hey, girl. I thought you were going to backslide, especially since you didn't call me last night." Candice extended a Holy Names prep girl hug, giving Jada three pats on the back. "I like the sexy style. You look like a woman in search of a new man. That's a good thing." Rambling on, Candice pinched the edges of Jada's jacket and peeped inside. "I'm scared of you, Ms. Thang, a split almost up to your clit. Terrell would never allow me to wear this." She released Jada's blazer. "But what's up with all the black? Are we mourning our loss?" Fanning the wind, Candice emphatically said, "Forget Wellington. He doesn't deserve you."

The little old man slowly walked by hunched over his cane, "She's got that right," he said.

What was that supposed to mean? Jada had taken enough of his insults, and if he wasn't seventy something, she'd tell him to go straight to hell. Sighing again, she thought, *Ms. Thang, not Mrs. Jones.* Maybe he was right.

Jada placed her computer bag in Candice's wavering hand and retrieved the waterless sanitizer from her purse. "Let's stop at Starbucks; I could use an iced frappuccino." Sniffing the freshness on her fingertips, she tilted her head back, lifted her smooth straight hair, and gradually released it behind her shoulders.

"How's Terrell?" Jada raised Candice's hand, tugged at her clothes, and pointed at her head. "Where are your acrylic nails? What's up with the Suzie homemaker muumuu dress? And why are you wearing that pent-up out-of-date hairstyle?"

Candice's flat shoes really made her every fraction of five feet, four inches. Her once lavish nails were now nubs so short her flesh protruded beyond the edges. A soon-to-be thirty-three-year-old diva was retired in her prime because the broom she was about to jump had already swept her raving beauty under the carpet. Candice had once dressed so provocatively she stopped everything except time.

Terrell wore muscle shirts whenever he wanted and smiled in the faces of gorgeous women, justifying his actions based on his professional image. The most sought after male model, in higher demand than Tyson, had landed his first acting role staring opposite Morris Chestnut, so he'd immediately postponed marrying Candice.

Jada remembered the days—less than six month ago—when she worked at Sensations Communications photographing the world's finest male models, including Terrell. But once Wellington's wicked aunt Cynthia landed Melanie a job as her boss, Jada typed up her resignation, handed it to the receptionist, and kept on stepping. As long as Candice Jordan catered to Terrell Morgan's needs, he was satisfied. That was exactly what Jada refused to do, compromise herself for the sake of having a man.

The airport was overcrowded. Travelers lined the walls and blocked the aisles. "Flight eighty-one has been changed to gate eleven." Outbound passengers grumbled loudly; some of them dragged kids along. Since Jada had experienced the inconveniences of LAX on numerous occasions, she anticipated the seemingly standard announcement.

Standing in line next to her, Candice replied, "My husband is fine. My husband didn't like the nails or the body-hugging clothes; but my husband loves this hairstyle, and he loves me." Candice fingered the chestnut-colored curl hanging alongside her face. "I have our wedding planner in the car. You've got to see the fabrics and colors. You're going to be the most attractive maid of honor." Candice flipped her wrist to display the diamond marquis her fiancé had recently bought.

Maid not matron. Jada was genuinely happy for her girlfriend. If Candice hadn't invited her to Will Downing's concert over a year ago, Jada probably wouldn't have met Wellington. Neither would Candice have met Terrell. They should have been planning a double wedding and reception. Tension throbbed at Jada's temples, so she pressed firmly, repressing the pain.

Handing Jada her drink, the cashier curled Jada's fingers over the ten-dollar bill. "The gentleman in the tan suit prepaid for you and your friend. What would you like?" she asked Candice, then turned back to Jada. "Oh, and he told me to give you this."

Jada flipped the card over and read, "Don't keep me waiting."

Lowering Jada's arm, Candice said to the cashier, "I'll have a café latte with steamed soy milk." Looking at her friend, she continued, "Terrell says I'm lactose intolerant and shouldn't consume dairy products. See, girl, you're reeling the men in already." Candice peeped at the front of the card. "Impressive."

Jada had already checked out the man with the immaculately trimmed beard. His teddy bear love handles seemed to snuggle under a sheer layer of confidence. He wasn't Wellington, but the brother was tall, sexy, and distinguished. He looked like money. Smelled like money, too, when he walked by and winked. His cologne wafted by her, alluringly fresh and clean; not harsh, bold, or like a cheap bar of soap. His nails were manicured. A watch and a ring adorned his left wrist and pointing finger. Diamonds and platinum. Not colored stones and gold. Casually scanning and assessing a man from head to toe was one of Jada's greatest diva techniques. Maybe she'd call him next week after her furniture was delivered.

Although her coochie, aka Lady C, craved affection, Wellington's semen was the only sperm Jada honestly wanted swimming inside her paradise. His lips were the only ones she wanted pressed against her lips, her breasts, and her clit. The idea of getting to know someone new sucked. New issues. Unbearable habits. Why hadn't she followed her first thought and rented a car. Now she was trapped with Candice for the rest of the day. With a sigh, she left the coffee shop and headed for baggage claim.

Helping Jada retrieve her luggage, Candice recovered the suitcase from the conveyor belt and rolled it to her car. "Stay with us until you get settled," she suggested as they got in the car and left the parking lot.

Homelessness was a better alternative than watching Candice mimic the housewife role of Florida Evans from *Good Times*. "I'd love to, but I can't. I need solitude." Jada paused for a moment, watching the cars in the fast lane zoom by. Lowering the visor to block the sun, Jada sipped her drink and said, "Candice, I know you dislike Wellington because he cheated on me, but you have no idea how much I love him. It hurts me when you brag about how perfect your world is while constantly reminding me how fucked up my situation is."

Candice's head snapped to the right. "Girl, where did that come from?"

Ignoring the question, Jada continued, "I'm not desperate to find another man, to get hitched, or to get laid." Okay, maybe the getting laid part wasn't true, because her menstrual cycle was due, and she was so horny the friction between her thighs could bring her to a climax. "Besides, everything I had planned for my wedding, you're using for yours, including exchanging soul mate rings. And what's up with the marquis diamond ring. That was my favorite cut, not yours. But not once have I protested, and I'm not complaining now. And another thing, you need to stop telling Terrell *everything* I tell you. Am I your daily soap opera topic of conversation? You know Terrell and Darryl are still friends." Finally Jada had said what she'd held in far too long. Slowly her migraine started subsiding.

Jada seldom heard from Darryl Williams, but he called—even if he was on the road with his NBA teammates—whenever Terrell updated him on her latest happenings. Friendships with her ex-men were common and important, but she detested when Darryl delivered a verbatim report to her about herself.

Candice had been her girlfriend since third grade, but ever since she'd met and moved in with Terrell, their closeness had become a triangle when it came to secrets. Candice boasted about Terrell's bedroom skills in such detail, Jada felt as if she'd fucked him, too. The head of his penis was smaller than the shaft. The base of his penis was thinner than his shaft, almost like the shape of green zucchini. His nuts were the size of two mouth-sized gumballs when they shriveled up. And his cum tasted natural, like vanilla extract, except when he drank beer. Now Jada understood why Daddy used to say, "Never tell your girlfriend how good your man is in bed because she will find out behind your back." Fortunately for Candice, Jada had access to dicks through her *reserve* list, to which Wellington had become her newest active reserve member.

"Whew! Girl, you are right. You do need solitude. I'll try not to be so happy when I'm around *you*." Faster than a stunt man on fire, Candice did a stop, drop, and roll. She parked in front of the hotel but didn't get out of her car. "I'll tell my husband you said hello. Call me tomorrow. Bye, girl." Candice drove away so fast the tailwind literally closed the trunk.

What was up with wearing out the word *husband*? They weren't married yet, and Candice was so blinded by love she couldn't see that Terrell was obviously content reaping all the benefits of a married man while maintaining a singles' lifestyle.

After checking in, Jada raced to her room. Before the frappé settled in her stomach, the chilled liquid poured from her mouth. Leaning over the toilet, Jada heaved repeatedly. She removed her clothes and showered, letting the water rinse the residue from her mouth. Then she turned off the water, stepped onto the rug, and dried her hands on the plush white towel. Admiring her dripping-wet radiant onyx complexion in the mirror, Jada punched in zero zero one on her cell phone, tossed back the floral comforter, pressed the talk button, and sprawled across the white sheets as her skin air dried.

"Hi, ba. I'm glad you made it in safely. It's so good hearing your voice. I miss you already." Wellington's captivating tone made her forget all about her pains.

"Yeah, I miss you, too." If not for the static in the line, their connection would have been undetectable. Dead silence. A million thoughts stirred in Jada's mind, but she didn't know what to say next. She'd terminated her relationship with Wellington. She wasn't going back to him, and she was tired of discussing his infidelity. But she also missed the hell out of being with her man. Ex-man.

"When are you coming back to Oakland?" His seductiveness drew a prompt response.

"Next week. To get my car." A coochie deluxe tune-up wouldn't hurt either because she loved experiencing those sex-released endorphins, those hormones that made her feel like dancing and singing. Wellington's lovemaking made Jada happy to cook breakfast, lunch, or dinner anytime of the day or night. Hell, sometimes she even vacuumed the whole house or jogged around Lake Merritt, waving and smiling at adults, kids, seagulls, geese, and the sparse flamingos. But Jada also needed to visit Dr. Bates to take a pregnancy test. Her sickness was never accompanied by vomiting, so Jada suspected the worse and prayed for the best.

"Call and let me know when you're coming. I'll help you drive back. And maybe you'll come over for dinner before you leave? That's if you're finished boycotting and egging my place."

Jada laughed. "Cheap shot. Anyway, the last time Chef à la Wellington charcoaled steaks into brittle bits, we ended up eating out."

"If I recall correctly, my Nubian—"

Covering her free ear, Jada screamed with laughter. "Don't say it!" Jada didn't want Wellington to remind her how her quasigourmet meal had been so horrid she washed her food and his down the garbage disposal. The salmon croquettes had been harder than hockey pucks, so Wellington had dropped one on the dining room floor, grabbed the broom, and handed her the sponge mop.

After Wellington's first bite of her pecan-orange bundt cake, he'd said, "Um, you've got to taste this. Close your eyes and open your mouth." Then he'd promised, "You're going to love this." When the dessert hit her palate, each of her five senses had protested. Jada had darted her eyes in search of a place to quickly spit it out because she definitely wasn't going to swallow a lump that tasted worse than earwax. They had then fallen to the kitchen floor laughing until their insides cramped, their saliva exchanged between hungry lips, and their knees became sore from making love on the linoleum all night long.

Jada pictured Wellington's dazzling smile, bald head, thick eyebrows, goatee, and his eight pack. Soft hairs outlined his chest and every crevice in his abdomen. His perfectly erect nipples were five shades darker than his caramel complexion. His gentle touch, sensuous lips, passionate kisses, and orgasmic lovemaking were unforgettable. His firm ass, two-hundred-and-twenty-pound, six-foot-four physique, and seductive mannerisms were etched in her brain forever.

Breaking their silence, he said, "Call me in the morning, ba. I'll talk with you later."

Melting at the hearty sound of his voice, Jada felt the words "I love you" suspend in air and surround her spirit. "What are you wearing?"

Wellington whispered, "A smile and a hard-on that's begging for your affection."

"Wet your fingers and massage the head for me." Jada eased her fingers into her mouth and did the same to her clit.

"Ooh, yeah. I'm stroking The Ruler. He's growing an extra inch just for you, ba. Open your chocolate thighs wide so I can taste you."

Jada missed how they used to role-play. Her fondest memory was when she'd dressed like a Jamaican and flirted with Wellington in a Caribbean accent at the Farmers' Market. She convinced him to buy exotic fruits that she'd feasted on, off of his succulent flesh outside by his swimming pool during sunset.

"I'm pulling your face in closer, Big Daddy. Trace Mama's rabbit ears with your juicy tongue. Nice and slow." Jada moaned into the receiver as she enjoyed the external orgasm continuously seeping from her clitoris.

"Damn, ba, all of this cream is for you. Your hairs are marinating in my cum. Rub it in," he commanded.

"I'm flowing with you. Sip in my last drops." Jada caressed the moisture between her inner lips and slid her index finger into her vagina, welcoming the strong pulsation accompanying her internal orgasm.

Deep inside, her pussy knocked hard like an out-of-control, overloaded washer machine on a fast spin cycle. That was the results of her daily vaginal weight lifting. The gold ben-wa balls were no longer a challenge, so one day while visiting the pleasure store, the owner had introduced Jada to the ceramic and smooth wooden eggs. Jada had charged both sets and the instruction manual to her VISA. At first learning muscle control to simultaneously move the ceramic eggs in opposite directions, left and right, and up and down, was difficult. But after Jada started stringing the one-pound weight into the bottom opening of the wooden egg and lifting and holding it with her vaginal muscles, rotating the ceramic eggs was a cinch. Jada's clenching drove Wellington so nuts his orgasmic groans intensified, sounding like The Rock lifting and then body slamming Stone Cold Steve Austin during a WWF Championship match.

"Say you love me."

"I love you, Wellington Jones." More than he'd ever know, and at the moment more than she was willing to admit. Her soul magnetically absorbed his spiritual energy.

"I love you, too, ba. I'm gonna go clean up this wonderful mess you've created. Don't forget to call and let me know when you're coming to get your car. Good night, my Nubian queen."

"Yes, it is a very good night." Jada recharged her cell phone on the nightstand and continued lying sideways across the jumbo-sized mattress. She cried hard into her pillow so the people in the adjacent room wouldn't hear her sobbing. Why did she keep crying over Wellington when she didn't want him? How long would her head and heart remain out of sync? The old man on the plane had given her a lot to think about. Should Jada abandon her pride in order to salvage their love? Or give up Wellington and maintain her dignity?

Chapter 2

Wellington loaded Jada's trunk with a portable battery charger, flares, a first aid kit, and an empty gas can. He double checked the spare tire and made certain his AAA roadside card was in his wallet.

All of his life was neat and orderly. Preschool. High School. College. Cynthia had overruled his plea to play football and enrolled him in golf lessons. On his first date with Jada, he'd thrown on his new rags, sagging his denim shorts and wearing his baseball cap backward. To impress Jada he'd adjusted his attitude to his attire and played it cool. He was always smooth, but seldom cool. Not as in calm. Slick. He wasn't the type of guy who could get caught fucking another woman, then convince his woman she was to blame or it wasn't his fault. If confronted, he told the truth or opted not to respond.

"We're all set." Hopefully this wasn't his last chance to spend time with his Nubian queen. "Did you phone your mother to make sure they're not *busy?*" Wellington recalled when Jada told him how she dropped by unannounced and saw her mother dressed in a bustier, garter, and G-string, waiting for Robert to come over.

"Yeah, she's packing. Robert is taking her to Las Vegas tomorrow. Those two are always traveling some place." Jada reached for the handle.

"Oh, no you don't. We may not be a couple, but some things haven't changed." Wellington opened and closed Jada's door. He checked the pressure in each tire. Then he adjusted the steering wheel and the mirrors, and pulled away from the curb.

"Thanks for driving my car to L.A." Jada affectionately rubbed her thumb aside his mouth.

Instantly he licked his lips, asking, "What was that?" He sucked her pointing finger into his mouth.

"Oh, toothpaste or something. Don't worry. It's gone now." She smiled, intertwining her legs until both feet rested atop opposite knees.

"Umm, I should have gotten it myself." He glanced at her feet. "Isn't that uncomfortable?" Wellington cruised Highway 1 South toward the San Mateo Bridge. He liked her new purple stonewashed unitard. Stretchable. Flexible. Sexy. The outline of her crotch stalked him, so he scratched the back of his neck. "Um. Would you please unfold your legs? You're distracting me. I've never seen you do that." He tucked in his lips to moisten them.

Placing her bare feet on the off-white mat next to her slip-ons, Jada answered, "After you abandoned me at the restaurant at Pier 39, I decided meditation wasn't enough, so I enrolled in yoga. It's the best mental and physical exercise I've done. You should try it."

Wow. Maybe he should. In fact, he'd enroll as soon as he got back, because if all the women in the class were that limber and peacefully centered—forget the church house—yoga class was where Wellington wanted to find his next mate. He thought about last night when Jada's iridescent-polished toenails had been cotton candy in his mouth.

"You think you'll ever relocate from Half Moon Bay?"

Jada opened the *Jet* magazine, reading the last page first. Eddie Murphy was on the cover without his wife and kids.

Wellington would sneak a peep when Jada turned to the centerfold. "Are you kidding? Never. The San Francisco Peninsula is one of the best places to live in America. You wouldn't believe how much I paid for my home ten years ago and what it's worth today." Maybe she was testing him to see if he planned on moving to L.A. Wellington wanted but refused to ask Jada for a chance to make things right between them. "How close are you to completing your business and operating plan?"

"Not very. In fact, I haven't even started. I'll work on it next week."

"You think your mom is going to let me in?" He hadn't seen Jada's mother since their breakup. Their separation wasn't completely his fault. But Jada acted as if her contributions were less important. Adam didn't pick the apple from the tree, but every Christian in the world knew he was just as guilty as Eve. So what if Jada hadn't initiated the threesome. She'd participated.

"Why wouldn't she?" Jada bypassed the Beauty of the Week. "Ah, ha. Gotcha."

Wellington smiled and nodded. "That's all right. You're sexier than all of them put together." He turned on 106.1 KMEL and passed the time with sporadic Dyad until he parked outside Mrs. Ruby's house in San Leandro. "Does Robert still sleep across the street?" he asked as they walked toward the front door.

Wellington envied how Jada's mother and her second husband had separate residences. Robert courted Ruby as if they were high school sweethearts. He bought Ruby flowers every week, ran her bathwater, and massaged her feet. She cooked his dietetic meals, watched his intake of carbohydrates, pricked his finger three times a day to test his sugar level, and clipped his toenails to make sure he didn't get an infection. Every story Jada shared about her mother had a happy ending, but she never talked about how her father had died.

Unfortunately, Wellington had never known the love, joy, or touch of his real mother. So he lived vicariously through the stories his older sister, Jazzmyne, shared about their mother, Katherine. Jazzmyne told him how Katherine had visited Cynthia every week for an entire year after he was born just to hold him in her arms. After Wellington's first birthday, Cynthia had insisted Katherine discontinue her visits, fearing Katherine might steal him away. Since Cynthia had become infertile during adolescence, she didn't want to risk losing Wellington to anyone, especially the sister who had supposedly stolen her man.

Wellington was pulled from his thoughts when Jada answered.

"Only when they have a disagreement, because they don't argue. Or when Robert is watching a game with his friends. Can you believe every room in Robert's house has a Raiders theme? His welcome mat, electrical plate covers, towels, and plates, you name it. Mama cooks for every game. Sets up the food at his place. Then goes about her business. She calls it his sanity time."

"That's a great arrangement." Wellington rang Ruby's doorbell, then softly kissed Jada's lips, remembering the intimacy they had shared last night. That was the first time Jada had slept in his bed since their ménage à trois with Melanie.

When Robert opened the door, the buttons on his Raiders cardigan sweater were unevenly matched, so one side hung longer than the other. "Hey, look a here. It's Homeo and Diamonette. What's up cat and catette? Come on in. Jada, Ruby in the kitchen. Homey, you can have a sit down with me. I spoke with your stepdad Christopher yesterday. We went to dat Super Bowl Mardi Gras down in New *Orleans*.

Man those 'Who Dat' cats party way harder than they work. You'd think they won the Super Bowl. And I could have sworn this woman at The Bottom Line was tryin' ta put a root on me, but Ruby wasn't havin' it. So y'all gettin' ready to hit the road, huh?" Robert smacked his hands together, dashing the right one in the air.

The Bottom Line. Wellington laughed. They really did get around. "Yeah, I didn't want Jada driving by herself." Wellington's cellular phone rang. It was Melanie, so he hit the end button to silence the musical tone. Then he leaned over to see if Jada was headed in his direction. "Man, Melanie won't stop calling me."

"You know the best way to stop a woman from calling you?" Robert burped. "Don't excuse me. More room out than in."

Shaking his head, Wellington asked, "Naw, what's that? I sure could use your insight, man."

Ever since his last visit to the hospital, Melanie was relentlessly blowing up his cell and home phones. And when he did answer, she acted as if the triplets she miscarried after her car fell from the cliff had never existed. If he hadn't read the doctor's report Christopher delivered to him personally, Melanie wouldn't have told him he had been framed. He wasn't the father. The ultrasound proved Melanie had been into her second trimester—fourteen weeks—when her body involuntarily aborted the kids. Less than eight weeks had passed between their first encounter and her automobile accident. Jada would have slapped fool all over his forehead if Wellington had told her. So he didn't.

"Sometimes you can't treat a woman like a lady. That's why Christopher left Cynthia. I don't know how he stayed with her as long as he did. Cynthia is half beast, half bitch. Says he's filing for his divorce, too." Robert reclined, elevating his feet. His black slip-on corduroy house shoes with Raiders patches sewn on the top fell to the floor. "Tell the bitch to quit calling you. Then block her numbers. She'll stop directly. Now, if you haven't asked her to stop, that means you still want her around. Eventually, she'll getcha at the right time when you're horny and bored. Then you'll get caught up in the moment. Next thing you know, you're rolling around in the hay with her again." Robert shuffled through the Sunday morning *Oakland Tribune*, retrieving the sports section. "The sports section isn't as exciting when my Raiders aren't playing. Let me see what these Warriors are doing."

Robert had a little OG, original gangster, in him. Wellington had never heard him cuss. "I guess you're right. I'll wait until she calls back. Then I'll tell her." And he would. He just wouldn't curse her out. What would using profanity prove? When he returned from L.A., Wellington would call his sister and confidant, Jazzmyne, for a second opinion. He already knew and was happy Christopher had walked out on Cynthia. The grapevine gossip had the facts twisted, claiming Cynthia kicked his stepfather out of the house.

"I know I'm right." Robert continued reading, shaking his head. "The Warriors are giving an appreciation party. What for? I should have brought back some of them brown paper bags the Saints fans wear to give them."

Robert stopped talking because Jada was heading his way.

"What are you two talking about?" Jada asked, lowering Robert's newspaper. Hugging his neck, she said, "Don't get up. We can see ourselves out."

"Be careful on the highway and call us as soon as you *tweetie birds* get in." Robert whistled like a bird.

"Bye, baby." Mama's eyes swelled with tears. "I sure wish you weren't moving so far away."

"Bye, Mama. I love you." Blowing her mother a kiss, Jada paused in the doorway.

Mrs. Tanner was a fox. Her silver precision cut was striking. Considerably shorter than Jada, she was five feet, four inches; almost average height for a woman. Maybe she'd shrunk an inch with age. The emerald green casual pantsuit accented her slender figure.

"Bye, Mrs. Tanner. Mr. Hamilton. Thanks for the advice, man." With the eighties, nineties, and new millennium, more and more women were maintaining their last names. Wellington was proud Jada had once wanted to carry his last name. No hyphen. No Jada Tanner-Jones. She was going to be Jada Diamond Jones.

"It's cool. But the next round will cost ya. Ya know what I mean?" Robert pointed his finger at Wellington's privates and said, "Bang!"

Walking to the car, Jada asked, "What was that all about?"

"Guy stuff. You know how Robert is. Relax. Take a nap. I'll get you home safely." Wellington reset the trip mileage to zero.

Jada retrieved her latest issue of *Upscale* magazine. "I'm not sleepy. I just woke up."

The sunrays dissipated behind the dusky gray clouds. Small raindrops beaded on the windshield. Wellington turned the wipers on low and merged out of the fast lane. "When was the last time you changed your blades?"

Defensively, Jada answered, "I never change my blades. The dealer—"

Boop! Boop! The cop couldn't be signaling him to pull over, because he was driving the limit in a fifty-five mile-per-hour zone. *Boooop!* Wellington merged again, and the patrol car followed.

"What's wrong? What'd you do?" Jada asked.

Wellington cut his eyes at Jada and gritted his back teeth as he pulled over, praying he wasn't a victim of Driving While Black. "I didn't do anything."

The Highway Patrol officer flashed his spotlight as if it was eleven o'clock at night. "Let me see your license, registration, and insurance."

Wellington remained silent and handed him the information.

"What did he do wrong?" Jada asked.

"I told you I didn't do anything wrong," Wellington grumbled angrily.

"Miss, be quiet. This is official business. You were traveling sixty-five in a fifty-five mile zone. I'm going to have to run your driver's license." The officer walked around the car twice with his hand steadily on his gun.

When Jada opened her door and stepped out of the car, he swiftly drew his pistol from the holster and aimed directly at her heart. "Get back in the car! Now!"

Jada eased into her seat and closed the door. She closed her eyes and took several deep breaths. Wellington's chest rose and fell, but he kept his eyes on the dirty cop, contemplating his next move. The officer resumed his walk. He zoomed in on the front bumper while suspiciously peeping over the hood at them. After about three minutes, he strolled to his car.

Pounding on the steering wheel, Wellington said, "I hate this shit! He knows damn well I wasn't speeding, so why is he treating us like fucking criminals?"

Jada buckled her seat belt and remained silent.

The officer returned and gave Wellington his license, registration, insurance, and a speeding ticket for doing seven miles over the limit. "I suggest you drive fifty in this area, boy. A person fitting your description was identified in a pedestrian hit-and-run." He slapped the roof of the car and said, "Have a nice day."

Wellington waited until the officer drove off first. "Can you believe this shit? He had the fucking audacity to call me boy, and he's blacker than me. I swear that's the kind of confrontation that'll land an innocent man in jail."

Staring straight ahead like a zombie, Jada whispered, "Baby, let's go back. I can get my car later."

"No. He does not intimidate me. I'll be okay." The small raindrops had grown to the size of quarters when they splattered on the windshield. Wellington drove twenty miles per hour. Not because of the officer, but because visibility was steadily decreasing, and his blood pressure was steadily rising. Gusty winds whistled about the convertible top. He glimpsed at his trip gauge. They had traveled fifty-two miles. Interstate 5 South was ten miles away, but it would take at least thirty minutes to get there. "Let's pull over and find a hotel." Wellington grumbled, "I can't believe I checked everything except the weather report."

"Okay," Jada calmly responded.

Apparently other motorists shared his view. The last available parking space was at the end of the lot. Wellington dropped Jada off at the lobby entrance and hurried to the vacant space. He didn't try covering his head or drying himself off once inside the lobby.

"We got the last room, too," Jada said, pressing two on the elevator. "Are you upset about the ticket?"

"Of course I'm upset. But I'm glad Christopher taught me by example how to keep my cool. That's why I hit the steering wheel after he left and before he returned."

The room smelled damp and stale. Wellington turned on the air, and Jada sprayed a dash of her perfume into the vent.

Jada turned on the TV. "We can watch a movie."

"What's on at eleven-thirty in the morning?" Wellington diagonally stretched across the bed. His arms hung over one edge and his feet over the other. "Come here. I want to hold you in my arms. I'm sorry, ba. I didn't know how to react when he pulled his gun on you. But I do know if he had pulled the trigger, both of us would be dead."

There was nothing Wellington could do to that asshole who made him feel less of a man in front of his woman. Friend. Whatever. Today was the first time Wellington realized he was willing to lay down his life to protect Jada.

Thankfully, he could quickly turn to her for solace. The scent of Jada's hair, the warmth of her body, and softness of her skin calmed and comforted him. He hoped he provided the same compassion for her.

Chapter 3

Three days of moping over Wellington after he'd left had practically driven Jada insane. The time had come for her to adapt to her new environment in Baldwin Hills, California. Spring's sunshine reigned outside. Snapping her fingers, swinging her hair, and dancing wildly, she sang ahead of Pattie LaBelle. "He's the right one baby. Sure nuff he's got the stuff . . ." A private victory because she'd decided earlier to call the good-looking guy who handed her his business card while she and Candice were at LAX Starbucks. Unbeknownst to him, he was going to cure her heartache and her coochie ache.

Jada skipped to the bathroom. She stopped and stared at the test tubes lying on the white marble vanity. Daddy used to say, "If you confess with your mouth and believed in your heart, your sins will be forgiven." On bended knees, Jada propped her elbows on the toilet lid and prayed, "God, if you let me out of this situation, I'll never do this again." The Lord must have been busy, or maybe He'd heard her whisper "Never again" once more since she'd made the same promise at twenty years old when she was in college.

From her five-pack First Response, the first, second, third, fourth, and last window each framed double pink stripes. Every damn test reminded Jada she'd not only fucked but also slipped up. One of her two lovers'—Wellington's or Darryl's—sperm had won a race and left her pregnant with a baby like a happily single female who had just reluctantly caught the bride's bouquet. And if Jada could have tossed her bundle to a woman who desperately wanted a child, she wouldn't have batted an eyelash.

"This can't be happening." Jada talked to herself in the mirror. "Okay, God heard your prayer. You've been late before and you weren't pregnant. Maybe you're stressed because of the move. Girl, what are you going to do with a baby if you are pregnant? Think positive. The home kit was defective. The only thing you're expecting is having a fabulous time with Mr. Wonderful."

When the phone rang, Jada dashed out of the bathroom, hoping it was her new acquaintance. "Hey, hey," Jada answered, grooving to the beat as she lowered the volume.

"Hi, Jada. This is Dr. Bates."

Picking up the remote, Jada turned off the stereo and said, "Tell me it was only a bad dream and my blood test result is negative." Slumping in the oversized chair, Jada stared at the ivy plant that hung as an accent across her living room drapes as she kicked her feet up on the ottoman. Then she crossed her pointing and middle fingers on both hands. "Lord, I promise. I really mean it this time."

"Negative. No can do," Dr. Bates replied. "You're going to be a mother, my dear."

"Thanks"—Jada paused—"for what? I'm not sure." Jada's voice was low and flat. Mother warned her about people who answered their own questions. They supposedly had psychological problems. Hell, sometimes it was appropriate to find one's own solution. Silent. Aloud. What difference did that make? Jada's condo had enough space for her, but her baby would need a backyard to roam around and play games. She'd focus on finding a new place later.

"Well, you know there are other alternatives," Dr. Bates commented.

Picking up her new beau's number, Jada ripped the card into tiny pieces, then dropped the pieces inside the burning candle on the tall brass stand. "Yes, there are. But not for me." A lump formed in Jada's throat as she swallowed. "I could never kill a living soul, especially not my own child. I guess I'll just have to fly back to Oakland for my checkups."

If she were going to have a baby, her mother was definately going to be involved. That meant Jada would have to temporarily move back to Oakland, but she could stay in L.A. a few more months then return after her baby was born. "I want you to recommend the best OB/GYN who freelances as a counselor. Oh, my gosh. A baby. Whew!" Jada followed with contrived laughter. Black folk didn't go to counseling, because that certified to their friends and family they were crazy.

"Are you okay?" Dr. Bates asked.

"I will be." One mesmerizing ivy leaf stood out above the rest, accented with more ivory than green. Jada tiptoed to reach the top of the blinds, plucked it off, and set it on her marbled coffee table. Mama had mentioned a pregnant woman should never reach above her head because she could strangle her unborn. No disrespect intended, but Jada believed it was a myth. She'd preserve the leaf, giving it to her child on the first day of school to represent his or her Ivy League college of choice. The sooner she planted the seeds of success, the better.

"Well, Dr. Carl Watson is the best in the Bay Area. I'll set everything up for you. You'll be just fine. I'll call you next week," Dr. Bates said. "Remember, Jada—"

Jada finished the sentence because Dr. Bates ended every

conversation the same. "Yeah, I know. Love myself first. Goodbye."

Just like that. Jada's whole life had taken a turn down the road she never envisioned traveling. Single parenthood. Daddy always said, "The things you fear the most shall come upon you."

Daddy was always afraid to go to the doctor. He said, "Once those doctors start cutting on you, they never stop." He feared going under the knife, so he suffered tremendously with his abdominal pains. Everything he ate came right back up, including his favorite vanilla ice cream. Mama couldn't take watching him suffer and lose more weight; so they drove him to the hospital, and sure enough, he had to have an emergency operation. Stomach cancer had destroyed Daddy's organs beyond salvation, so the doctor stitched him back up and sent him home to live out his last days. Seeing her father slowly deteriorate was so disturbing, Jada decided to only reminisce about the good times and never talk about how her daddy might still be alive if he hadn't delayed going to see his doctor.

Jada dreaded and debated whether to tell Wellington or Darryl. The one person Jada knew she could tell—the person who wouldn't judge her—was her mother. "Baby, if you don't know which one is the father, you've got to tell both Wellington and Darryl," Mama insisted. Mama's advice was honest and direct. Unlike Robert—who comically judged everyone—Mama never labeled anyone. Robert said, "What you crying for Diamonette? They both rich."

Jada instantly decided to defer her dream of opening the doors to her company until after her child started school. Between her Mutual Funds and her inheritance from Henry Tanner, she and her baby could live a moderate lifestyle on the interest income. Within five years she could complete her business and operating plan and lease adequate office space downtown. Black Diamonds' mission statement, "To build a better America one community at a time by insuring low-income areas become educationally, technologically, and financially sound," had been developed before she moved from Oakland and would remain the same.

Not mentally prepared to tell either of her exes face-to-face, and writing a letter seemed so distant, Jada did the next best thing—she phoned Wellington and then Darryl.

Nervously Jada dialed Wellington's number. Heartbeats pounded in her throat as though something was trying to escape—that was an outward sign of pregnancy, Mama had explained. Immediately after he said hello, Jada blurted out, "Wellington, I have something to tell you." Jada didn't wait for a response. "I'm pregnant." At first it didn't seem real, but Jada could no longer pretend. Her pregnancy was very real. So real, it frightened her. Not having a child, but having someone totally dependent upon her. Shitty diapers. No husband. Soiled bibs. No man. Sleepless nights. No lover. Well, theoretically she made love to Wellington, in her dreams.

Jada sighed, but not from relief. She became quiet. If Wellington didn't say something soon, she wouldn't be able to tell him anything else, because her body was on the verge of lying horizontal and unconscious.

Wellington's silence seemingly lasted forever. He finally whispered, "Ba, that's great." Wellington gasped for air. Then he shouted with joy, "Yes! We're going to have a baby!" He never questioned the paternity.

No easy way existed for Jada to tell her soul mate—the man she would have married had it not been for that bitch Melanie—the truth. So she didn't. Wellington's vote of confidence gave Jada the comfort she needed, realizing he'd be there for them.

Before Wellington spoke another word, Jada hung up the phone, fearing she might provide too much information.

Jada reclined in the chair and imagined "The Ruler" between her soft thighs. That was what had gotten her in her predicament in the first place. Her libido. High. Wellington was nine inches. Darryl was ten. The thought of Wellington made her juices flow. Tugging on each end of her drawstring, she slipped her hand inside and massaged her clit. Her index finger rotated in tiny circular motions. The lubrication saturated her G-point. The apple spice scent of her candles became an aphrodisiac. Partially spreading her legs, thoughts of Wellington's strong hands massaging her breasts brought Jada to the edge of orgasm. She envisioned him clinching her nipples. One between his teeth and the other inside his fingertips. Jada's vagina pulsated from the inside out.

"Yes." Jada spoke the word that continued her groove. Again she said, "Yes," softly but a little louder. By the time Wellington put the head in all the way, Jada could feel the uncontrollable throbbing along the lining of her uterus.

"Yes, that feels so damn good, baby." Jada removed her hand and tasted herself. Her mama said, "Never feed a man *anything* until you've tasted it first." Her last memories of Darryl left a bitter tang. Thankfully it wasn't in her mouth.

Jada took a deep breath as she dialed Darryl's cellular phone. It was now or never, and she truly wanted the moment behind her.

"Hi, Darryl."

"Yeah, who is this?" he asked as if he were screening his calls.

"Ja-da." She was pissed he needed to ask.

"Hey! I didn't catch your voice. You sound um, different. Where've you been? Have you moved yet? Are you in Oaktown? Or in La La Land?"

He'd perked up, probably because he thought he was going to get laid. Never again. Darryl was officially and permanently moved to her inactive list. "I called to tell you I'm pregnant." Jada tapped her foot and waited for his response.

"And?"

"And, what?" Jada's forehead wrinkled. Instantly, tension built up from one temple to the other like a rainbow, but this one didn't bear good fortunes. Perhaps her blessings lay behind her soon-to-be potbelly.

"So who's the father? Not me." Darryl's voice escalated and deepened. "I know because I pulled my snake out of your pussy the last time we fucked."

Jada moved the phone away from her ear. She wrapped all eight fingers and both thumbs around the receiver. Her grip was so tight her knuckles cracked. The back-and-forth motion should have been Darryl's neck. Was this the same person she'd known since high school? She spoke into the receiver so close her cinnamon-colored lipstick filled the opening.

"Well, I'm not one hundred percent sure it isn't yours!" Jada responded with an equivalent volume. "Maybe your venom had already poisoned my womb."

"Well, look-a-here. Call me when you're ninety-nine point ninety-nine percent sure. I know the routine all too well. I thought you were different, but all you bitches are just alike. I'm glad I didn't marry you! Better yet, don't ever call me again! I can't believe you're trying to stick me with a kid. I know your rich ass don't need my money, but if you want child support, you're going to have to pawn the engagement ring I left at your house. I've just been hit for child support up the ass for two kids that I just found out are mine. This shit will not come in threes. You'd better call Wellington—mister lover-boy financial advisor—Jones and let him foot the bill." Then Darryl mumbled, "I don't believe this bullshit. Pregnant?"

Instantly she hated Darryl's guts. If Jada never saw him again as long as she lived, it wouldn't matter. Two kids. Damn, that was a hell of a way to discover Darryl had children. As her heartbeat quickened, Jada's breasts moved up and down. Her eyes filled with tears. Her baby definitely didn't need an asshole for a father, and Darryl had obviously lost his frickin' mind. Or had she? Otherwise, how could she rationalize such bizarre behavior? In the midst of Darryl's relentless outrage, Jada slammed the phone on the base so hard it cracked, snapped, and pinched her thumb.

"Shit!" Jada became so enraged she snatched the base from the wall and slammed it to the floor.

That was the day Jada independently concluded the paternity of her unborn child. There were some things a woman knew but didn't tell. Darryl had pulled out before cumming, and Wellington had not. But based on the rhythm method, her window of conception was definitely during her affair with Darryl. Unless the embryo growing inside of her was a miracle baby, Jada disappointingly knew that Wellington was not the biological father.

Chapter 4

"Not so deep, you're poking the baby in the head." Jada held her stomach. Each of her orgasms accompanied a mild contraction. Wellington's body curled into a fetal position behind hers.

"I'm trying not to, ba, but this feels so warm and wonderful I could stay inside of you forever." The fellas weren't lying when they said pregnant pussy was top shelf. Wellington kissed the nape of Jada's neck and rubbed her cocoa-butter-saturated belly.

"Feels like the baby is punching and kicking. I think you should pull out." Jada tried stretching her legs.

Wellington nestled into the groove so The Ruler wouldn't slide out. "Okay, ba. A few more strokes, please. I'm almost there." When he squeezed Jada's breast, milk expressed from her nipple. He massaged her breast until he released himself. Then Wellington rolled her over, snuggled into her bosom, and breast-fed himself.

"Leave some for the baby," Jada laughed and pushed his head backward.

Wellington mumbled, "I'm just sampling."

When Jada sat up, Wellington's lips detached, making a smacking noise. Placing her feet on the floor, Jada used both hands to push herself up. "I'm going to shower."

In the bathroom, a stream of amniotic fluid trickled down her inner thighs all the way to her feet. "Wellington!" Jada froze as the flow of mucus continued. "Get me a towel."

Wellington sprang from the bed. "Damn! Did I do that? Are you okay?" He wiped from her ankles all the way up to her vagina. "Ba, you're bleeding!"

"Call my mama first and then the doctor. I'm going to take a quick shower." Lifting her foot, Jada yelled, "Ooooooo!" sandwiching her fetus between her breasts and thighs.

Wellington grabbed the cordless phone and speed dialed the number. "Mama Ruby, I think Jada's in labor. She's leaking and bleeding. Is she supposed to bleed? She said she's getting ready to shower, and we'll meet you at Alta Bates in an hour." He listened. "No, the blood isn't heavy." He paused again, shaking his head. "No, there are no thick clots falling out." Wellington was quiet, then said, "Okay," and hung up the phone. Something had told him to let Jada spend the night at her mother's, but no, his dick begged her to stay.

"Your mama said no shower. I've got to get you to the hospital right away. She'll bring your bag."

"This hurts too much," Jada cried, doubling over, holding her stomach. "Nobody said it would hurt so much. I feel like I'm gonna die."

Wellington tossed Jada's bath towel on the shower bar. He eased her arms into his thick black cotton robe. Then he hurried into his pants and shirt so fast he bypassed putting on underwear. "Let's go."

"I'm not leaving the house like this. Look at me. I'm all slimy, nasty, and naked except for this heavy-ass robe." A series of *ooooooos* turned into *oooooows*.

Kissing her temple, he said, "You look lovely. Now let's go." Wellington coaxed Jada down the stairs and to the car.

"Shit! I locked the keys in the house." He picked up a cobblestone from his front lawn, broke the side window, and unlocked the front door. Returning with the keys fumbling in his hand, he helped Jada into the car. "Hang in there, ba." The tires screeched against the driveway, generating a smoke cloud that reeked of burnt rubber. Wellington shifted into drive and sped down the hill.

"The baby isn't due for another two weeks," Jada said, taking short, quick breaths like her Lamaze and yoga instructors taught her. "I'm ready to push! Get it out of me, I'm scared!"

Monday morning rush hour in the Bay Area was hectic, especially along Interstate 880 with more eighteen-wheelers than automobiles. The two-passenger car-pool lane provided minimal relief.

"Uhhh!" Jada strained.

"No! Don't do that! Don't push. We're almost there," he lied, hoping Jada was too preoccupied to notice the truth. Maybe since she was sitting, the baby would stay inside. Wellington flagged the Alameda County Sheriff in the next lane. The police owed him restitution from issuing that bogus citation. He lowered Jada's window and shouted, "My wife is in labor! Can you help us get to Alta Bates in Berkeley?"

Rocking in her seat, Jada screamed, "Pleeeeeeease! Help me!" so loud Wellington almost pissed in his pants.

Merging in front of Wellington, the officer fired up his siren, motioning for him to follow.

Tailing the dark blue car, Wellington said, "Hang in there, ba. We're on our way."

Wellington parked in front of Alta Bates' emergency sliding glass doors and waved goodbye to the officer who kept on driving.

Mama Ruby was waiting in the lobby. Her hair was combed, and her earth-tone lipstick matched her outfit. She must have been dressed when he phoned.

Wellington raced to the counter, signaling for Mama Ruby to go to the car. "My wife is in labor."

"Who is your doctor? And what's your wife's full name?" the assistant asked.

Wellington stamped his foot. "Damn! I knew I was forgetting something. I forgot to call Dr. Watson." He rubbed his head and told the assistant Jada's first, middle, and last names.

"Okay, Mr. Tanner"—she smiled—"you're in luck because the doctor has been here all night, and he's here this morning. He's napping in one of our rooms. I'll notify Dr. Watson right away. Where's your wife?"

Pointing at the entrance, Wellington said, "She's in the car."

"We'll get a wheelchair and take care of her. Park your car in the garage and come up to labor and delivery."

By the time Wellington arrived in the birthing room, Jada's legs were in stirrups, and Dr. Watson had his fingers stuck up her vagina, pressing on her stomach. "You've only dilated two centimeters. Nurse, intravenously induce her labor. I'll be back in a few minutes."

Jada's contractions grew closer, some within the same minute. "I can't take anymore. How much longer do I have to suffer?" A series of quick, short breaths followed.

Dr. Watson returned and asked, "How is she doing?"

The nurse held the brown clipboard in front of him.

"Prepare Mrs. Tanner for an emergency cesarean. I'm going to check on my other patient. I'll meet you in the operating room in ten minutes."

"No!" Jada cried. "I can push." Jada held her breath, and her entire face contracted.

"Stop! Don't push, because the baby can't get out." The nurse rubbed Jada's hand. "You're only two of ten centimeters, sweetheart. Your baby's heart rate has dropped, and if we wait for you to fully dilate, your baby may suffer brain damage. Or even worse, he might not make it at all. Trust me. You'll both be fine, but we must take you to surgery immediately. We can put you to sleep or give you an epidural and numb you from the waist down. The choice is yours, but you have to decide quickly."

He. Did that mean he was having a son? Wellington smiled.

Jada reached for her mama and Wellington. "Can they come with me?" When Wellington tried to kiss Jada, she snapped her teeth, almost biting off his lips, so he held her hand instead.

"Yes, they can come, but they have to be sterilized first." The nurse instructed the staff and left the room.

Wellington vigorously cleaned his face and hands. The disposable scrub long-sleeved shirt and pants squished whenever he moved his arms or legs. The white face mask covered his nose, mouth, and goatee while the cap shielded his bald head. He squeezed his fingers into the yellowish gloves, making a popping sound like the doctor.

In the operating room, the anesthesiologist pressed his forearm across Jada's back, restricting her movement. "Don't move," he insisted.

"Ouch! You're hurting me. How am I supposed to stay hunched over while having contractions?" Jada attempted to force his burly arm away, but he pressed harder.

Wellington frowned. Mama Ruby looked at Wellington and whispered, "Don't speak. She's fine. If she moves, and he hits the wrong spot, she could become paralyzed."

Dr. Watson entered the room a few moments later and pinched Jada's legs and stomach. "Can you feel that?"

"No," Jada said. "But I'm watching you."

Dr. Watson repositioned the mirror. "Don't watch me. Just relax and tell me if you feel any pain."

An aqua-colored plastic screen blocked her view as the assistant shaved Jada's pubic area cleaner than Wellington's head. A bright lamp beamed toward the lower half of her body. Jada was covered from head to toe with linen except for her stomach.

Mama Ruby held Jada's hand while Wellington focused on Dr. Watson cutting through several layers of Jada's stomach tissue. Blood oozed with each cut. When the doctor sliced through the last layer, the assistant soaked up the blood with gauze, stretched Jada's incision to opposite ends of her pelvis, and clamped her flesh on each side.

Damn. Wellington covered his mouth guard as his body swayed. He definitely had a newfound respect for women. Just when he was about to pass out, he saw his baby's head emerge sideways between Jada's flesh. With another tug, the slimy body slipped out, and Dr. Watson announced, "It's a boy," and handed Wellington the scissors. "Cut the cord and welcome your son into the world."

"Yes! It's a boy!" Wellington's hand trembled as he cut the umbilical cord. Darius Henry Jones had arrived: seven pounds, fourteen ounces, and twenty-two and a half inches long. If it were a girl, they had agreed to name her after his biological mother, Katherine. The assistant held Darius close for Jada to see.

"Hey, sweetie. Your eyes are closed, but I know you can hear me. Grandma is here. Daddy is here, and your mommy is here, too." Jada smiled at the bundle wrapped in a blue receiving blanket, stared at Wellington, then cooed at Darius, kissing his tiny fingers.

"We need to take him now," the assistant said, easing Darius away.

Jada looked at Wellington and said, "Go with them and make sure they put the right tag on our baby."

Wellington laughed.

Jada pointed toward Darius and said, "I'm serious, Wellington. Go with them."

He'd go in a minute. What were the odds their child would be switched at birth or kidnapped from the hospital? Jada was overreacting.

While Dr. Watson was stitching Jada's bikini cut, Wellington said, "My boy needs to be circumcised before we leave the hospital."

"I don't do circumcisions, but Dr. Lenoir does."

That was the second time Wellington thought he'd pass out. Watching his son strapped down like a frog on its back. Dr. Lenoir performed the surgery, clipping and stitches, without any anesthesia. Darius screamed so loud and cried so hard Wellington wanted to push Dr. Lenoir aside and comfort his son. After the surgery, Wellington visited the cafeteria, then returned to the recovery room to check on Jada.

The nurse was instructing Jada on—what Jada already knew—how to properly breast-feed Darius. Mama Ruby sat nearby. Wellington recalled the Lamaze instructor emphasizing the importance for a nursing mother to breast-feed her child immediately. "Some infants refuse to nurse after receiving a bottle because they have to work twice as hard to get half the milk. So make sure you tell the nurse not to give your child a bottle. No matter how tired you are. You must nurse your baby as soon as he or she is ready to feed."

Jada held Darius in the football position, tucking his wrapped frame under her arm as she held his head. She protruded her nipple between her first two fingers and tickled the side of Darius's mouth until he opened wide enough for her to place the entire nipple in his mouth. They were also taught that if the baby didn't latch on properly, the mother's nipples would crack and possibly bleed. Sensing instinctive behavior, Darius aggressively latched on to Jada's breast and started sucking. After five minutes, Jada eased her pinky finger into the corner of Darius's mouth to properly break the suctioning. She burped her son, then fed him again. Darius was destined to become a breast man just like his father.

Chapter 5

Everything happened for a reason, including how Wellington met Simone Smith. Thirty-three-o-six. Lakeshore Avenue. Oakland, California. The Jahva House. Wellington's preferred coffee house because everyone was down to earth like the owners, D'Wayne of Tony, Toni, Tone, and his wife, Michelle. Wellington pulled out a stool, turned the back to the counter, and sat with the guys: Rich, Marshal, Kojo, Mike, and Michael.

Rich started their usual Tuesday morning philosophical discussion. "Why did Socrates say, 'A good man cannot be harmed'?" Most mornings one could find Rich sitting in the last seat at the end of the counter, wearing his Kangol black leather cap, blue jeans, and a sweatshirt, with his silver peace sign dangling around his neck on a thin, twenty-four-inch black suede cord.

Rich was retired. Marshal prepared and circulated the monthly community calendar. As an artist, Kojo worked whenever he wanted. Mike was like Tommy from the *Martin Lawrence Show,* because no one knew exactly what he did for a living. Michael was an entrepreneur like most Jahva House morning patrons.

Kojo responded immediately in his native St. Vincent Caribbean accent. "If you are man or woman, you can be harmed." Whenever Kojo got excited, he stood and twisted one of his long, exotic dreadlocks.

"Kojo. Good is the operative word," Rich said, sipping his coffee.

"Like me." Michael patted his chest. "I'm a good man, and I have a good wife."

Rich looked at Michael and responded, "But you still haven't answered the question." Rich bit his buttered croissant. "Mike. Maybe you can answer the question."

Wellington interjected. "I can answer the question. I agree with Kojo. Any man good or bad—" Wellington paused. "Um, um, um." He stared and rubbed his goatee.

The fellas followed pursuit. Kojo tilted his head. Rich leaned over his chair. Mike scratched his beard. Michael nodded. Then they all turned to Rich because he not only knew every regular customer on a first-name basis, but he also knew, with the exception of Mike, what they did for a living.

"Don't look at me. I don't know her. But she is a cutie. Hee, hee." Rich chuckled, wiping his lips with a paper napkin.

A sky blue mat was rolled into a sack strapped across her back. Black Lycra pants clung to her wide hips, thick thighs, and well-toned calves and disappeared inside her ankle boots. The safari waist-length jacket was zipped low, exposing magnificent cleavage. Her hair was smoothed into a short bobtail that slightly curled under, highlighting her gold hoop earrings.

"I've seen her before." Wellington smiled. "She attends the yoga class across the street."

"How do you know that?" Kojo asked, deepening his voice.

"Because, sometimes I take a class after I leave here." As

she walked up to the counter, Wellington approached her and said, "Let me order for you."

In slow motion she nodded and lowered her eyebrows. "Sure." She paused, then asked, "Haven't I seen you somewhere?"

Wellington turned and winked at his friends. "Casper, two organic house coffees for here, please." Leaving the fellas, Wellington sat at the piano with his lovely prospect sitting close behind on the love seat.

D'Wayne's family photos were lined atop the black piano. An antique cedar chest functioned as one of the coffee tables while six of Kojo's original oil paintings adorned one side of the wall. Patrons lounged in the nearby old-fashioned high-back chairs, munching on Casper's breakfast bagels and pastries. Banging on the keys, Wellington mimicked Jamie Foxx's imitation of Stevie Wonder. She fell on her side with laughter, which was exactly what he'd hoped for, a woman with flexibility and a sense of humor. Just like Jada.

"I'm Wellington Jones, and you are?" Wellington passionately pressed his moist lips on the back of her hand.

"Simone Smith. Your pleasure." The gentleness of her glimpse lingered.

Joining Simone on the love seat, Wellington noticed her plump thigh felt nice and soft against his. Her voluptuous figure resembled Jill Scott's. Simone's cleavage was speaking to his tongue. How she packed all those goodies into a tank top should qualify for *The Guinness Book of World Records*. "I know I'm not supposed to ask, but how old are you?"

Simone looked directly into his eyes. "Old enough to make my own decisions, work a nine-to-five, and pay my own bills. What you really want to know is if I'm free, single, and available for a date Friday night."

Well, she certainly wasn't shy. And at the moment, she

was engulfing his senses. Simone's mouth was twice as wide as Jada's. So wide that when she laughed, he verified she had all thirty-two teeth and her tonsils. Thankfully, the guys were too far away to hear her comment. He'd ask her out, but not so soon. Wellington was enjoying the chase. "I've seen you at yoga."

Simone snapped her fingers and nodded. "Right. Right. That's where I've seen you. You look different in regular clothes. Sexy. But different." Simone leaned her head back on the cushion, elongating her neck and awakening The Ruler.

No woman had managed to conjure up a tingling sensation since Jada. Hopefully Simone was on her way to and not from yoga. "Are you going to class today?"

Simone's succulent lip movements made his saliva glands overreact as she mouthed a simple, "Yes."

Fortunately, The GAP store across the street opened early. He refused to miss out on sealing a date with Simone. Wellington held his breath to control his breathing pattern and slow down his heartbeat. Exhaling, he asked, "How old did you say you were?" He was thirty-nine, almost forty, and she appeared at least fifteen years his junior.

She scooted to the edge of the cushion and said, "I didn't." Simone moved until her face was so close Wellington inhaled the organic aroma of beans. "Thanks for the coffee. Hopefully, I'll see you in class. Peace and blessings, my beautiful black brother." If he responded, his mouth would touch her honey-covered, luscious lips. So he remained silent. Simone stood, zipped up her jacket, and sashayed out the door.

Wellington remained seated on the love seat, allowing Simone enough time to walk across the street, down the block, and up the stairs to class. On his way out, he waved goodbye to the guys.

"You're leaving already? You just got here," Rich said.

"Yeah, man." If he stayed, Rich would engage him in conversation about Simone and Socrates. Sometimes four hours whisked by talking about any and everything at the Jahva House. Meeting Simone was the best thing that had happened to Wellington since the birth of his son and his breakup with Jada. "Gotta go to class, man." Wellington laughed and jaywalked across Lakeshore to the GAP.

Chapter 6

What did the lonely do at Christmas?

The past four years Jada, Wellington, and Darius had spent Christmas together. One of the six annual times they pretended to be a family, celebrating each of their birthdays, and Mothers' and Fathers' Day. But this year was depressing. Once Wellington started dating Simone, Jada stopped making love to him, and that wasn't because he'd quit trying. Jada couldn't fathom being the other woman.

Simone's influence altered their holiday activities one hundred and eighty degrees. None of the stockings Jada had decorated would hang by Wellington's chimney, including his. Although she didn't want him, she'd never envisioned him with anyone else. She had imagined that if she remained single, he would, too.

Mama phoned and insisted she and Darius spend the holidays with Robert and her in Oakland. Another time Jada wished she'd followed her first instinct. Paying for a luggage cart at the Oakland International Airport and selecting a rental car from the premier isle were disheartening because until now, every year Wellington had picked them up and carried their bags. If it wasn't for Darius, Jada would have stayed in Los Angeles.

"Mommy, where's Daddy?" Darius dragged his red, blue, and green child-sized suitcase with the wheels facing up.

"He made other plans this year, sweetie." Thanks to Simone. She looked around. Too many happy people were on the plane, at the airport, and at the rental car pickup.

Darius tugged on her knee-length crimson sweater. "Let's call him!"

"We can call him later, honey." Jada said as they found their rental car and left the airport. "Mommy has some last-minute shopping to do, and the stores close at six o'clock today. So I'm going to drop you off at Grandma's." Jada wasn't anxious to tackle the task of wrestling with last-minute shoppers who would grab everything she stared at for more than fifteen seconds. Most of the time they didn't really want the item; they merely wanted first consideration.

"Why do you sound so sad, Mommy? I love you." Darius's eyes drooped, and his mouth curved downward as teardrops soaked into the Raiders jacket Robert bought for Darius's birthday.

Since Darius was in the backseat where his mama had insisted he would ride until the auto dealers made air bags safe enough for children to ride in the front—and couldn't see her face, Jada changed the inflection in her voice. "Mommy's not sad," she lied. "Would you like to see a giant Christmas tree tonight?" Jada beamed with excitement.

"Yes!" Darius's eyes lit up as he clapped.

Why could a child's sadness be eradicated in a matter of seconds but not an adult's? Over development of the billions of brain cells perhaps?

They soon reached Grandma's house. When Jada opened the door, Darius hopped out and ran up the stairs.

"How's our big boy?" Mama asked.

"Whatcha feedin' this rugrat? Miracle growth?" Robert

jokingly gave Darius a one-two punch to the ribs and tilted his chin. "Boy, looks like you been crying. Crying is for girls and sissies. Remember that." Robert straightened his back and asked Darius, "Are you a girl?"

"No! I'm not a girl." Darius stood like Robert.

"Are you a sissy?" Robert saluted Darius.

"No way!" Darius saluted back.

Mama said, "Robert, don't go filling Darius's head with nonsense. Boys have feelings, too."

"Hi, My Dear! I miss you. I love you." Darius hugged his grandma's neck and kissed her cheek. "I brought some cookies for Santa." He unzipped his suitcase and pulled out a huge bag of gingerbread cookies. "You got milk, My Dear?"

Robert snatched the brown bag. "I got milk, and now I have cookies."

Darius kept jumping and grabbing, but each time Robert held the bag higher.

"Mama sure is glad y'all came, baby." Mama embraced Jada and said, "Jazzmyne, Candice, and Terrell are in town. They're stopping by tomorrow for a little holiday cheer. Can you believe the wonderful weather we're having this Christmas Eve? Sixty-five degrees. Y'all come in. Robert, give the boy his cookies before they get all crumbled."

As fast as they had come outside, Mama and Robert must have been sitting at the window, waiting.

Jada thought about her friends, whom she would see tomorrow. Respectfully, Candice had stop divulging their secrets; but four years had gone by, and Terrell still hadn't married Candice. Every year she set a date, and every time Terrell had an excuse to change it before she mailed the invitations.

"Mama, I'm going to the mall. I'll be back."

"Okay, baby. We'll wait 'til you get back before we eat dinner."

Darius ran inside with his cookies. Mama and Robert followed.

Everything Jada wanted to purchase at the San Francisco FAO Schwartz—one of the world's largest toy stores, standing four stories high—was either sold out or the lines were too long. Deviating from her list, Jada shopped at Embarcadero Centers One, Two, and Three for presents. Jada found the perfect gift for Wellington, a crystal heart with a two-by-two glass mirror so whenever he looked at her heart, he could also see his heart. Straight, gay, and lesbian lovers cheerfully strolled along Market, Powell, and Embarcadero Streets, clinging to one another as Jada wrestled with the oversized packages. Children dressed in black and white with red ribbons and bow ties merrily sang carols while spectators gathered and listened, another group for Jada to maneuver around.

After tossing the neatly wrapped boxes on the backseat, Jada hurried to her mom's house to pick up Darius before sunset.

"What'd you do? Buy up the store?" Robert asked, taking several gifts.

"Of course not. Where's Darius?" Before Robert answered, Jada yelled, "Darius, honey, let's go!"

Darius came running with his black-and-silver jacket in hand.

"Mama, we'll be back in an hour. I promised Darius I'd take him to see the Christmas tree."

"One more hour won't hurt me, but Robert needs to eat a little something now," Mama said.

Darius pulled Jada's hand until they were out of the house. As they drove, he shared how his My Dear let him bake a cake and how it had sunk in the middle because he kept opening the oven door. Parking in Jack London Square's garage, Jada realized she was so preoccupied with her own thoughts, she hadn't listened very well to Darius. The giant tree near Barnes and Noble Bookstore stood so high all Darius said was, "Wow!" Then he raced, circling the pine branches until he was breathless. Catching his second wind, Darius pointed and said, "Mommy, look, there's Daddy."

Darius scurried over to Wellington and whom Jada presumed to be Simone. Wellington was giving the valet attendant in front of Scott's Restaurant a claim check for his car.

Jada's body felt weaker than it had the day she gave birth to Darius. This was the first time she'd seen Wellington with a date. *Oh, no, he was not bringing her over.* Divas didn't duck, dodge, run, or hide, so Jada instantly masked a phony smile.

Extending her hand, Jada said, "Darius, honey. Come to Mommy."

When Wellington embraced Jada, she lovingly rubbed her hand up and down the back of his trench coat. She even held on a little longer than usual. "It's so good to see you. Darius asked about you earlier."

Wellington nervously stepped back and said, "Jada, this is Simone Smith. Simone, this is Jada."

Introduction of the last name was a dead giveaway. Good. Wellington had no intentions of marrying Simone. She was cute and all, but it wouldn't hurt her to shed fifty pounds or more. What did Wellington see in Simone?

"Hi." Jada gave her best Colgate smile and extended her hand.

Simone stared at Jada from head to feet and back to her face, then said, "Ba, we'd better get going. I haven't given you your surprise yet." Simone slipped her arm inside Wellington's and turned away.

No she did not just call him ba!

"Yeah." Wellington bit his bottom lip, and puckered a kiss at Jada. Then he turned to Darius and said, "Daddy will see you tomorrow morning, fella. Take care of your mommy for me."

"Okay, Daddy. Love you," Darius said.

Wellington smiled at Darius, "I love you, too, son."

Whistling like Grandpa Robert had taught him, Darius spread his arms like a bird as he glided back to the tree.

Wellington looked at Jada and mouthed, "I love you, ba."

Oh, no. She was not going to be the joke of the day. Jada responded, "I love you, too," loud enough for Simone to know Jada could easily take Wellington away from her if she wanted. For the first time Jada realized she didn't have an endearing name for Wellington. As Simone turned around, Jada walked away. Her breath short-circuited like one of the bulbs on the pine tree, but who had noticed? Who cared? Ol' Saint Nick had dumped twelve tons of coal in her heart.

Chapter 7

A night plagued by insomnia and filled with sex left Wellington restless. Unlike Jada, Simone constantly tossed and turned in her sleep. Maybe she was still upset about him saying, "I love you, ba," to Jada. He'd never make that inconsiderate mistake again. Wellington gave up on tugging the king-sized covers, slipped into his pajamas, and made his way to Simone's couch. It was three o'clock in the morning. If he masturbated, that would knock him out for sure. After rubbing and stroking for ten minutes, he realized Simone had extracted all of his sap. The next four hours the flat-screen television watched him while he gazed at the ceiling, counting backward from a thousand and creating stock portfolios in his head.

Making his way to the shower, Wellington tiptoed, trying not to awaken Simone. The steamy water relaxed his muscles so much he wanted to tuck himself inside the comforter as if it were a sleeping blanket and take a nap, but there wasn't enough time. He'd promised to pick up his son early, and knowing Darius, he'd already opened all of his toys and was ready to go. Jada had probably stuffed the ripped Christmas paper and tattered boxes into hefty trash bags. In the midst of putting on his brown knee-length socks, Wellington stopped, retreated to Simone's guest bedroom, and closed the door.

As a family in the eyes of God, the last three years Wellington had led the prayer on Christmas morning reaffirming for Darius the true meaning. This year he knelt alone and prayed as if they were together. "Oh, Heavenly Father, we give praise to You on Your birthday. We thank You for Your many blessings throughout the year and especially today. Thanks for keeping us healthy and safe as we realize many families are mourning the loss of their loved ones. We ask that You let not their hearts be troubled. In light of the holiday spirit, Lord, our family gave generously to the Battered Women's Organization. We pray the season will be joyous for them. Please, Lord, bless them with the courage to love themselves, as You love them. Before we open our gifts, we pray that You open our minds and hearts with appreciation for each card and every present. Amen."

Wellington felt strange as he stood. He was full of praise, but the void in his heart could be filled by only one woman. Simone was still asleep, so he slipped on his brown slacks and his tan tapered—but not too tight—long-sleeved sweater that vaguely outlined his biceps, chest, and abs. He picked up his keys and headed to Jada's mother's house. When Jada opened the door, Wellington expected the heartbeat in his chest to drop below his waist. Instead, his heart skipped a beat.

Every Christmas since they had met, Jada had changed stunning outfits at least three times Christmas Day. Last year, nighttime was his favorite because they had dressed up for each other, danced under the moonlight on his patio, and then skinny-dipped in his heated pool.

Today her eyes were noticeably red and puffy. Her silky strands of hair were uncombed and tangled together. The only time he'd seen her in pajamas was when she wore his top with her legs exposed, or his bottoms, showcasing her beautiful breasts.

"Hey, come on in. Darius has been waiting for you." Jada closed the door and walked to the rear. The red-and-blue plaid pajamas were too big and too wrinkled.

Darius raced by, bumping into Jada. "Hey! Daddy is here!" Boing. Boing. He jumped as if he were on a pogo stick.

"Hey, son! Looks like Santa's elves worked overtime this year." He hugged and kissed Darius, then peeped to see if Jada was coming back. Instead, Wellington saw Robert.

"What's up, Homey? Merry Christmas. Jada give you your gifts?"

Flatly, Wellington answered, "Naw, not yet."

"Well, we can take care of that," Robert said as the white ball of his Santa's cap bounced off of his right ear. "Have a sit-down."

"Merry Christmas, Wellington," Mrs. Tanner said, handing him the packages. She was cordial but didn't say much to him this year, and she didn't call him son.

Wellington glanced at his watch, wondering if Simone had called, since he'd conveniently turned off his phone. "Wow, four presents."

"Open mine first, Daddy." Darius shoved the decorated box in his lap and sat at his feet.

Unraveling the package, Wellington looked toward the back of the room again. "Hey, just what I wanted. A remote control car."

"Yep, just like mine!" Darius scooted to his remote and said, "Put your car on the floor, Daddy. Let's race!" Darius's car flipped over Wellington's and kept rolling.

Wellington also received another nice sweater from Mrs. Tanner, a Raiders cap and scarf from Robert, and a crystal heart with a two-by-two inch square mirror plate from Jada. He knew Jada had an explanation he probably wouldn't get.

"It's almost ten; we'd better get going. Darius, put on your jacket. Go give your mom a kiss for me and tell her you'll be back by six."

"Okay, Daddy." Darius zipped and came back. "I'm ready!"

No return message from Jada. Why did Wellington feel as if he'd done something wrong? Wellington cruised back to Simone's place.

"Daddy, where were you this morning?" Darius asked.

Wellington looked in his rearview mirror. "Stop kicking the back of the seat. I was at Simone's, son." Darius handsomely wore the blue fleece outfit Wellington had given him before Christmas.

"Is Simone and Mommy friends?"

"No, son. They're not."

Darius kicked the seat again, then stopped. "Daddy, what's a home wrecker?"

"Whoa, you're too young for that conversation, fella."

"Do you still love Mommy?"

"Of course I do." Wellington turned and glimpsed at Darius.

Darius leaned forward. "Do you still love me?"

"What kind of question is that? I will always love you." Wellington looked at his son again.

Darius sat back and asked with teary eyes, "Did I do something wrong, Daddy?"

"I don't know. Did you?" Wellington's forehead wrinkled as he exited Interstate 680 into Danville.

"I think I made Mommy sad, because when I walk into the room, her eyes don't light up no more."

Wellington took a deep breath and pulled into the nearest gas station. He sat in the back of his four-by-four with Darius. "Mommy just has a lot on her mind, and it has nothing to do with you." Taking his time, Wellington talked and listened intently, giving Darius his undivided attention.

"I'm holding in my tears because Grandpa Robert said crying is for sissies and girls." Darius blinked repeatedly.

"Son, there's a big difference between crying and being a crybaby. Everybody's got to cry. And it's okay to cry sometimes; just don't cry all the time." Once Wellington had answered all of Darius's questions, he dried Darius's eyes and changed the subject before he became emotional, too. "Let me see your muscle pose," he said as he returned to the driver's seat.

Darius grunted, balled up his fists, and threw up his arms.

"That's my boy." Wellington drove off and said, "You're going to need that strength to open the rest of your presents." Simone had gone overboard with buying gifts for Darius. Even Simone's mother agreed.

When they arrived at Simone's house, Darius ran inside and slid under the tree, almost tipping it over.

"Well, hello, Darius. Merry Christmas." Simone poured hot chocolate into mugs with real bells strung on the stained-glass candy cane handles. "Go ahead. They're all yours." Simone sat about six feet to Darius's right and snapped pictures with her computerized digital camera.

"Wow!" Darius unwrapped a hand-held video game, stuffed animals, an identical remote control car to the one Santa gave him, a helmet for which Simone had bought a bike and in-line skates, and more. . . .

"Next year invest some of that money in stocks for him," Wellington said.

"That's your job, Mr. Investor. I work for the phone company, remember. I just want Darius to have fun. Don't you think we should have one of our own?" Simone's eyes became hazy.

"I already have stocks." He knew where Simone was going, but Wellington wasn't ready for another baby. But one day he'd love to have a precious little girl. And if a guy ever broke her heart, he'd have to answer to him.

"I mean a child," Simone said, picking up the mugs.

"Oh, let's wait a while," Wellington insisted.

"Darius, wouldn't you like to have a baby brother or sister next Christmas?" Simone asked.

Darius focused on his hand-held computer. "No girls. And only if Santa brings my baby brother his own toys."

Wellington laughed.

"Well, think about it." Simone brushed her black velvet pants against Wellington's shoulder as she carried the empty cups into the kitchen.

"And don't try to sneak one in on me." Wellington stood, stretched, and yawned.

Simone yelled from the kitchen, "I am not Melanie or Jada. I've already told you what you need to do."

"Don't mention that in front of my son, Simone." Wellington stood, walked into the kitchen, and stopped directly behind Simone. He wrapped his arms around her, squeezed her breasts, gently kissed the nape of her neck and said, "You're my baby. And if you really want a child, let's start making plans."

Simone faced Wellington and pressed her lips against his. Her eyes brightened then shifted focusing on his left eye then his right and back again like she had just received the best Christmas present of her kife. "I love you Wellington Jones." She rested her head on his chest.

Wrong choice of words. Wellington instantly thought of when Jada used to speak those words to him. He slapped Simone on her butt. "Yeah, I know. Look, I'm going to take Darius to the park and teach him to ride his bike."

"Well, am I not invited?" Simone asked placing the clean mugs in the cabinet.

"Don't take it personal. I need to spend some quality time with my son."

Simone raised her eyebrows.

Wellington squinted and said, "He *is* my son, Simone." He returned to the living room. "Son, get your jacket and your helmet. Daddy's going to teach you how to ride your bike."

"Yes!" Darius dropped the remote to his car in the middle of the floor.

Pointing at the object Wellington said, "Oh, no you don't buddy."

Darius placed the controller under the Christmas tree beside the car and raced outside. Looking back at Simone, Wellington easily lifted Darius's bike with one hand and said, "I'll call you later." Then he walked out of Simone's front door.

After three hours at the park and two more hours at the restaurant, Darius slept all the way home.

Wellington carried Darius to the door. Simone needed to leave that paternity test nonsense alone or she was going to find herself alone.

"Can't hang, huh. I'll take him," Robert said, laughing.

"It's okay, I can carry him." Maybe Wellington would have a chance to speak with Jada.

"Jada's not here, man. Ruby took her out. Said she needed some fresh air. But they should be back soon. You can wait a while if you'd like."

"Oh, that's okay. I just wanted to know how she liked my gift," Wellington lied, handing his son to Robert.

"You mean the last one under the tree. Unless she has X-ray vision, I'd say she doesn't know yet." Robert laid Darius's head on his shoulder.

Wellington nodded and walked away. "That's cool. Merry Christmas, man."

The Whispers' voices resonated through his surround-sound auto speakers as Wellington drove home. "People really need one another: man, woman, boy, girl, sister, and brother . . ." A year ago after their dip in the pool, he had been cuddled in front his fireplace with Jada listening to their favorite holiday song by The Stylistics, "When You've Got Love, It's Christmas All Year Long." This year didn't feel like Christmas at all.

Chapter 8

Jada Diamond Tanner discovered love happened just like shit. Unexpectedly. For the past year, after Wellington met Simone, she and her son, Darius, had managed quite well by themselves. She had two trustworthy baby-sitters—Candice lived on the other side of town, and Jazzmyne Jones resided in her neighborhood—and visits from her mother allowed a decent social life. Mama traveled to Los Angeles monthly and stayed one or two weeks each time. Mama would spoil Darius so badly it took Jada another week to retrain him. Whenever Darius asked for anything, Mama answered, "Yes, my dear." Darius learned how to change things to his advantage before he even understood the effect. As a toddler, Darius had begun calling Mama, My Dear.

School started at eight-fifteen, and the drive was less than ten miles. Jada had Darius dressed, fed, and out the door by seven-thirty. Jada glanced at her baby in the passenger seat. Sporting a fresh low haircut, he was handsomely dressed in beige khaki pants, brown loafer shoes, a white polo-style shirt, and a navy blazer.

Focusing on the road ahead, Jada asked, "So, are you excited about your first day of school, sweetie?"

"Um, I don't know," he said, hunching his shoulder pads higher. "They got girls?" Darius's bright eyes widened and shifted to the corners as he mischievously bit his bottom lip.

Tapping her brakes, Jada glimpsed down at him. "Now, Darius. You're going to school to get an education, honey. Don't worry about the girls." He was only five. Jada had figured girls wouldn't be a distraction for at least another eight years.

"Daddy said I should worry about them." Darius nodded, looked up at his mother, and froze. His brown eyes lingered in silence. When Jada parked in front of the building, Darius pointed and said, "Wow! That's my new school! I like this one. No more preschool crybabies. May I go play, Mommy? Ooh, may I?" His seat belt sprung into its socket.

Since other kids were playing, Jada said, "Sure, sweetie. But don't leave out of my sight."

Switching the radio to her favorite station, KJLH, Jada heard Cliff and Janine interviewing Karen E. Quinones Miller. Her new book, *I'm Telling,* had recently been released. "Well, Ms. Miller can tell all she wants, but I'm *not,*" Jada remarked, then whispered, "Some things are better left unsaid."

A black Mercedes sedan parked directly behind her car. Jada adjusted the rearview mirror, looking first at her dazzling hazel-colored eyes which flattered her ebony complexion, then at the man exiting the Mercedes. Running her hand alongside her head, behind her ear, and across her neck, Jada gathered her long, dark hair in front of her right breast and said, "Ah sooky sooky." Now that was a chocolate superman, at least he looked the part. A little girl sat patiently and waited until he opened her door. Hopefully, he treated his spouse as well. As stunning as he was, a woman or two had to be in the picture. Now, how committed was he? That was what she intended to find out. Jada cracked her front windows. Suddenly, it was too damn hot, so she pressed the rear buttons, lowered all four windows, and centered herself, using a yoga technique to clear her mind.

"Thank you, Daddy," the little girl said while flattening the pleats in her blue, black, and white plaid skirt.

Jada settled down and waited until they were inside. She checked her makeup, then hopped out of the car. Eight o'clock sharp. The play area was swarming with kids.

"Darius, honey, let's go inside." She also gestured for Darius in case he couldn't hear her calling him above the cheerful noises.

"A few more minutes, Mom." His little hands clung to the monkey bars.

Jada responded, "*Now.*"

When Darius let go, his feet hit the chipped wood. He squatted, paused, and then trotted to her. She was definitely going to enroll him in drama. Jada brushed his jacket and pants and grabbed his slim hand, almost completely covering it with her long fingers.

Inside the hallway, Jada stopped within speaking distance of the man she'd noticed outside. The gap between him and the competition standing behind him was just enough to slide in with Darius.

Jada sang, "*Good morning.*"

Implementing flirting technique number one, Jada smiled. The woman, now to her left, cheesed a phony grin, but Jada beamed as though she were posing for the cover of *Essence* magazine. Keeping her focus, Jada thanked God for peripheral vision. Luring method number two was her peek-a-boo glance. His up-close image did not disappoint. Maintaining her smile, Jada said, "You have a lovely daughter." Then she pretended to straighten Darius's clothes. Jada knew flattering him would have scored a field goal, but complimenting his daughter was a guaranteed touchdown.

Facing in her direction, he said, "Why, thank you, and good

morning. My beautiful daughter, Ashlee, is starting kindergarten."

Another key factor Jada had learned was not to correct a man. If he spoke the obvious, she'd let it slide since she was interested in getting to know him better. Of course Ashlee was starting kindergarten. Either that or he was in the wrong line.

Exuding confidence, he said, "My name is Lawrence Anderson."

Oh, damn. He sounded exactly like Hawk on *Spenser for Hire*. Not remembering the last time she'd seen the TV show, that voice was still unforgettable. Nice smile. Wide. Perfect teeth. He must have used whitening strips, because God didn't bless any man with teeth so marvelous. The waves in his voice melodically rolled and faded gently into her eardrums.

Breathe in. Breathe out. At thirty-nine, her snapper was snapping at practically every man that appeared halfway decent and had a pulse. Jada twitched to suppress the sensation. She'd grown tired of casual sex. Occasional escapades with her vibrators were hardly enough to satisfy her growing appetite, but being a single parent definitely limited her sexual activities. Children were very impressionable, and she never wanted to give Darius the wrong idea about women.

"Hi, Lawrence. I'm Jada Diamond Tanner, and this is my son, Darius Jones. He's starting kindergarten, too." After scoring a touchdown, Jada went for the extra point. "By the way, that's a fabulous tie you're wearing. Very tranquil." The compliment was meant for the sexy tight ass she pictured concealed under his jacket, but as a true diva, she was rarely straightforward.

"Hey, thanks." Lawrence straightened his tie and flashed his pearly whites.

Prim and proper, Jada reached into her lavender backpack purse and retrieved her gold card holder. Snapping it open, she removed her black business card and gracefully handed it to Lawrence. The diamond logo sparkling prominently in the upper left corner cast a twinkle in his smile.

Everything was in place for Jada to launch her company tomorrow. Six years had been a great sabbatical and sufficient time to secure the perfect office space inside the KPMG building in downtown Los Angeles. At an angle, the skyscraper appeared as flat as a platinum credit card, although bronze was more the color.

"Impressive." Lawrence reciprocated and extended his one-by-two pallid card on stock paper.

A glance at his card was all Jada needed. Delicately she tilted her head and commented, "Attorney, huh. That's interesting. Anderson, Anderson, *and* Anderson?"

Standing proud like a U.S. Marine with his chest swelled, he replied, "That's right. Three generations."

Was he blushing? Wow. Trés. That reminded Jada of her favorite tequila, the drink she'd ordered at the bar in San Francisco the night she'd met Wellington.

"Does your company have a firm on retainer?" Lawrence asked.

Okay. There goes that delightful grin again. He'd probably won lots of clients with his charming ass. Lawrence's suggestive influence rescued Jada from herself. When was she going to let go of Wellington? Did he think of her as often?

"Yes, and thank you," Jada lied. She was not mixing business with pleasure. The door was slammed shut, and she hoped Lawrence wouldn't inquire any further.

Interviews for legal representation were being held next week, and her primary staff was already hired. Ginger was twenty and the youngest division director, and Zen was the oldest, thirty-five. Miranda and Heather were twenty-five and thirty, respectively. Jazzmyne, Wellington's full sister—who was at one time believed to be his half sister—and one of Jada's best friends next to Candice, was hired to handle public relations for Black Diamonds. Theo. Yes, Theo was destined to be exactly like *Huggy Low Down*. Huggy could dig up more dirt than a bulldozer could shovel in a week. Then he spilled his guts over the air during Donnie Simpson's morning show with Chris Paul and David Haines. Theo's job was to thoroughly check out her competitors and report back to her. Occasionally she might hire him to get the inside scoop on folk for personal reasons. Maybe Mr. Anderson required a background investigation.

"How about dinner tonight? You can tell me all about Black Diamonds." Lawrence held the card in one hand and pulled Ashlee's spiraled curls back out of her creamy-colored face with the other.

"How about lunch instead? I'm having dinner with Darius to celebrate his first day of school." Conveniently omitting Wellington's name, Jada glowed. Actually, he was flying into town to take them to Darius's favorite place, Dave & Buster's, the restaurant with an arcade and pool tables.

Darius tugged on her purple sarong. "And Daddy, too, Mommy. Don't forget Daddy's coming."

Jada's sarong came untied. Lawrence's eyes widened; then he covered Ashlee's eyes and stared over and beyond Jada's shoulder. Quickly Jada caught and retied the ends. Looking at Darius, she said, "Be careful, honey."

"Sorry, Mom." Darius tied the knot in Jada's sarong tighter.

Uncovering Ashlee's eyes, Lawrence said, "Lunch it is." He laughed at Darius and then smiled at Jada.

"My mommy is taking me to dinner tonight, too. We're going to Dave & Buster's," Ashlee said, poking her tongue at Darius.

"So. That's where we're—"

Jada lightly jerked Darius's jacket and pierced a glare into his eyes. Darius tucked his lips in as if trying to swallow them and looked away. Not believing "Spare the rod. Spoil the child" was logical, Jada never beat him. She'd reared him to behave with just one die-hard stare.

"Ooh, oooh," Darius sang and turned to Ashlee. "You want to see my leaf? My mommy gave it to me this morning. I'm going to Duke University."

Ashlee frowned. "What's that?"

Jada looked up at Lawrence and resumed their conversation, "The View? Is that okay?"

"Malibu?" Lawrence asked.

"Yes, Pacific Coast Highway," Jada clarified, "down from Gladstone's."

"Then, you mean Pier View Café and Cantina. How's noon?" Lawrence asked.

The old familiar sound of the bell rang throughout the school. "Fine." As soon as the classroom door opened, Jada clutched Darius's hand and attempted to escort him inside.

A stout, friendly-looking light-skinned woman with round cheeks and eyeglasses blocked her entrance. "I want each of my students to line up according to height on the left side of the hallway. And their parents on the right."

Jada felt as if she were back in elementary school.

"This is so I don't have to repeat myself. I'm Mrs. Allen. Welcome to St. Boniface. Students, I want you to quietly enter the room and take your assigned seats. If you can't find your name, *silently* stand in front of the room." She pressed her pointing finger against her pale lips. Peeping over her narrow silver-framed glasses, she scanned the line of parents and said, "I'll see each of you on Back-to-School night. This is my class. Your children are now my students. Have a good day." Then she closed her door.

Jada turned to Lawrence and said, "I guess she told us. I'll see you at noon." Her walk-away model twist—one foot directly in front of the other—with a subtle jiggle in her booty, left the most intelligent man dumbfounded. Jada chuckled to keep from crying. Her baby had started school.

* * *

Lawrence requested a table for two outside. Jada's size twelve shapely hips leaned against the wooden rail as she watched the white sand wash away with the undercurrents and return with the waves. The seascape at The View was breathtaking. That was what Jada and Wellington had called the café for years, and she refused to change their nickname for Lawrence's sake.

Once seated, they ordered two strawberry lemonades, then Lawrence asked, "How do you feel about love at first sight?"

Jada rested her vision on his long, thick fingers—hopefully a good sign of what he packed in storage. She studied the tips, base, and middle sections. There was a direct correlation between the shape of a man's fingers and his penis.

"I used to believe in love. Now I'm a firm believer in happiness. Love comes and goes, but I can be happy forever if I choose. It's all in my attitude." Jada opened both of her hands.

"Okay. Then, I'll admit. I was happy as a kid on Christmas Day when you stood next to me." Lawrence laughed.

Of all the holidays in the year, why did he have to mention Christmas? Damn, his sex appeal divided her attention, so Jada eased on her sunglasses. Lawrence's mannerisms were fluent, suave, and inviting, three positive signs of an experienced lover. Not to mention his kissable lips that always displayed a hint of moisture. "Why? You don't know anything about me." Jada stared out over the Pacific to calm her out-of-control hormones which were yelling, "Charge!" A group of youngsters trotted onto the beach. The tall redhead wearing a yellow bikini carried the volleyball.

"Oh, on the contrary. I can tell you're a loving mother. You work out. You eat right or at a minimum, well. You dress impeccably. Your lavender bodysuit matches your shoes, and your purple wrap has highlights that match your top. *Most* importantly, you're well groomed. Manicure. Pedicure. Your anatomy is delightful, and you have long, silky hair that I'd love to—"

"Yeah, but those are external qualities—"

"But it's a great place to start," Lawrence said.

The waitress interrupted, "Excuse me. Are you ready to order?" Lawrence gestured toward Jada.

Jada looked up at the waitress and said, "I'll have the crab Louie."

Lawrence said, "Make that two;" then he smiled at Jada.

"So tell me about Lawrence."

"Okay. We can focus on me if you prefer."

Jada learned Lawrence was going through a divorce. He claimed his biggest mistake was marrying a woman who needed more time than he had to offer. He had thought if he bought his wife the home of her choice, lavished her with expensive gifts, and gave her full access to a six-figure joint bank account, that would adequately supplement the small amount of time he spent with her. According to Lawrence's side of the story, in the beginning Ashley had been the perfect wife. Later she'd begun nitpicking about every little thing: "How late are you working tonight? Why won't you be home for dinner? Where are you going? When will you be back? Who else is going?"

Raising an eyebrow, Jada made a mental note. She nodded, interjecting an occasional, "I see," or "um hum." She listened intently, knowing it was best, especially when dealing with lawyers. The well-tanned redhead on the beach had just spiked the ball. It bounced off the blocker's arms and landed in the ocean.

Lawrence continued. *He* figured it was time for them to have a child. *He* felt that should have been perfect, too. But it still wasn't enough for Ashley. *He* even named their daughter Ashlee in honor of his soon-to-be ex-wife. In the gospel according to Lawrence, that seemed to have made matters worse. When Ashley firmly stated she wanted out of their marriage, Lawrence said he thought she was kidding, saying, "What woman in her right mind would walk away from a good man?" With his hectic schedule, Lawrence admitted, no judge would grant him custody of Ashlee unless he called in a favor, and that wouldn't be to either of their advantage because he'd finally admitted he was a workaholic. The shocker had come when Ashley told him they were moving to Texas after Ashlee graduated from kindergarten.

Jada nodded and said, "Behind every challenge there's an opportunity, if you want it." Jada told Lawrence about her vision for her company. How she'd ended up branching out on her own because Melanie had become her boss. "Black Diamonds may have never evolved had it not been for Melanie. And I would not be sitting here with such a handsome gentleman." Fine as hell was what she wanted to say. Snap. Snap. His tinted, lightweight, rimless eyeglasses made Lawrence look even more distinguished. Lady C did a somersault between her thighs, so Jada crossed her feet at the ankles and cheesed. Lunch with Lawrence was Jada's one-year anniversary of celibacy.

"I know you're the woman for me. We're equally yoked. Look, you're a busy woman. Right? You already have a child. You own your own company. So instantly we have a lot in common. Unlike my first wife, who was exclusively a housewife, you're a perfect fit." Earlier he'd vowed never to marry another woman who was incompatible.

"Far from it. Besides, you're not even divorced," Jada said, turning to watch the volleyball game. Obviously the redhead was a professional. Every time someone was successful enough to block her serve, instead of the ball crossing back over the net, it landed in the water. Her opponents appeared tired of swimming to get the ball.

The waitress had finally arrived with their order. "Sorry for the delay. Would you like anything else?"

Jada shook her head as Lawrence responded, "No, thanks." Lawrence reached for Jada's hand, bowed his head, and said grace. Several moments later he said, "Amen." He sampled, seasoned, then immediately started eating his salad while picking up the conversation as if they'd never been interrupted.

"Men know these things. We don't have to spend years deciding whether to marry. It's like buying shoes."

Jada redirected her attention toward Lawrence. His goatee reminded her of the one Wellington had recently shaved. Damn, he smelled edible. His navy designer suit wore him well, and his mocha brown complexion heated Jada more than Mother Nature's golden circle percolating in the sky.

Curiously, Jada asked, "Shoes?"

"Yes. For example, I'm six-foot-five, two-ten, and wear a size fifteen." Lawrence flashed her that smile again.

If Lady C didn't stop acting like a 49ers cheerleader at the Super Bowl, Jada was going to need a chastity belt to put her ass on lockdown. Concentrating on Lawrence's comment, Jada nodded. His size was good, but the feet had fooled her once. Actually, twice.

"Now, a woman will know she wears a size nine, but will ask to try on an eight and a half *and* a nine. They pick men the same way. Always unsure of what they really want. Never in tune with what they need." Lawrence shook his head. "They buy a pair of high heels knowing their feet are going to hurt. They date a man knowing he has all the traits for warranting four legs instead of two."

"Ha, ha, ha. That's a good one," said the man seated at the next table.

Two of the kids had resorted to swimming since they were in the water so often.

Lowering his voice, Lawrence said, "Now, you see a man, he'll buy that comfortable size fifteen every time. Why? Because a man knows what he needs and likes, no ifs, ands, or buts. That's until a woman convinces him otherwise; then it's downhill from there. Because then you have two people who don't know what the hell they want."

"Brother, I wish I would have overheard this conversation before I got married." Patting Lawrence's back, the stranger said, "Good luck, man."

Ignoring the intruder and staring directly at Lawrence, Jada quietly said, "And your point is?" Maybe they were a good match since he didn't hesitate to answer this last question.

"Closing argument." Lawrence smiled seductively. "You are going to be my next wife. I already know. Just like you already know if we're going to be intimate. The truth." Lawrence raised one eyebrow and lowered the other simultaneously. "You already know. Don't you?" Then he ate the last of his salad.

A smirk crossed Jada's face. Lady C gave her a high five.

"Case dismissed. Pick out your wedding dress. And as far as Darius's father is concerned, he must have been a *fool* to let you go."

Jada sharply responded, "Foolish, maybe. But he's nobody's fool." Jada looked at the waitress. "Check, please."

After one year of dating—only one month after his divorce was final—Lawrence formally proposed. Jada accepted, but wasn't ready to set a date. Since well-established men remarried much faster than women of the same caliber, she wasn't surprised Lawrence was serious. His offer was her opportunity to forget her past. Jada never wanted to feel that pain—the way Wellington had hurt her—ever again. A walking zombie, there had been a time she couldn't eat, sleep, or think. She'd definitely be happy with Lawrence. How long? That was a question she simply could not answer.

Chapter 9

February 14. Relieved Mama had agreed to fly to Los Angeles and baby-sit Darius, Jada moisturized her skin with shea butter. Robert refused to travel on anything that left the ground, so he had stayed in Oakland. Exposing her legs and covering her breasts, Jada eased into her black, brown, and tan leopard dress that stopped midway between her hips and knees. No stockings. Form fitting. Long sleeves. A dab of perfume caressed her ankles, wrists, cleavage, and behind each ear. The three-way mirror cast a gorgeous reflection from every angle.

When her phone rang at five-thirty that evening, Jada hurried, taking the shortcut, crawling across her bed to answer before Mama or Darius could. "Hello."

"Hi, ba. Happy Valentine's Day." Wellington's sensuous tone tingled her nerve endings.

Chill bumps covered her butter-smooth skin quicker than microwave popcorn bursting through the hull. "Thanks. Same to you." Sitting on the edge of her bed, Jada crossed her legs. The eight-by-ten family portrait she'd taken with Wellington and Darius was removed from her dresser and stored somewhere in the garage along with her other photos with and of Wellington. One eleven-by-fourteen of Darius, Wellington, Mama, Robert, and Jada remained in the family room.

"You received my delivery?" Wellington asked.

Three bunches of red roses each accompanied by a single yellow rose was overkill. One arrangement would have sent the same message, reminding her of the night they fell in love. "Yes, and thank you." After Jada started dating Lawrence, she'd stopped sending Wellington gifts: birthday, Valentine's, and Christmas. The only day she acknowledged was the one she had every reason not to: Fathers' Day.

"Did you receive my invitation?" Jada asked, fumbling through her jewelry box for a pair of earrings that wouldn't make her a hoochie look-alike. Lawrence had scratched Wellington's name off the guest list, saying he didn't want any man she'd slept with at his wedding. It wasn't just his day, so Jada had personally mailed Wellington's invitation. If Wellington showed up, she'd blame the wedding coordinator.

"Yes." Wellington was so quiet, Jada pressed the down arrow lowering the volume on her television. Judge Mablean was trying to convince Kendra not to divorce Kevin because he was good man.

Jada couldn't go wrong with diamonds, so she braced the phone between her shoulder and ear, inserting the three-carat stud. What she really wanted were the huge solitaires Oprah was wearing in her ears and around her neck. "So, are you coming to my wedding?"

Wellington sighed. "Maybe. Not sure I can handle seeing you marry someone else."

So now he had a problem. There hadn't been a problem when he'd introduced Simone to her. Or when Simone had come to her house in L.A. with him to pick up Darius. Jada had started to make Simone wait outside, but bitterness wasn't characteristic of a genuine diva. "You can bring Simone."

Bring her ass so she could see Lawrence's fine ass. Would Kendra go on and give poor Kevin a chance? He seemed like one of the few brothers who apologized from his heart. Jada wished she had the number to Judge Mablean's chambers so she could talk some sense into Kendra.

"That's not the point," Wellington softly responded.

"You love Simone, right?" Jada was confirming what she'd already known.

"Yes." Wellington became silent again.

"And I love Lawrence, so both of us should be happy and happy for each other. Let me ask you a personal question. Where did you meet Simone?" At forty-three, Jada realized Simone was slightly more than half her age. "The truth or don't answer the question."

Suddenly, Wellington spoke louder. "What difference does that make?"

"None. I'll talk with you later. Goodbye." Jada hung up the phone because that was the third time he'd evaded the question. The first time he'd changed the subject. The second time he'd pretended he didn't hear her. "Five. Four. Three. Two."

Jada answered, "Hello," as if the caller ID hadn't displayed his name.

Wellington said, "I met her at a coffee shop in Oakland, and she's in my yoga class."

What! "I don't believe you. Yoga? How long have you been going?" Jada switched ears because the friction irritated her left earlobe. She should have waited to put on her earrings.

He politely answered, "Since you moved to L.A."

Jada's voice escalated. "You mean since I told you I was going to yoga? And you probably went to my instructor on Lakeshore. Didn't you?" Jada tossed her long curls behind her shoulders.

Clearing his throat, Wellington said, "Yeah, something like that. What about you and Lawrence?"

Jada knew he'd ask and couldn't wait to answer. "On Darius's first day of school." Uh! Why had she told him about yoga?

"You mean the same day, four years ago, when I flew to L.A. and took you guys to Dave & Busters?"

Right about now, Wellington was either rubbing his head or pacing the floor. Jada casually responded, "Yeah, something like that."

"That's cool. But you know our feelings for each other run deeper. I have a question. Can I make love to you one last time before you get married?"

She wanted to say hell yeah. "No. We tried that for four years after Darius was born, remember?"

"Yeah, but you only set a date because you're trying to prove you don't love me when you know you do. I told you. I used poor judgment and made a mistake. I'm not like that anymore."

Mistakes. Plus, his begging and pleading hadn't made him leave Simone. He probably called her Princess or something close to that. "I know. It's not you. It's me. I have to do this for me. Listen, I'm running late. Lawrence will be here shortly. Thanks for calling."

Enunciating every syllable, he said, "I love you, ba. For real."

Oh, really. A couple of please, please, please, pleases, a wig, and a cape and he could go on stage as James Brown. She probably didn't cross his mind when he was eating Simone's pussy the way he used to eat hers.

Mama knocked on the door and said, "Jada, Lawrence is here."

Yes! Kendra saved her marriage; now Jada could turn off the T.V. "I've got to go. Call me tomorrow." Prancing into the living room, Jada asked, "Where is he?"

Acting as though he had a secret he was itching to tell, Darius said, "He's outside, Mom."

"Come here, sweetie. Give your mother a hug." Jada embraced Darius, but didn't have to bend far because he was nine years old and almost her height.

Mama said, "Have a good time. We won't wait up for you."

"Have fun, Mom. Hurry." Darius pushed her toward the door.

Jada tilted her head and waited. "Well, I guess I have to open the door myself." She pressed down on the gold lever. A big red helium-inflated heart crossed the door seal. The doorway was stacked to her hips with enough gifts to host a Valentine's Day sidewalk sale. Lawrence leaned against the black stretch limo, holding a dozen roses as if the four dozen the florist had delivered to her earlier weren't sufficient. Jada had hidden Wellington's flowers in Mama's bedroom just in case Lawrence came inside. Maybe the former Mrs. Anderson was hiding Lawrence's flowers from her man, too. The driver moved the eloquently wrapped packages indoors.

Anything Jada didn't want to know, she didn't ask, so she never inquired about Ashley, before or after Lawrence's divorce. If he volunteered information about his ex-wife, she listened but didn't comment. When his ex-wife moved away, he handled it well. The first six months, he flew to Dallas every other weekend, taking Darius with him. Later, he started sending for Ashlee to visit them.

Smiling all the time, Lawrence was reserved, mellow, and nonchalant. His photographic memory made him one of the best civil attorneys in California. "Happy Valentine's Day, honey. You look great." Lawrence smiled, kissed Mama on the cheek, and massaged Darius's head as if he were juicing an orange. Darius frowned and stumped to his bedroom. Lawrence laughed at Darius and said, "Kids." Then he hugged Jada's waist. "We'd better get going if we're going to be on time for our dinner reservations. Bye, Mrs. Tanner."

"Where are we going for dinner?" Jada asked, holding

her hemline, preventing her mini from becoming micro while scooting along the air-conditioned limo seat.

"No questions. Just enjoy the element of surprise." Placing a dissolvable mint strip on his tongue, Lawrence knelt before Jada. He spread her thighs, pushed her thong to the side, and held his tongue against her clit. His lips surrounded hers; then he blew cool air through his mouth three times.

"Damn, that feels refreshing," Jada moaned.

Licking or sucking would unpleasantly alter the sensation, so he slowly glided his tongue into her vagina. When Jada grabbed the back of his head, he stopped and sat next to her. Lawrence tilted her flute and poured the champagne. "A toast to us." He tapped Jada's glass, kissed her lips, and said, "I love you."

Jada gazed into his eyes and listened to the melody in her heart. "I love you, too," she responded.

The restaurant host greeted them at the door. Jada laughed and pointed at the huge disco ball centered over the small dance floor. Every table was covered with a red cloth. The women were dressed in red from head to toe: shoes, purses, and outfits. The men wore black tuxedos.

"Aren't we a little out of place?" People were either gawking or admiring their attire. Lawrence's suit and collarless shirt were black, but he didn't have on a bow tie.

"Mr. Anderson, your family is waiting. Follow me." A short, heavyset woman, with patent-leather shoes so tight her feet looked as if they would double in size if she took off her one-inch heels, escorted them to a group of tables.

When Jada looked closer at the people there, she noticed Lawrence's parents, siblings and their spouses, grand and great-grandparents were all seated at the tables. "Do y'all do everything together?" Jada mumbled.

"No. But we do share Valentine's Day so no one in the family feels alone or lonely. My great-grandmother started this tradition during the Depression. No one eats until everyone arrives, so sometimes we party first and eat and clown around with one another over dinner later. And as usual, I'm one of the last to arrive." Lawrence held Jada's chair until she was seated at the table with his parents. "We'll bring the kids next year after we're married."

Lawrence's great-grandfather proceeded to bless the food. The waiters served home style, placing platters and casseroles on each table. Jada picked at her greens, cabbage, and succotash.

"Lawrence, you need to feed your fiancée; she's not eating," Lawrence's mother said.

His mother reminded Jada of someone who kept her wig on a stand and false teeth by her bedside.

Smiling, Lawrence said, "She's fine, Ma. I love her just the way she is."

During dessert Lawrence slipped another strip on his tongue and smiled at Jada. She clamped his hand between her heated thighs. He fondled her clit, dipped his finger in her coconut cream pie, then sucked it slowly.

His mother's eyes shifted from Jada to Lawrence. She grumbled between her teeth, "Stop that. Use your fork."

Lawrence leisurely placed Jada's napkin in her seat and escorted her to an empty chair under the disco ball.

Jada whispered, "What are you doing?" Everyone already knew they were engaged.

"No questions, remember?" Lawrence smiled.

Brian McKnight's "Back at One" resonated throughout the restaurant. Jada covered her mouth with both hands, watching Brian as he sang a few lyrics at each table. Brian handed Lawrence the cordless microphone, and Lawrence picked up the song where Brian left off.

Okay, Lawrence must be lip-syncing like Millie Vanillie.

Lawrence gestured for her hand, gave Brian back the mic, and continued singing in her ear as couples joined them slow dancing on the floor.

"Wow, I didn't know you could sing like that." Jada laid her head on Lawrence's shoulder.

Stroking her hair, Lawrence spoke tenderly, "There are a lot of things you don't know about me. Yet."

"Baby, you sound so good, I had an orgasm." Let the family party without them. Jada was ready to make love to her man.

"We're just getting started. Wait until I get you back in the limo." He kissed her hair.

Wait until she got him back in the limo was more like it. "How much longer are we staying?" Jada asked, hand dancing to The Temptations.

"Are you ready to leave?"

Jada responded quickly. "Yes."

"Okay. Let's go." Lawrence said goodbye to his family and escorted Jada to the limo.

As soon as the door shut, he doused her hair in champagne and pulled her dress below her breasts. He teased her nipples with ice cubes, filled his mouth with bubbly, and sucked hard as he fucked her with his index finger.

Jada ripped open his shirt. Several buttons flew off. Vigorously her hands raced about his chest. She licked his left, then right nipple. Unbuckling his belt, she slipped his erection into her mouth. Moving his pants down to his knees, she pushed her thong aside, teasing her clit as she squatted on his dick. Each time her muscles tightened, Lawrence held her ass against his pelvis.

"Don't cum yet," Jada commanded, squeezing his penis with her vaginal muscles. Changing positions, she tightened her hand around his shaft until his head became enlarged. Controlling the flow of his cum, she hungrily sucked the head. Bobbing repeatedly, she stroked the shaft. Bringing Lawrence to his peak, Jada pressed his thighs together and straddled her legs outside of his. With her hands braced on his knees, she rotated up and down until she got all Lawrence had to offer for round one.

They culminated the night at Lawrence's house, where he had her silk and lace lingerie laid across a red-and-white picnic cloth in front of the burning fireplace. A bottle of bubbly was chilling next to the giant dark- and white-chocolate-covered strawberries. And the Jacuzzi water was pleasantly hot. That must have been the urgent phone call he needed to make before they left the restaurant. Their all-night foreplay exploded with passion that outlasted the sunrise.

Chapter 10

Darius was officially a sixth grader because the last day of school was yesterday, but tomorrow the movers were coming for all of their things. His mom was serious about marrying Lawrence, and there wasn't anything he could do to change her mind. Darius didn't want his mother to stay single forever, just until he went off to college. Mom said the movers would pack and unpack their belongings. "They'd better not break my trophies," Darius had said, admiring his recent MVP memento that stood four feet high. The National Junior Basketball League wasn't as competitive as the AAU league, but he was. He wanted to win every game by a twenty point margin so his opponents were clear which baller dominated the courts.

Bored, he double-checked to make certain his bedroom door was locked and dialed Ashlee from his home computer. "Can you believe I'm ten years old and Lawrence still massages my head like I'm a kid." Darius spoke into the built-in microphone on his desktop.

"I'm sure my dad doesn't mean it like that. He does that

to me, too," Ashlee said, blankly staring into the camera. Imitating her dad, she rubbed her head. "Ask him to stop."

"I have. He just laughs and goes about his business. The next time he tries that, I'm going to grab his hand." Darius raised his arm and grabbed his wrist in front of his camera so Ashlee could see how serious he was.

Shaking her head, Ashlee said, "I wouldn't do that if I were you. He does have really big muscles. He almost slapped my mom once, but my mom said he wasn't serious. They were horseplaying or something. What do you like most about school?" Ashlee blew a huge pink bubble that blocked her lens until it popped, covering her nose and mouth.

Darius stuck his chest out. "If he ever hits my mom, I don't care if he is playing, he's going to have to deal with my dad and me." Relaxing, he said, "I like girls and basketball of course. How about you?"

Two girls in his fifth grade class had real breasts, and he couldn't wait to see them again when school started in September. One day they approached him on the playground and said, "Darius Jones. We've decided to be your Valentines. So you can either have your boring girlfriend *or* both of us. But if you choose us, you have to bring us the same gifts." Darius had no idea what he was supposed to do with two girls; but two sounded better than one, and since they had volunteered, he spent his money on two large, pink heart-shaped boxes of assorted chocolates. Each box was decorated with white lace and a silk red rose with a green plastic stem.

"Science, math, and drama. But drama is extracurricular." Ashlee made a serious, silly, and cute face.

"I thought about drama. My mom wanted me to enroll, but basketball consumes most of my time." He alternated between the number four and five: forward and center. Forward was his preferred position.

"What do you want to be when you grow up?" Ashlee stood on her hands and walked across her bedroom and back.

"Hell, I'm already grown. I'm going to the NBA. I'm going to be a combination of Shag, Jordan, Kobe, Iverson, and Wilt the Stilt Chamberlain mixed together." Wilt was a certified player. After doing the math, Darius calculated he'd have to have sex with a different woman every day for over twenty-seven years to break Wilt's record. He'd have to get started soon because old people like his mom and dad probably didn't do it anymore. The girls he gave chocolates to on Valentine's Day had kissed him on opposite cheeks, so maybe he'd had sex twice already.

"I believe in you, Darius. You can do anything you set your mind to. You coming to visit me this summer in Madrid?" Ashlee sketched on her pad with long strokes.

"Yep. You the only friend I have. And you're going to be my half sister. So I guess that'll make you my sisterfriend. My mom said she has to renew my passport. What are you drawing?" He envied how Ashlee could do so many things in a short period of time.

"Yeah. But let's leave out the half stuff. I'm your sister and you're my brother. Make sure your mom hurries up because I'm not going to Spain without you. It's a surprise. I'll show you when I'm done."

Darius needed Ashlee's opinion on what had bothered him for quite some time. "Honestly, I don't want my mom to marry your dad."

"You, too. I wanted my parents to get back together, but my mom keeps saying I'm dreaming. I hate living in Texas. It's so far away from my dad. And it's too hot."

"We can dream if we want to." Darius spread his arms wide. "But if our peeps do get married, at least we'll have each other. When you come back to L.A., we're going to all the theme parks."

"Okay." Ashlee's pink lips curved up. Her top teeth were

perfect, but the bottom row was a little crooked. She was so nice and sweet it didn't matter. And her hair had grown longer, too.

"I've got a plan," Darius said, moving closer to the camera. "We can run away from home."

"Yeah, and divorce our parents," Ashlee agreed. "Maybe then they'll take us serious."

Darius spoke firm. "Make sure you pack a toothbrush, and lots of clean underwear and socks."

"Is that all?" Ashlee asked. "What about food?"

"I don't know. My mom always says, 'Darius, you got your toothbrush? And extra underwear and socks?' so I guess that stuff must be pretty important. She never mentions food because we always have money, I guess."

"Okay. Let's run away right before the wedding," Ashlee suggested.

"Great idea! I've got to go. My mom is calling me."

"Yeah, and we know what happens if she has to call you twice. Hey, here's your surprise."

Darius laughed. Ashlee had drawn a caricature of him with a basketball head. "Bye, Sisterfriend."

Chapter 11

December 31 Jada stood behind the doors of the First African Methodist Episcopal church, waiting to walk down the aisle. Mama had told her, "Honey, you have to shit or get off the pot. This man has patiently waited for you. If you're not going to set a date, let him go." Why couldn't they stay happily engaged forever? Marriage ruined a lot of good relationships. But Mama was right. Lawrence was tired of her procrastination and had handed her an ultimatum, so Jada had chosen the last month of the year. For the first time, at forty-four, Jada Diamond would carry the title Mrs. while her last name remained Tanner.

Lawrence was the perfect fiancé. No matter what he was doing, he stopped precisely at eight o'clock every night and called her. And each weekend they would set aside thirty minutes to candidly discuss their likes and dislikes about each other and their relationship. Sex on a regular basis with a man who knew how to hit all the right spots without being coached didn't hurt either. They agreed never to say no, except during illness. Always satisfying her man, Jada didn't understand why women withheld sex, because the supply well exceeded the demand.

Their wedding plans started out plain and simple. By the time Lawrence's friends and family—immediate and extended—got wind of the wedding, the list grew from seventy-five to three hundred. Lawrence argued and won because his parents were paying for everything, including their honeymoon.

Being an only child and the offspring of parents who also had no siblings, Jada's family consisted of Darius, Robert, and her mother. Her girlfriends Jazzmyne and Candice were there today along with her staff. Terrell still hadn't married Candice, but Candice hung in there with him.

"You know I'll marry you. Please don't do this." Jada heard Wellington's voice echoing in her ear.

Lifting her gown, Jada twisted halfway around in slow motion. A cool breeze swept across her face. Jada still heard Wellington's voice.

"What?" She whispered.

As soon as the doors of the church opened, Jada turned back and scanned the room for Wellington. Maybe marrying Lawrence wasn't a good idea. Was she supposed to think about another man on her special day? Was it normal? Perhaps everyone had second thoughts but kept them private. Although Jada found herself searching for Wellington, thankfully he wasn't there. Wellington was the only person who could speak, not hold his peace, and she would change her mind. Maybe secretly she wanted him to talk her out of marrying Lawrence.

Simulated snowflakes trickled from the ceiling. Jada, Lawrence, Darius, and Ashlee usually spent the Christmas holidays in New York City. Snowball fights, snow angels, warm cocoa, and lots of joyful moments taking in Broadway plays and watching the ball drop in Times Square were shared amongst all.

Guests seated in the pews covered in white specks did a one-eighty and stared at her. They weren't the only ones spellbound, so were the bridesmaids, groomsmen, and Lawrence. The pianist stopped playing. Jada suddenly realized it was too quiet. White rose petals were scattered along the white floor runner. The flower girl stood near the altar, holding an empty basket. The coordinator, Denise, stepped in front of Jada and closed the doors. As soon as they were shut, people started mumbling.

"It's okay, darling, lots of brides get cold feet. I want you to take a deep breath. Inhale." Denise held her hand against Jada's stomach. "Good girl. Now release." Denise pressed Jada's abdomen in slightly. "One more time," Denise instructed. "Now, this time when the music starts, I want you to start, too."

Jada looked at Denise and said, "What are you talking about?" Jada pointed toward the church doors. "I'm waiting for him to play 'Here Comes the Bride.' " The song wasn't her preference. Lawrence's mother was old-fashioned and requested the traditional tune. Jada's selection was an instrumental version of "Ribbon In the Sky" by Stevie Wonder, but that was another battle not worth fighting.

"Honey, it's already played from start to finish. Twice. You didn't move a step. Let me get some water and touch up your makeup. Don't move."

"But I don't want any water," Jada responded. "I'm fine. Just tell them to start." Jada refused to say start again, because she couldn't believe she stood in the doorway so long. That part of the video would be clipped and destroyed along with any incriminating photos.

Returning with a paper cup in her hand, Denise said, "First of all, the water isn't for you. It's for me. You can't mess up your lipstick. Secondly, we will not start again until I'm convinced you're ready to walk down that aisle." Denise took a sip of water and handed the floral-printed cup to the usher.

Holding the powder puff in one hand and a handkerchief under Jada's chin to make certain the foundation didn't stain her Vera Wang original, Denise patted gently. White. Halter. Low back. Long train. The beauty of Jada's black-velvet skin radiated a wonderful contrast to her gown. Lots of exposed cleavage was hidden behind her veil for Lawrence's view only. Fresh white roses were added to the lower half of her gown to match the flower girl's petals.

Something old: the pearl necklace her father had given her before dying. Something new: a diamond anklet Mama and Darius bought. Something borrowed: Jazzmyne's silver hair clips. Something blue: her spirit. Conspicuously absent.

Denise fluffed Jada's hair and asked, "Ready?"

"Yes, I'm ready," Jada whispered.

"Great. You'll be fine this time. Just take small steps." Denise gently placed the veil over Jada's face.

Jada flashed a fake grin. This time she didn't hesitate. Resembling an outdoor wedding, hundreds of gardenias graced each pew, the altar, and the podium; Denise had definitely outdone herself and would be compensated accordingly. From the corners of her eyes, Jada watched the faces of too many strangers. Candice and Jazzmyne smiled as they stood with her wedding party. Jada stepped on cue until she arrived at her fiancé's side.

Darius gave her away. Lawrence's nephew acted as ring bearer, and Lawrence's childhood friend, Doug, was the best man. The one thing Jada wouldn't compromise on was her minister performing their ceremony.

"Do you take this woman . . ." Pastor Tellings's lips moved slowly.

Ashlee made a beautiful junior bridesmaid. Her complexion resembled her mother's, almost milky white. Except for her beautiful big brown eyes, Ashlee scarcely resembled Lawrence. Jada glimpsed at Darius and wondered if she and Ashlee's mother harbored the same secret.

"I do," Lawrence said, gazing deep into Jada's eyes.

Jada glanced over her left shoulder at her mother seated in the front row. Mama nodded and swirled her finger in tiny circles, so Jada turned and faced the pastor. Darius was thrilled, and Jada knew exactly why. Mama was spending the week with him while they honeymooned in London. Knowing her mother wouldn't establish a list of rules for him to follow, Darius was certain to find a new limit.

"Do you take this man . . ." Pastor Tellings hadn't changed much. His hair still resembled Don King's, except now it was all silver. The train on Jada's gown lay twelve feet behind her. The wedding vows she had written for Wellington were now in her safety-deposit box. Had he kept his? Lawrence didn't want to exchange any sacred messages, and that suited Jada just fine.

Taking a deep breath, Jada replied, "I do," as she exhaled. She was still uncertain but now committed. Lawrence looked handsome and smelled great. His tailor-made black tuxedo was flawless.

Pastor Tellings cleared his throat and said, "I now pronounce you man and wife. You may kiss your bride."

Their wedding was more beautiful than Jada had envisioned. She had wanted to be a bride ever since she was a little girl pretending to match and marry her dolls. The next day flights to their honeymoon destination from Los Angeles to New York and then into London's Heathrow airport was tiresome. After they checked into their hotel, Lawrence swept Jada off her feet and carried her from the lobby, to their room, then across the threshold.

"I want to make love to you like never before. Like there's

no tomorrow." Lawrence had reserved the finest suite at their hotel near Buckingham Palace. Not permitting Jada to go farther than the living area, he said, "But before I do, I want to blindfold you."

Memories of when Melanie blindfolded Wellington resurfaced. Sexually sharing her man with another woman had seemed innocent and fun at the time. That was until Melanie had announced she was pregnant with Wellington's baby. And being a gentleman with morals, values, and principals, Wellington had married Melanie. In contrast to Wellington, Lawrence was all hers, and Jada wasn't making the mistake of sharing him with anyone, ever.

Eyeing the black satin mask and silk scarf, Jada said, "Okay." She closed her eyes and patiently waited. "Are you planning to use both of those?"

Lawrence kissed from her shoulder up to her ear as he undressed them both. "Trust me. You're my wife now."

True. After signing her marriage certificate, she felt closer and more dedicated to Lawrence than before. Jada took baby steps on the plush carpet, erased everything from her mind, and totally submitted. The nakedness of Lawrence's body pressed behind hers made her nipples harden.

The man standing behind her was her husband in both her eyesight and God's. No more fornication. Romance. Love. Sex. Jada didn't want one without the other. Lawrence's pubic hairs grazed the small of her back as the tip of his head momentarily lay between her firm cheeks. Jada paced her steps so theirs became one. Lawrence held her hands and continued to lead her.

"Where are we going?" The suspense emitted sexual hormones that made her heart rate quicken.

"Sssh." Lawrence traced her inner earlobe with his tongue as though it were a maze. He paused, then lightly blew into her ear and whispered, "Tonight, no questions." His moist lips pressed softly against her nape and lingered.

"Oooooh." Jada trembled in his arms. Her knees weakened. Whenever Lawrence told her no questions, there was an unforgettable adventure ahead.

"Don't stop. We're only a few steps away. Trust me to lead you. Today. Tomorrow. Always."

Jada's voice trembled, "I will," and her body followed in motion. Surrendering her heart and soul to the man she loved felt heavenly. She did love Lawrence. Otherwise, she would have let someone else marry him.

"Now step up," Lawrence instructed. "Again. Once more. Stop. Now step down and slowly sit. "

Bubbles galore floating on warm water surrounded her. Lawrence removed the blindfolds. Covering her mouth with both palms, Jada gasped. The black marbled Jacuzzi with gold fixtures was lined with red, yellow, white, pink, peach, and lilac roses. The jet stream created so many suds they overflowed onto the black granite floor. The flower bundles were connected with clusters of gardenias. Aromatherapy candles burned in every corner of the unbelievably spacious bathroom. Although no stars were outside the windows, so many fireworks exploded inside her heart they could have celebrated Independence Day.

"Oh, my gosh! This is too much." Jada looked around the room. The familiar sound of John Coltrane's *For Lovers* CD filled the air.

"Don't speak. I want every sense in our bodies to express our love without words. That's how I want to remember our wedding night." Lawrence motioned for a toast. Their quietness heightened her other senses as she internalized the essence of feeling versus speaking. Jada focused on the sounds of water and music. His touch made her hot. His scent made her hotter. His smell made her even hotter. His taste made her famished and hungry to feast on his love. This sight of her husband, naked and vulnerable inside and out, made Jada appreciate Lawrence.

Handing Jada a chilled glass, he removed the champagne bottle from the gold metal ice bucket and filled it halfway. After pouring his own, he held his crystal in the air. Jada mimicked his movement. Her energy twirled inside and escaped through tiny bumps of excitement.

Picking up a soft, white sponge, he stroked her feet. As he cleaned, he massaged every crevice between her toes. Ankles. Calves. Knees. He delicately washed inside her thighs. Butt. Back. Waist. Breasts. Nipples. Neck. Spreading her lips, he fondled her, stimulated her clit, and inserted his finger into her vagina while using his thumb and pinky to tease her clitoris and her anus until Jada released herself. Then Lawrence lathered her hair, widened her legs, and slid his penis deep inside of her, making her cum again. Jada lifted her body, took a deep breath, held it, and sank under the water. When she came up, she unequivocally returned his passion with the same persistence.

Afterward, Lawrence carried her to the bedroom. She felt as if drifting on air. Lawrence's pole was solid and stood north. As he braced her back in one arm and her legs in his other, Jada felt his erection touching her ass. Love. Peace. Happiness. Different words were sewn on so many pillowcases she hardly saw the white linen sheets. Red rose petals accented the bed and the floor.

Laying her across the cushions, he positioned his lean body next to hers. Holding her in his arms, her husband kissed her lips for at least an hour. Slowly, Lawrence moved down to her breasts and teased with his fingers, tongue, hands, and lips. By the time he finished loving every inch, Jada was a burning inferno.

Tenderly, he turned her onto her stomach. Jada's now favorite fragrance—tropical-scented shea butter—filled the air. Lawrence had ordered it from Sacred Thoughts across the country in Jersey City, New Jersey. Shondalon RaMin knew exactly how to mix the cherries, berries, and fruits into a delectable blend.

Lawrence's hands traveled from the arch in her back up her spine to her hairline. Penetrating her, his head maneuvered in and out. The softer he rubbed, the deeper he traveled. Occasionally, he blew air over her back. His chest and stomach flattened against her vertebrae, while sweat dripped onto her face.

Jada thrust against his movement, wrapping her insides around his shaft. With each downward motion, the pace quickened to squishing perspiration. Lawrence plunged so far his penis slipped into her cul-de-sac. Attempting to prolong their orgasms, Jada used her vaginal muscles and pushed down so hard she almost ejected Lawrence completely. Tightly, he embraced her shoulders, holding her virtually motionless while he rotated along her spot.

Panting, Jada said, "Oh, damn, baby, I can't hold back anymore." The thickness of her secretions liquefied as their orgasms combined.

"Sssshh." Lawrence instinctively moved in tempo to her beat. Nature's fluids abundantly flowed. After Jada was one hundred percent satisfied, Lawrence tossed the wet pillows on the floor.

The last moment Jada remembered before dozing in her husband's arms was Lawrence delicately running his fingers through the wetness of her hairs.

In the beginning, Lawrence expressed pleasure whenever Wellington spent quality time with Darius, thereby providing Lawrence more time with his firm. But immediately after they had married, he didn't want another man around his wife and stepson, so he made himself available and took Darius to Texas when visiting Ashlee and Ashley. Lawrence and his ex-wife became friendly again, while Darius and Ashlee ultimately became best friends.

Sometimes a woman had to let a man be manly, but Jada

knew Lawrence had no power over her relationship with Wellington. Hell, she couldn't deny the truth. She didn't have any control her damn self. Wellington still made her spirit dance every time she saw him. Why couldn't she erase those feelings?

Chapter 12

Watching his mother marry Lawrence was saddening. Why couldn't *his* parents get married and the three of them live happily ever after together? Why did they have him out of wedlock, birthing him into this world a bastard? Technically, he was an illegitimate child. Sometimes he wished he'd never been born.

Darius could neither understand nor forget how Wellington had shown the audacity to punch him in the chest for almost ruining his mother's wedding. Ashlee had received a spanking from her mother. They only ran away to the guesthouse for two days. Actually they had a pretty good time sharing scary stories, drinking apple cider, and catching bugs for pets. Darius had concluded his dad was taking out his frustrations on him, since Wellington had been in town and hadn't shown up at the wedding or the reception.

Darius tied his basketball shoe and shot his orange sponge ball into the plastic hoop mounted on his bedroom wall.

Jada yelled from the foyer, "Darius, your game starts in ninety minutes, sweetie. We've got to go!"

Yeah. Yeah. Darius dunked the ball and watched the orange rim flutter so fast it left shadows in its tracks. Glancing in the mirror, he admired his fresh twists. Maybe growing dreads would be easier and less time consuming. "I'm coming, Mom." If his mother had to call him twice, she'd lecture him all the way to the gym, and at the age of fifteen, he'd heard every speech his mom had at least ten times over.

Lawrence was a good guy and all. He bought Darius's mom flowers and candy and showered both of them with gifts and trips for no reason. Lawrence didn't miss many of his games, and he played escort to and from practice whenever he had time. Lawrence even shot the ball with him and helped to perfect his skills. But Darius couldn't wait until he got his driver's permit. His mom had reneged on letting him get it as one of his birthday presents this year. His urgency was predicated on the fact that California was considering raising the legal age limit to get a permit from fifteen to eighteen.

Lawrence and Mom never argued; at least he'd never heard them. And Lawrence had bought the family season tickets for the Lakers' games just because Darius had asked. His sisterfriend, Ashlee, was jealous because Lawrence had seldom made time for her and her mom when they were a family. But Lawrence's generosity couldn't replace Darius's love and need to reside with his own father.

Darius's average was ninety percent from the free throw line and eighty percent as a three-point shooter, and though he didn't play the number one position of point guard, he called all of the shots on the court. Hopefully, his leadership abilities would increase his chances of going to the NBA. At six-foot-five he prayed he'd grow at least another three inches to increase his possibility of being drafted into the pros on the first round. This was his ninth year playing CYO, but he preferred AAU because the kids were tougher, the referees didn't call as many fouls, and the girls that came to the games were finer than the Catholic school girls—like his future prep girlfriend Maxine. Today was AAU.

Closing his door so his mother wouldn't see the mess he'd created in his room, Darius grabbed his NCAA basketball and dribbled to the front door.

"Darius Jones!" his mother shouted.

When he got to the door, his mother gave him "the look," so he spun the ball on his pointing finger. Once outside, he dribbled in the driveway while she got the car from the garage. They already had a gymnasium; but Lawrence had bought him an expensive outdoor goal, so all of Darius's friends came to his house on the weekends to shoot hoops.

Darius hopped in the back of the car and dropped his ball between his feet. Shuffling it side to side, he asked, "Is Dad coming to my game?" He already knew the answer. He just needed to occasionally remind Lawrence that he couldn't replace Wellington. He knew Lawrence made his mother happy, but didn't anyone care about his feelings? Evidently not, since they had been together over ten years and never asked. He realized his situation could have been worse, because Lawrence could have been a jerk.

"Yes, sweetie. He'll be there," Jada answered.

Darius liked that his mom still called him sweetie. "You think he can come over for dinner afterward?" Darius was pushing his luck, but why should he be considerate of them?

His mom glanced at his image on her front windshield. That meant she'd had enough of the questions. "We'll see. Just concentrate on mentally preparing for your championship game."

Darius loved his mom's new car, but with the new projector, she could watch his every move without turning around. If it were a weekday, he could say, "*Oprah*'s on," and his mother would instruct her voice command to change to channel seven. He flipped up the cover of the screen on the back of his mother's headrest and popped in the DVD music video *Area Codes* by Ludicrous. In a way that was how he was already living, because every trip he'd taken over the past year he'd met a new female. And if an opportunity was presented, he sexed her, too. Shanté had permed him on his fourteenth birthday, so Darius was no longer a virgin. Shanté was a preacher's daughter, so his mom trusted her to come up to his bedroom. As soon as his mom put the car in park, Darius turned off his video.

"Open doors," Jada voice commanded, and all four doors opened automatically. Darius waited, then got out. His mother went ballistic if he unlocked the door while the car was in drive or the engine was still running. "I'll see you guys inside."

Darius strolled past the snack bar and into the gymnasium. The head coach signaled for him to come join his teammates. Coach yelled so much Darius had become immune. He liked coach's rule that all ballers had to wear a suit and tie to and from each game. Darius's black designer suit made him feel like a professional player. Shanté made him feel that way, too, giving it up whenever he asked or offering when he didn't ask.

"Hurry up and get over here, Jones!" Coach gave the same speech each game, and although Darius appeared distracted, he listened intently. Paying attention to details and working really hard was why his coach had made him captain. Most of the time Darius scanned the bleachers; he was looking for Wellington, checking out the honeys, and sizing up the scrubs he was getting ready to whip up on. He spotted his dad and waved. If his dad showed up late, Darius had to work harder to concentrate on his game.

Nobody understood his frustrations, because he never complained. Whining was for sissies and females, so he released his anger on his opponents during his games. In a few years, he'd be on his own. Instead of feeling special, he felt odd being the only player with three parents in the bleachers. His dads usually sat with his mom seated in the middle. They expected material items to compensate for his happiness. In fact, he used to give CDs and video games to teammates whose parents couldn't afford them. He even gave away his PlayStation2 and asked Lawrence to buy him another one.

"Hey, Darius." That was one of his ladybugs giving him a shout out.

Coach would bench him in a heartbeat if he answered. Huddled in a circle, Darius led his team, "Dragons on three. One. Two. Three."

The whole team yelled, "Dragons!"

During the game, Darius earned each of his four fouls and the championship three-point shot that sealed the lead. The crowd went wild cheering with excitement. That was another reason he preferred AAU. The fans weren't quiet like at Catholic high school games. AAU fans, especially the ladybugs, let a player know right away when he'd messed up.

Darius's teammates and Wellington paraded him on their shoulders. But the best ride he could remember was the last one he got from Wellington when he was ten. Riding high on his dad's shoulders had made him feel like King Darius. Suddenly, all the players lowered him to the floor and swarmed around this giant man handing out autographs.

Darius followed pursuit. "I'll be right back, Dad." He raced over to the pack. Running back to his mom, Darius was so excited he could hardly speak. "I—I—I need a piece of paper. Quick. Darryl Williams is signing autographs." Although Darryl Williams had hung up his jersey a few seasons ago, he was still one of Darius's all-time favorite ballers.

Jada frantically fumbled through her purse, then handed Darius a credit card receipt and a pen. "Here, honey."

Darius zoomed over to the crowd. When he stood before Darryl, Darryl asked, "Where's your uniform?"

Darius was speechless, but rumbled to dig his cover-up out of his bag. Darryl signed it and said, "I've got my eyes on you, DJ. You keep ballin' like that and I'll make sure you get a scholarship and starting position at GT." Then he handed Darius back his shirt.

Darius raced back to his parents and said, "Man, that was the highlight of my day. Darryl Williams autographed my uniform! Mom, you're going to have to pay for this."

"Pay for what, sweetie?"

"The uniform. I can't give it back. Darryl Williams signed my uniform! And he said if I keep on playing like I'm playing, I can start for him at Georgetown." Darius handed his mom back her receipt and ink pen. "Just imagine if he were my dad. I could be six-nine or taller!"

Chapter 13

Six feet, seven inches, seventeen years old, and college bound, Darius packed his bags, preparing to travel east. He had accepted the four-year full scholarship to attend Georgetown University in Washington, D.C. His mother had tried convincing him to go to Duke, but his visit to Duke's campus didn't measure up to Georgetown. Ashlee chose Spelman, and his high school sweetheart, Maxine, stayed local and enrolled at the University of California at Los Angeles.

Darius had declined his mother's offer to host a going away party, knowing she wouldn't throw the type of party he wanted and include his boys from Compton. His mother would send invitations to her family, friends, Lawrence's relatives, and of course, Ashlee and Maxine. Boring like all of his teenage birthday parties. No freaks. No DJ. His last three birthdays she'd played Lawrence's horrid classical music and called it culture. Darius called it torture.

Inventorying his bag, Jada asked, "Darius, are you *sure* you've packed everything?"

"For the fourth time, Mother, yes, I'm sure." Darius closed his suitcase.

His dad didn't approve of him piercing either ear, but his mom supported his decision. She also bought his diamond studs. His dad also didn't care for the dreadlocks he wore, and his mother said they were stylish as long as he kept them neat. As he'd gotten older, his parents seldom shared the same view, so Darius usually got whatever he wanted.

"Jada, you have to let the boy grow up. He's going to college," Wellington said, sitting at the foot of Darius's bed. "He'll be fine."

Jada folded her arms. "I'm not babying him. I just don't want him calling back asking me to send whatever it is he's going to forget."

"Then, don't send it. He'll manage without," Wellington said.

"Yeah, Dad's right. I'll manage," Darius said, hoisting his bulldog sweatpants over his waistline because his dad started staring at his boxers. The taste of independence was on the tip of his tongue.

Jada sighed. "Darius has never lived on his own, and he's moving so far away."

"And? So?" Wellington said. "The sooner he learns to take care of himself, the better. Otherwise, he'll be living with you the rest of his life."

"Fine." Mom threw her hands in the air and blinked her teary eyes. "I'll be in the living room with Lawrence. Darius, let us know when you're ready to go to the airport."

"Have a seat, son," Wellington said.

Darius spun his computer chair around and sat with his elbows on his knees. "What's up?"

"Son, your mother is happy and sad. But college is different from high school. Your biggest challenge will be time management. I know you; you'll try to make every party. Hang out late. Get up early. Be the star athlete. And have women in and out of your dorm." Gesturing like a referee signaling no basket, Wellington said, "Don't do it.

Don't waste your time or the school's money. Stay focused."

Grown-ups must have thought teenagers were brain dead or something. "I've got my schedule all figured out, Pops."

"Yeah, right, and you haven't even got there yet. That's what I'm talking about. It's easy to get off to a bad start, and if you do, you'll spend the entire semester trying to catch up. You've got to stay ahead of everything. Study. Practice. Tests. Everything."

He'd forgotten to mention females. "Y'all worry too much. Chill out like Lawrence. He's the only one not sweatin' me."

"I'm your father. Don't expect me to chill out, ever," Wellington said. "I'll call you tonight." His dad slapped him on the back and said, "Let's get going."

Great. Darius was traveling alone by request. What was all the fuss about? He could handle himself.

Since only ticketed passengers were allowed past security, Darius said his goodbyes at curbside. His mother was in tears, so he swiftly disappeared beyond the sliding glass doors.

How did he get a quiet, nerdy bookworm for a roommate and teammate? If they got the same classes, maybe his new friend could cover his assignments while he roamed Wisconsin Avenue. Darius loved the colonial-style buildings in Georgetown and how the stores and restaurants were open late at night.

The first month was a breeze. Frat parties. Drinking. Basketball practice. No games. And lots of females. The greatest thrill and disappointment of freshman year was his head coach, Darryl Williams. If he was late for practice, Coach wouldn't let him start. How could he bench his number one fan and best player? Wellington had come to several games, but Darius never saw his mother or Lawrence in the stands.

Damn, she'd cried at the airport, but the only time he saw her was when he went home on holidays. Obviously, they couldn't wait to get rid of him. That was cool, because he didn't want them to see him bench warming. At the end of the season, Wellington gave him the "I told you so" speech about too much partying.

Forget them. Darius spent spring break in Miami by himself. Florida was on point with lots of beaches and chicks in bikinis. By the end of his freshman year, Darius had lost his starting position. Early in the season scouts were checking him out, but after losing his starting spot to his nerdy roommate, Darius decided to ride out the remainder of his scholarship stomping with his frats, the Omegas.

Chapter 14

Jada relaxed on the white cushioned lounge chair at her beachfront Malibu home. Wide blue waves quietly washed up on the private shore. On numerous occasions, residents of the county had unsuccessfully petitioned for publicizing the entire oceanfront. Jada couldn't imagine strangers loitering outside her residence, so she refused to sign the petitions and voted against the propositions. Quietly, she stood and placed the cordless phone on the leatherlike seat. Although leather and saltwater wasn't a good combination, vinyl felt too harsh.

Rising from his chair, Lawrence said, "Honey, I'm going to cook dinner."

"Oh, great. Surprise me." Jada reached for his hand, pulled him close, and licked his lips.

"Keep that up and you'll be served up on a platter." Lawrence smiled and went inside.

She knew he meant what he'd said. Jada rolled up her pant legs. Thirty steps later sand and water meshed underneath her feet and seeped between her toes. At times her mango polish sank so deep the color was buried and all she saw was wet white sand. The light wind caressed her high cheekbones and softly weaved throughout her hair. Dying out the first strands of gray had subtracted almost ten years from her appearance. Besides, gray was Jada's least favorite color. The warmth from the sun covered her face as haunting memories flooded her mind.

How was she to know Darryl would be at Darius's game signing autographs? That was all Darius talked about. He framed his uniform and hung it on his bedroom wall. Then for Darryl to surface as Darius's basketball coach, too. How could she show her face at Darius's games and risk Darius finding out the truth? Obviously, Darryl already knew. Offering Darius a scholarship was probably his way of making up for lost time.

Continuing her walk, the cotton outfit with a matching pink jacket protected her. Aerosols and other products humans couldn't or wouldn't live without may have been breaking down the ozone layer, but not her silky skin. On the other hand, her secret was eating away her insides like maggots feasting on a dead cow.

Gazing at the sky, she saw the huge yellow circle had begun to descend behind the clouds. Her wavering hand swayed in the air, volunteering to trade places so she'd have a new spot to hide her information. Amazingly, no one discovered the truth, because as a child playing hide-and-go-seek, she was always the first found. Hypnotized by bright orange streaks blending to create red ones, Jada stood still and relived the moment of discovery when she'd received Dr. Bates's phone call.

Some things hadn't changed. The same ivy plant from her Baldwin Hills home now decorated her ceiling-to-floor patio windows. Invisible walls of glass surrounded the backside of their Malibu home, providing a cozy indoor/outdoor feeling. Guests routinely walked past the four inside columns and almost into the windows, so Jada had attached the plant to clear plastic suctioned hangers to avoid being responsible for any accidents.

Returning to her beach lounge chair, Jada exhaled, wondering why she'd been so careless. She picked up the cordless, sat, and placed the phone in her lap. Her long, dark chocolate legs caressed but didn't cross each other. Clumps of sand fell from the bottoms of her feet. The aroma of Lawrence's cooking made her hungrier.

While searching for a new home for Darius and her, Jada had instantly fallen in love with Malibu and its beachfront homes. Despite the temptation, being pregnant made her think twice about living too close to the water, so Jada had sold her Baldwin Hills condo and moved to Orange County near Wellington's sister, Jazzmyne. Once Darius turned ten and Jada married Lawrence, her husband had bought her a Malibu dream house situated on one-point-five acres.

Their ten-thousand-square-foot home included six bedrooms, eight and a half baths, a gymnasium, a guest suite, staff quarters—although they rarely requested workers stay overnight—a four-car limo garage, a wine cellar with a tasting room, a pool, a spa, a lighted tennis court, and not to mention the master suite with a fireplace, a sitting area, and spacious his and her baths with separate walk-in closets. Lawrence didn't tell her the price, and she never asked. Jada's only wish was that everything wasn't on one level, but Daddy always said, "Never nag a man who puts his family first."

Looking out over the ocean, Jada's head swiftly moved short distances to the left and right, trying to erase the past. When her phone rang, Jada realized both the moon and the sun were exposed. Her hand roamed across her lap as the ring tone repeated. Her stomach growled so loudly it could have answered for her. She picked up the cordless. Every time she mentally regurgitated her secret, her palms became clammy. Without looking at the caller ID, she sensed it was Wellington.

Drying her hands on her jacket, Jada solemnly answered, "Hello."

"Hi, ba. How are you?"

"Great, as always," Jada stated. Not that she was feeling that way, but that was what Wellington was accustomed to hearing. After Jada married Lawrence, they created codes for phone talk. Great meant they could speak openly. Fine was for keep it clean; Lawrence or Simone was within ear range. Okay indicated it wasn't a good time for conversation.

"Is everything all set for Darius's birthday party Friday night? Can you believe our son is going to be twenty years old? Do you need me to do anything?" Wellington offered.

Jada pressed the mute button. After twenty years did it matter? She'd planned on telling him when Darius was born, then after Darius turned five. Again, she'd contemplated doing so when Darryl autographed Darius's uniform, but that wasn't a good time either. "Lord, show me a green light for perfect timing." Would it be another two decades before she revealed the truth? Or would Jada remain silent the rest of their lives?

Turning off the mute, she said, "No. Thanks. Denise volunteered to coordinate the party, and she has everything under control."

"Okay. Great. I fly into L.A. Thursday evening around six. You think your should-have-been husband can borrow you away from your husband for an hour or two?" Wellington laughed.

"I'm working late Thursday. But I'll meet you at our usual place at say eight o'clock." Yes, indeed. After all this time—ten years of marriage included—Wellington still made Jada feel the same way as the night they had met in San Francisco. Just as Rachelle Farrell had sung the last song of the evening especially for them, the lyrics inevitably true: "Nothing Has Ever Felt Like This."

"Great. I'll see you at the Beach Café at eight. Hey?"

"Yes, Wellington." Jada smiled, because she knew he was getting ready to earn it.

"Wear a bikini underneath your business suit."

"Bye, Wellington." The Beach Café was the best hideaway in Malibu. With wooden chairs and tables right on the water, patrons could swim while waiting for their food.

"Bye, my Nubian queen."

Jada walked into the kitchen, returned the phone to its cradle, and joined her husband in their dining room for dinner.

Chapter 15

Wellington packed his suitcase and little Wellington II's diaper bag. Simone would arrive soon to pick up their son. Fortunately, everything went in the bag except diapers, mainly a change of clothes and toys to keep Junior occupied while in his car seat.

Looking at Junior's smiling face, Wellington's lips parted as his son's cheeks rose higher; then he said, "Everybody loves JR."

Junior chimed in on cue, "It's like I'm 'ma mobie star."

"That's my boy. Give Daddy a hug."

At the age of two, Junior's speech had improved. Junior benefited from Darius's upbringing in many ways. Jada insisted on correct pronunciation from day one. Darius was never taught da-da, always daddy. His *r*s and *t*s were clearly pronounced. Since being proper wasn't cool with the current hip-hop generation, Wellington noticed when Darius spoke with his peers he often rolled his *r*s saying, "Herrr," instead of here and, "Therrr," versus there. Darius was a faster learner than Junior, not that Junior was slow. Darius's IQ was off the chart, but he was also arrogant and overconfident. Junior was potty trained at twenty-four months and Darius at eighteen. Junior still pissed on the floor, but at least he'd learned how to go to the bathroom. Just like Darius, Junior had the best worlds from both parents, but Wellington remained hopeful that one day he and Jada would unite in holy matrimony.

Wellington loved both of his sons. He also adored Simone Smith-Jones. But the ugly divorce from Melanie had left him with cold feet, and sixteen years had passed before he remarried. The fact that Jada had moved on with her life years ago still bothered him.

Wellington and Simone dated off and on for thirteen years before their private wedding ceremony almost three years ago. Only their family and closest friends were invited. Wellington's father Keith, Cynthia, and Melanie surprisingly came together. Simone could plan everything her way as long as his sister, Jazzmyne, was matron of honor. Simone liked Jazzmyne and was honored to have her in their wedding, but refused to send Jada an invitation. Little did Simone know Melanie was the one she needed to watch.

The moment Wellington said, "I do," Simone started saying, "No, you won't." Since when did a grown man need permission to leave his own house? Six months of asking himself, "Who is the woman?" ended with a divorce. Better safe than sorry. The out-of-court settlement to his first wife, Melanie, definitely cost more than she was worth—ten thousand dollars. Wellington quickly decided they were all better off living apart, so he evicted Simone's tenants and moved her back into her home in Danville.

After the phone rang twice, Simone's name flashed across the caller ID. Wellington picked up the handset and said, "The door is open." Simone seldom knocked, because after she moved out, he changed the locks and declined her request for a key. Simone tried to slip him her house keys by leaving them on his nightstand, but Wellington politely returned them via U.S. Postal Service insured mail. Certified mail held a lower priority, and he wanted to be reassured Simone's keys wouldn't get lost in transit.

Simone stepped into the living room wearing a sleeveless, mustard yellow dress and no pantyhose. Wellington gently put his arms around her. Gliding his fingers through her honey-golden shoulder-length hair and softly kissing Simone's neck, he said, "You look nice." Slowly he rocked, and Simone instantly swayed in unison. Simone's youthfulness was refreshing. "You smell good, too," Wellington said. Suddenly the pitter-patter of Junior's little feet sounded, so they stopped.

"There's my little man. How's Mommy's baby?" Simone stooped, and Junior ran as fast as he could to give her a hug. Simone caught him in midair. Junior wrapped his chubby legs as far as he could around Simone's waist. Simone's 38DD breasts and forty-six-inch hips were disproportionate to her thirty-inch waistline, but as far as Wellington was concerned, everything was in the right place, especially Simone's heart.

"Hi, Mommy." Junior pecked Simone on her lips.

Admiring his woman, Wellington shook his head and said, "Um, um, um." Simone was a large, sexy woman, five feet, seven inches and two hundred pounds solid, no flab. Women would flirt with Wellington and then turn their noses up at Simone as if to say, "What does he see in her?" He could have answered them, but there was no need. Simone was confident and had every right to be so. Next to Jada, she was the most creative woman Wellington had experienced in and out of the bedroom.

"Lucky for you he's awake." Simone winked and flicked her pink tongue. Then she made that smacking sound when her tongue suctioned against the roof of her mouth and released. "I'll hook you up after you get back from L.A." Simone teased with a pucker of her lips, then asked, "Darius's party is tonight?"

Wellington and Simone managed to remain an item and

continued dating after their divorce. Jada had taught him how to be a true friend, which made the growth of his relationship with Simone easier. When they first met, Simone was twenty-one and definitely no virgin. After their first year together, all she wanted was for Wellington to father her child. Although she was of legal age, he felt she was barley out of the cradle herself. At the time they decided to become parents, Simone was thirty-three and worried about her biological clock. Afraid she was only after his money, he delayed fathering another year, feeling Simone out. The love, comfort, and support she gave him reassured Wellington she definitely wasn't chasing his wallet.

After Simone became pregnant, marriage was Wellington's idea, believing family unity was best. As often as he confided in Jada, she knew very little about Simone—until they married—but Simone certainly knew all about Jada *Diamond* Tanner from week one.

"The party's tomorrow. I'm just going early to help out. I'll be back Monday." Wellington squeezed Simone's breast while Junior wasn't looking.

"Monday, huh?" Simone put her hand on her curvy hip, held Junior on the other side, blocking his access, and said, "She's married, Wellington. Diamond is a married woman and has been for ten long years."

"I'm not staying because of her," Wellington said, hoping Jada would be able to get away for more than just tonight. Two black suitcases sat at the door. One oversized bag contained his clothes, and the other carry-on had Darius's birthday presents. A remote control car, video games, a digital watch that kept time in every country, and a stock portfolio, amongst other items, filled the smaller bag, which would accompany him on the flight.

Simone had never found her soul mate, so Wellington knew she couldn't relate. Understanding how one could unite with and depart from one's soul mate and then spend the rest of one's life longing for that person was like trying to solve ten Rubik cubes in two seconds. Wellington looked at Simone and said, "Stop talking crazy in front of Junior before his terrible twos roll over to three." Time was truly his friend. Wellington could easily pass for forty-five and double as an older Morris Chestnut. He still shaved his goatee, maintained his mustache, and continued to shave his head bald. A few crow's-feet had developed around the corners of his eyes, but they showed only when he smiled or squinted.

"Seems like he's not the only one suffering from the terrible twos. You are too stuck on Miss Goody Two Shoes. How many times have I told you that Darius is probably not your son? But no, you don't believe me. I had to take a blood test, but not Miss Perfect. Just wait and see. But I love you anyway." Simone abruptly kissed his cheek.

"Brother." Junior smiled. "He's on the plane, Mommy. He's coming to see me?" Junior clapped and kicked his feet.

"I told you to stop saying crazy things in front of our son."

Simone had met Darius, and Darius had met Junior, but Simone didn't want Jada anywhere near Junior. If Wellington told Darius how Simone felt, then Darius would tell Jada, and then Wellington would have to explain. So he made up excuses each time Jada asked to see his son. Some things were better left unsaid. If only he had believed that when he cheated on Jada with Melanie, maybe Jada wouldn't have left him.

"Okay, you're right." Simone placed Junior on his feet. "Junior, go to your playroom," Simone instructed. Wellington's downstairs family room had been converted so their son would have play areas on both floors. The paneled walls were replaced with clear fiberglass so they could watch Junior from the living room.

"Okay, Mommy." Junior happily ran off, saying, "Brother's coming."

Simone sat on the sofa next to Wellington. "Ask her if

he's your son. What are you afraid of? *If* he's your son, then we can introduce her to Junior. The child looks exactly like her but nothing like you. Ask her this weekend."

There went Simone making demands again as though she was in control. "There is no *if* as far as I'm concerned. Darius will be twenty years old tomorrow. I'm the only father he knows. If someone else was his father, Jada would have told me."

"Baby, listen to me." Simone sighed heavily. "It's time you know for sure; that's all I'm saying. It isn't fair."

What was this conversation really about? Why was Simone being so persistent? Since he was getting older, maybe she was concerned about Junior's inheritance. Wellington responded, "Life isn't fair."

Simone slapped her thighs. "I knew you were going to say that."

"Well, let's say hypothetically Jada did lie and Darius isn't my son. That's the worse that can happen. Right?" Wellington nodded in response to his own question. "I'll assume she did it because his real father is an asshole like mine—"

"Don't you *dare* try to justify her actions! So you're basically saying even if she's lying, you've already forgiven her?" Simone leaned back, folded her arms, and frowned.

"Basically, yes. If that's the worst thing she's done, I can live with that. I've hurt her before, and she's forgiven me, so why can't I do the same? Besides, Jada wouldn't lie to me about being the father. I love her, and no matter how hard I try to deny it, the shit is real, Simone." Wellington moved to the edge of the blue custom-designed plaid sofa. All shades of blue had become his favorite colors: royal, dark, sky, aqua, and pale.

"But you love me, too, Wellington." Simone fluttered her eyelashes.

"True, but not like Jada, and you know that. Hear me out, Simone." Wellington scooted closer to Simone, lowered his voice, and spoke deliberately. "Have you ever met someone for the very first time and instantly felt you wanted to share the rest of your life with that person? The moment I laid eyes on Jada, my heart damn near stopped beating. We exchanged phone numbers. I was hanging out with my buddy Walter, probably had one drink too many, and couldn't find her number the next day. I tore up this house upstairs, downstairs, and my Benz, desperately searching. It took nine days. Actually, the woman at the dry cleaners found it. You don't know how happy I was to get that card."

Simone sarcastically said, "If you gave her yours, why didn't she call you?"

"Because she's a lady. And she's always made me feel like a man. Some women are so independent they want to control everything and reduce their men to being boys. They have the answer to every question." Wellington slapped the backside of one hand into the palm of the other each time he said, "What? When? Who? Where? Why? How?" He opened his palms faced toward Simone, squinted, shook his head, and continued, "Men hate that shit with a passion. That's why Christopher divorced Cynthia. And Cynthia still hasn't changed, but I guess she's too old now. Anyway, Diamond, she wasn't like that at all. She was different." Wellington smiled as he flashed back on their first date in Carmel. He knew he had an outdoors-chic, bona fide indoor-freak type of woman the moment Jada paused Chris Tucker's video and said, "It's intermission. What would you like?" Then Jada broke out the strawberry whipped cream and squirted it all over her breasts.

Wellington stared off into a daze at the memory.

Simone asked as she snapped her fingers two inches from Wellington's nose, "What does this have to do with Darius?"

Wellington was thirty-five when his sister, Jazzmyne, had told him he was adopted. He shook his head and said, "Everything. When a man loves a woman, he accepts her child, even if it's not his. Hell, everybody would be single if we refused to raise someone else's kid. That's why I don't care, Simone. As a person that's been adopted, I feel an obligation to give back. At this point in our lives, if Darius isn't my son, he'll be the main one hurt. I won't do that to him." Wellington pounded his chest and said, "A real man raised me, Simone, and he raised me to be the man my biological father, Keith, wasn't." Keith was spineless, always running away from his obligations. Anyone who cost him time or money, Keith dismissed with quickness. Wellington was no exception.

Now that Keith was growing old and feeble, he called almost every day, pretending to check on Junior and asking about Darius. Really, he just wanted Wellington to keep paying his bills and giving him an allowance. Keith had never held a steady job, so he had no retirement income. Social Security gave him a stipend, but he'd have to feed on dog food and choose between buying his blood pressure medicine and having a roof over his head.

God had blessed Wellington with so much to give, and he gave selflessly. Keith gave nothing. He didn't give a damn about Keith's wanting his money; he just wanted his father to love and accept him. Wellington chose to live his life like his stepfather, Christopher. Always willing to give more than he received. Especially when it came to Jada, Darius, Junior, and Simone.

"The worst day of my life was when I walked out of Jada's penthouse for the last time. You know why?" Wellington blinked repeatedly to wash away the tears before they could stream down his face. "It wasn't because she was moving to L.A. It was because I thought I'd never see her again. And that shit hurt like hell. I cried long and hard. But the difference between a man and a woman is a man can't let anyone see him shed tears. If so, he's weak, a wimp, or a punk. So when she called and said she was pregnant, I said, 'Yes! We're going to have a baby.' Jada Diamond was back in *my life* to stay. And if she confesses he's not mine, I'm not going to abandon them. Just like I wouldn't have left you if Junior wasn't mine."

"Bullshit and you know it. What the hell!" Simone threw her hands in the air. "Is her pussy dipped in platinum and trimmed in gold? I give up." Simone rubbed her baby-oiled legs with both hands and sighed heavily.

"Let me do that for you," Wellington offered as he placed Simone's legs across his. Using his manicured fingers, he massaged Simone's calves. Soft. Smooth. Freshly shaved. Wellington slipped off Simone's yellow sling-back shoe and glided his fingertips through her toes. Simone had every right to be jealous. Wellington had never loved her the way he loved Jada. No woman who walked the face of the earth compared to Jada Diamond.

"I hope I find my soul mate soon so he can protect me like you protect her ass. My hat is off to you, Mr. Jones." Simone saluted Wellington. "You are the first man I've met that honestly loves someone unconditionally." Simone moved her legs, placed her foot inside her shoe, and stood. Wellington watched Simone's ass shake from side to side like a seesaw as she walked into the playroom. She picked up Junior and his diaper bag, walked into the living room, and said, "Give your daddy a kiss goodbye."

"Bye, Daddy. Bring me something back from your trip." Junior kissed Wellington on the cheek.

"You know Daddy will." Wellington returned his love, then whispered in Simone's ear, "Bye, Simone. Thanks for listening. I love you, baby." His lips pressed against her forehead; then he kissed Simone's thick lips. He knew she'd keep her word and take care of him when he got back. Simone had no problem rotating, gyrating, or stretching during sex. The last time he made love to Jada had been right before he started dating Simone, hoping it would keep her from tying the knots in his stomach even tighter.

* * *

Initially, Wellington had subtle doubts about Darius, but he wasn't alone. The thought crossed every man's mind immediately after any woman said, "I'm pregnant." Refusing to admit Simone was right, somehow deep down inside he felt he should have asked Jada about Darius, but every question Wellington had faded away when Darius slid out of Jada's stomach covered in slime. Although he nearly fainted in the delivery room, he'd hung in there once he heard Dr. Watson pronounce, "It's a boy!" Video taping Junior sliding out Simone's uterus was also incredible. Wellington was shocked at how Simone's vagina had stretched during delivery.

Darius's birth had empowered Wellington. Those feelings returned when Junior was born. As he watched Junior grow up, Wellington noticed his and Junior's baby pictures looked identical. Eyes. Nose. Ears. Seemingly Simone had only *carried* Junior for him. Wellington suspected Darius might not be his as the only features they shared were their complexions and physiques. Perhaps he was just being foolish since Simone brought up this nonsense, because often ladies would say, "Oh, he's so cute. He looks just like his daddy. Yes, he does." When they would reach for Darius's cheeks, Wellington stopped them before they made contact.

Having a child together had helped Wellington and Jada trust each other again. Jada needed him, and the feelings were mutual. His stepfather, Christopher, had never reunited with his soul mate, Sarah. It was too late. Sarah had made her transition before Christopher divorced Cynthia. Wellington prayed he'd have his time on earth with Jada before they faced the same inevitable fate: death.

Chapter 16

Ginger. Miranda. Heather. Zen. Darius glimpsed at his counterparts seated around the rosewood conference table at Black Diamonds. Everyone must have forgotten today was his twentieth birthday, because he hadn't received any gifts or acknowledgements. After a disappointing freshman year at GT, the option of earning six figures to work full-time for his mother was irresistible. Plus every time he mentioned giving GT another shot, his mother suggested he stay close to home and help her run their company. Dropping out of college completely was unacceptable, so he promised his parents he'd enroll at UCLA. Instantaneously, Darius found his entrepreneurial passion, so formal education would have to wait, at least until his fiancée, Maxine, received her bachelor of arts degree next semester. The two of them at the same university at the same time would definitely cramp his style.

Darius desperately wanted to run the business, and his mom supported him; but Wellington insisted he wasn't ready, saying, "Son, you're brilliant. You have the capability to run the company, and when that time comes, you'll do well. You need more experience, and that can only happen with time." How could his father have said that when he'd started Wellington Jones and Associates while he was in high school? And he'd never had any associates.

The fact that Darius was fucking four of the top-level executives in the room meant he was very mature. And as soon as his mother promoted him, he'd wean each of them off his chocolate dipstick.

Dreadlocks neatly grown in the pattern of a high top fade were long on top, but Darius shaved his scalp clean on both sides and the back. Then he meticulously twisted his locks and let a few dangle loosely to complement his twenty-four carat nickel-sized hoop earrings. An invisible line highlighted his manly jaws and squared his masculine chin. Lighter than his mother and slightly darker than his dad's caramel complexion, Darius's natural tan resulted from his newly discovered, cherished pastime, jet skiing. At six-foot-seven with a well-defined chest, roller coaster, rock-solid abs, and a slim waistline, Darius was quick to let brothers know he was an MSW—a man having sex with women—not an MSM. He didn't care how many categories society created—down low, bisexual, in the closet—he was straight.

With his hands casually clasped across his stomach, Darius sarcastically said, "Zen, so you think one of your clients will win first place again this year?" His elbows rested on each arm as he relaxed in his chair. No matter where he chose to sit during a meeting, Zen religiously sat to his left. Out of twenty-seven women working for his mother, Zen was the primary person his mother relied upon whenever she had a management crisis.

Hunching her small shoulders, Zen said, "Um, you know me. I just do my best and dim sum." Then she laughed. Zen's short bob haircut covered her ears but didn't touch her neck. Shaking her head, her hair whipped from her face to reveal her tight, slanted dark eyes. "A little extra goes a long way.

Maybe you should try doing *extra* sometimes." Zen grinned at Darius.

Yeah, like Zen's thick black lashes with matching lines under her narrow lids. To hell with that; more wasn't always better. Eventually, he'd be her boss, so he had to conserve his energy to keep her scintillating ass in check. Zen worked hard enough for everybody.

Positioned across from him, Ginger snickered.

"What about you, Darius?" Miranda asked, tugging the collar on her red power suit. "You've been working with us for two years, and none of your clients have made the top five."

Right now Darius wished he could speak Spanish, because his words would slash through that Mickey Mouse blazer. Locking his fingers tighter, he answered, "They say the third time is a charm, and since I'm a charming mutherfucker, I'd safely say I'm taking the number one spot this year." Darius propped over the table and stared directly at Miranda.

Heather jumped in, "The only reason you're here is because of your *mommy*."

The white girl always slipped in her remark. Heather claimed it kept everyone in the dark about their affair. Over the last year she'd shortened her hair and dyed it blond. A few wrinkles had sprouted above her lips like whiskers, and they weren't sexy. Darius remembered when his mother first hired Heather. Her brunette hair, catlike gray eyes, and really soft legs had landed him in her office since he was five years old. While she hadn't lost her figure, the firm texture of Heather's skin had loosened, and age spots had started filling the gaps.

"Your peeps invented the system. I'm perfecting it. And *do not* forget"—Darius plucked a paper football in Heather's direction—"they stole this country, after they were ostracized from their homelands." Between the *ooh*s and *ah*s, Darius held his hands in the air like the extra point was good. "What we need in this firm is more men. You know you can't expect a woman to do a man's job *and* do it well." Twenty-seven women in the company and the only four he was fucking happened to be at his level. Or was he on their level? It didn't matter. But what concerned him the most was he was the only man working at his mother's company.

Entering the room, Jada asked, "What was that I heard you say, Darius?"

Jada's tailor-made black pantsuit was tapered to her hourglass figure. Her hair was slicked back and neatly tied into a bun with two handcrafted oriental sticks poking through. His mother had talked about cutting her hair for years, but couldn't convince herself to do it. His father claimed he preferred it long. Since she was married to Lawrence, Darius didn't understand why Wellington's opinion mattered. Darius smiled. His mother's scheduled exercises four times a week kept her finer than some women his age. She also treated her masseuse to the pleasure of giving her a full-body massage every Monday morning at six o'clock, believing if she started the week out right, the projected ending would follow suit.

Darius coughed, then said, "We need more mints." Candid conversation often flowed when his mother wasn't present. His mother strongly believed in equal rights and pay for women, and if she'd heard his comment, a long sermon over family dinner was mandatory. He was the only man ever hired to work internally for Black Diamonds, so he had to represent his brothers. Darius couldn't lie; the women did have their act together, but he'd never openly admit it, especially not to Zen. The bottom line was they needed more testosterone, and as soon as he got a controlling position, manes and tails would fly out the door, window; it didn't matter how they left as long as they got out of his firm.

Observing his mother, Darius never could figure out why his parents hadn't stayed together. They seemed to get along better than most married couples. His mother said she loved his father, and he confessed the same. Yet, they aggravated him by living apart. As a child, he had prayed daily for his family to reunite. Whenever he questioned his mother, she'd say, "Because we wanted to give you the best we had to offer. And that meant going our separate ways, sweetie. One day you'll understand." Which day? Hell, today he made the big two-oh.

No mention of a celebration from either of his parents was unusual. No vacation package. No gifts. My Dear had called him this morning, and all she'd said was she might not make it to L.A. this weekend. Well, if they were planning something, they had better speak now or forget about it. Kimberly was his appetizer, and Maxine Moore, dessert. Ashlee, who had earned the honor as his very best friend because—even though she was the top person on her high school debate team in Texas—she refused to compete with him, hadn't called either.

Maxine had become Darius's fiancée a year ago, because she always placed him upon a pedestal. In this confused world, a black man needed a woman to uplift him. Plus, she was perfect marrying material. Black and beautiful just like his mother. Ladylike. Soft-spoken. Maxine was the one woman who blew up his cellular phone three times a day, but so far he hadn't heard from her once. His mother never forgot. She was as proud of him as he was of her. Darius watched the smile on his mother's face as she spoke.

"Good morning. Did everyone have a fantastic workout?" Jada asked as she sat at the head of the table. Jada strongly encouraged them all to fully utilize their corporate-sponsored fitness memberships. Since exercise stimulated the brain, she said the earlier they hit the gym, the better. A *yes* response was received from all, except Darius. He simply alternated flexing his chest muscles underneath his Brian McKinney designer suit.

Ginger Browne pretended she wasn't watching. She loved his body, and he couldn't resist hers. Scrutinizing his coworkers, he recalled how each of them had seduced him as soon as he turned eighteen, because they believed he'd convince his mother to promote them to vice president. Claiming her mouse was stuck, Ginger had solicited help with her computer and motioned for him to come into her office. Quite taken with Ginger's womanly features and refusing to appear inexperienced, he had gone.

Loose satin curls that curved under only at the end never touched Ginger's shoulders or covered her ears. Small opal-stud earrings complemented her clean, fresh face. Her only makeup, brown spice lipstick. As Ginger's hands roamed, she said, "You're an adult now, Darius. You don't need anybody's permission." Ginger's luscious lips grazed his. As they held her mouse, he froze like the mime at Venice Beach. She positioned her lips less than an inch away from his. Darius heard himself breathing. Then Ginger whispered, "Kiss me. You know you want to." So he did. The first kiss of an older African-American woman practically caused a volcanic eruption. That was the best lip locking he'd ever done.

Unlike Miranda, Heather, and Zen, Ginger was divorced. Twice. Two men had played tug-of-war with Ginger for as long as Darius could remember. Her ex-husbands? Forget those amateurs. Darius wanted more, and Ginger gave it to him. His body heat turned up, and his blue cotton sweatpants plunged frontward. Just when his dick became rock solid, Ginger cut him off, but not before her hand squeezed and sized him up. Her smile was all the approval he needed. "Come over to my house. Tonight. Seven o'clock sharp and don't be late."

She was thirty-three then, but thirty-five now, and still a pro.

"Excellent!" Jada said. She was so perky he couldn't

gauge his mother's real mood. "We have several agenda topics to cover. The first being one not on the list." Jada smiled at Darius. He shifted his eyes to the right as though he were a kid again.

No surprise, just pleasant. There sat Miranda Gonzalez, the finest Latino in all of California and south of the border. Her approach had been different from Ginger's, but her timing was the same. Miranda frequently brought him home-cooked meals. Since she had four children and a husband, it wasn't as if she went out of her way. Contrary to Ginger, sex in the office was acceptable for Miranda. Two big titties sat at attention with or without a bra. Miranda always wore low-cut everything. Tops. Sweaters. Dresses. One day she called him into her office:

"Close the door. I have something for you." Her tone aroused him, so he obliged her, anxiously desiring to finally see the boobs he'd drooled over for thirteen years.

Miranda seated him behind her desk. Removing the blue lid from the Tupperware container, she fed him. "You must promise not to tell. Okay?" Darius nodded. The remaining sour cream and taco sauce clung to Miranda's finger. Slowly. Meticulously. Miranda's finger disappeared into Darius's mouth. Impatient to try the new skills Ginger had taught him, he sucked her clean. Before he finished, Miranda buried his face in her bosom. The next thing Darius knew his penis was joyfully sliding between her twins. If Miranda ever got lost, the missing persons' bureau would have to show a photo of her breasts. As beautiful as Miranda was, Darius doubted anyone—man or woman—noticed her face first.

"I have a special announcement to make." Everyone sat up straighter and moved in closer. Jada smiled again and continued focusing on Darius. "This coming Monday, Darius Henry Jones will assume the posi*tions* of corporate executive officer and senior vice president." Jada had spent twenty years hiding the truth from Darius and she still couldn't confess. Promoting Darius was the best way she could keep him from returning to school at Georgetown.

Hell, yeah! It was about time. "Whoa! Thanks!" Wanting to do somersaults, he resisted. Darius beamed brighter than the day he had received his first car—a metallic gold Escalade. Sporting his Cadillac, he had instantly become the most sought after guy in high school. All the females had gawked as if he were a celebrity. The fellas had been envious. Darius would bet money that each of his coworkers was resentful.

If Darius were handing out awards for assuming positions, Heather Hartzford would have topped his list. Heather's mouth was her greatest asset. Articulate. Sharp. Yes, she was attractive, married to an *African*-American, and wasn't afraid to play race to her advantage. He remembered back to their first time.

Boldly, she asked, "Have you ever made love to a white woman?" If woman *was the operative word, then the answer was no, since the twin girls were seventeen at that time. Darius played along with Heather, wondering how she'd compare to Miranda and Ginger. In a class of her own, she didn't. Her approach was straightforward. She offered a blow job, and he accepted. Heather's collagen-filled lips swallowed all eight inches, causing his bodily fluids to vanish without a trace.*

Four of his mother's division directors had earned international notoriety. Promoting him to such prestigious levels was brilliant, but Darius also wanted his birthday gifts. In order to avoid jealousy and controversy over promotions, clearly she had to light his torch. If the women weren't so preoccupied with trying to persuade him to put in a good word for them, they would have seen his promotion coming. Fortunately, his mother didn't take sides with his father's delaying his well-deserved advancement. Any one of his subordinates could name their price and Black Diamonds' competitors would hire them on the spot, especially Zen Chin.

Zen was five feet, one inch, Asian, and worth her weight in platinum. Aggressive. Confident. Overachiever. Merely getting the job done wasn't enough. Darius didn't know where she found the time or energy. Married. Three kids. Fifty. Zen never lingered. In. Out. That was her style with her clients and with him.

During their first encounter, Zen's hands massaged his neck, shoulders, back, ass, and hard-on in ten minutes tops. "You cum too fast. Next time you go slower." Orgasm timing was one thing Zen eventually made him master. His entire being—mind, body, and soul—was so relaxed he didn't move well after Zen had left her office. The family picture on Zen's desk stared at him, so he placed it facedown.

Dressed in an earth-tone leisure suit, Jada's assistant, Shannon, quietly entered the room. Shannon's hair was combed into two afropuffs—one on each side. Her style was cool. Shannon was fly but not his type. The number one rule of "Darius's Law" was never gamble with anyone who had nothing to lose, so each of his women had intangible valuables as well as monetary wealth. Maxine's parents owned several floral shops around the country, so that made her legit.

"Mrs. Tanner," Shannon bent over Jada's shoulder and said, "excuse me for the interruption. Ms. Ruby is on line one." Shannon's whisper was the volume most people spoke normally. Darius knew his mother wouldn't keep My Dear waiting. Why hadn't My Dear phoned him instead?

"Thanks, Shannon." Jada's hazel-colored eyes gazed in his direction. "Darius, take over until I return."

Great. Now he could strong-arm his staff. Maintaining eye contact, his bodybuilding physique rose simultaneously as he strolled to the head of the asymmetrically shaped table. Darius stood adjacent to his mother, flashed a million-dollar smile, and softly stroked his well-trimmed mustache and his irresistibly thick, milk-chocolate lips. Darius slid into his mother's seat and firmly said, "Black Diamonds' Fifteenth Annual International Cultural Convention will be held in Manhattan exactly three months from today." His pointing finger bounced on and off the desk four times for emphasis.

The corners of Jada's mouth partially spread while her coffee-colored lips pressed together to conceal her smirk. Her eyes glistened as she watched in amazement, then exited through her private door.

Focusing directly on Miranda's forehead, Darius said, "Miranda, I need your updated status report on the Mexican, Latino, Panamanian, and Puerto Rican participants ready for posting to the website by eight o'clock Monday morning." As Darius turned to Zen, he stared dead center at her nose and said, "Zen, let's review your budgeted expenditures for the Asian, Chinese, Japanese, and Korean telecommunications requirements . . ." As Darius spoke, he made contact with Ginger's temples and Heather's eyebrows.

Variety had always spiced his life, so why should his sex life be any different? Why did women falsely accuse him of cheating when they were the perfectionists of seduction? Like vultures, those females swarmed, waited, and then practically raped him as often as he permitted. Why did he crave sex every day like it was food? Was that normal? Not even My Dear could help him if his mother ever found out about his dealings. That would unquestionably be the day he'd die or wish he were dead.

He smiled softly, knowing it secretly turned his women on. Sex had become an academic sport. At least, that was what he learned while in high school and college. Emotions were for nerds who had sugar in their tanks, like his foe, Rodney Banks. Once Darius's heart was involved, he was vulnerable to losing control, and by no means would he allow that to happen. Only weak men relinquished their power. Maxine was the only exception to Darius's law, because she'd never hurt him. And he would love her as long as she allowed him to dominate their relationship.

After dictating for half an hour, Darius peeked his head into his mom's office. "Ma. Is everything all right?" Darius whispered, since his mother never left a meeting for more than five minutes.

Mama answered, "Yes, baby," and her entire face smiled back at him.

When Jada stepped back into the room, Darius immediately relocated to his seat. Everyone was so silent, Darius heard air blowing through the vents.

"Darius, I need you to accompany our potential client, Mr. Barnes, on his business stops today. Shannon has his schedule."

Damn. Why now? Mom knew he hated receiving a special assignment during an important meeting. Jada nodded, so he squared his shoulders and silently exited. Those bitches had better not say a word about what just happened.

Chapter 17

After leaving work on his birthday, Darius dropped off Mr. Barnes and picked up his friend Kimberly Stokes. She was the type of woman who didn't care if he phoned her the day after having sex or a month later. When he'd called her yesterday morning, she was en route to work.

"Hey, Kimberly. What's up?" Darius used her whole name because Kimberly hated when people called her Kim. The first time he shortened her name, Kimberly had politely said, "If you're too lazy to use the name my mother gave me, then don't call me again."

"Darius, baby, what's up? I miss you, dawg."

If a woman called a man a dog long enough, eventually he'd bark. Why was Darius really marrying Maxine? Better yet, why was Maxine marrying him? She knew he wasn't faithful. The only commitment he'd ever kept was sitting courtside at the Lakers' home games.

Although *dog* sounded sweet coming from Kimberly, Darius knew she had the 411 on his modus operandi. Having pledged Omega, he was a pure breed in more ways than one and had the brand on his left arm to prove it. But Kimberly didn't trip, and that was what made her special. "Let's hook up for a few hours for my birthday tomorrow. I'll pick you up at five."

"Sounds like a plan. Now, you know I'm going to use your credit card and shop my ass off today." Kimberly had laughed.

"That's my girl. See ya tomorrow." Darius hung up the phone. Kimberly was generally upbeat and ready to go with a moment's notice. If more women were like Kimberly, he'd be happier. Hell, they would, too. He didn't mind wining and dining ladies, but he refused to pay for headaches when he got that crap for free. Willingly, he paid the monthly maximum on the platinum VISA account he'd opened in Kimberly's name, because she kept him satisfied.

As he parked in front of his condo now, his cell phone vibrated. Looking at the display, he answered, "Hi, Mom."

"Darius, where are you, sweetheart? I need you to stop by the house ASAP."

Darius pulled his keys out of the ignition. "Can't it wait until tomorrow?"

"No, it cannot," she said firmly.

Picturing the expression on his mother's face, Darius restarted his engine and said, "Fine, I'll see you in a minute, but I have plans, so I can't stay." His mother lived on the same block, and they could have walked, but Darius didn't waste any time since he had made plans with Maxine later that night.

"Thank you, sweetie."

He heard the smile in her response. His mom was a trip. As long as she had her way, she was happy as hell. But when she didn't, and things went his way, she made him feel guilty. Darius noticed she did the same with Lawrence and Wellington. Hanging up, he said to Kimberly, "I have to zip by my mom's, but we won't be there long." Finally, somebody remembered it was his birthday.

"Cool." Kimberly refastened her seat belt.

Zipping into the driveway, Darius parked and opened Kimberly's door. Entering their home, he heard his mother call from the banquet room.

"Darius. I'm in here, darling."

He didn't want Kimberly standing in the spacious white marbled foyer alone, so he motioned for her to follow. *Click. Click. Click.* Kimberly's red stilettos tapped on the tiles and dissipated into the carpet. Darius peeped his head into the dark room. "Mom?"

As the lights came on, everyone yelled, "Surprise!"

Oh, shit! Michael Jackson didn't have brighter lights during the Pepsi commercial when his hair caught on fire; Darius wanted to shift into reverse and moonwalk his ass back out the door. Like a vampire exposed to the sun, Darius covered his face and stood in the doorway. Slowly, he placed his hands by his sides. His head remained motionless as he viewed the well-known faces. Unfortunately, he knew too many of them intimately.

Maxine was dressed in a black strapless minidress. Savvy haircut. She must have gotten that done today. The style resembled the singer Eve's, but he was pleased she hadn't changed her natural black color, because that would have required a trip back to the salon. Maxine was outright edible. Her sensuous expression vanished when Kimberly stepped beside him and smiled as if the surprise were intended for her. Maxine clinched her teeth and stretched her cocoa brown, succulent lips so far Darius saw doubles. Thinking of which, two fingers of cognac would surely help right about now. Maxine's eyes bulged and squinted at the same time as if to say, "Your ass had better be able to explain!" If looks could kill, he'd be in transit to ICU. But God must have blessed him with nine lives. Seven of which he'd already used. So at the speed of light, Darius closed his eyes and prayed for nine more.

Kimberly stood five feet, four inches. Slender and completely nude under a red leather coat that scarcely covered her voluptuous ass. Ah man, he hadn't even licked her marshmallow nipples or seen the new strip dance she'd created as his gift. Darius had serious plans to finish what Kimberly had started while he drove on the freeway. An erection stirred in his pants just thinking about her pierced tongue. She'd seriously made him consider pulling over to side of the road. Now he wished he had an emergency exit lane to aid in his escape. Kimberly hid her body behind his and wrapped her arms around his waist. Electric sliding, Darius glided forward and broke Kimberly's grip.

Walking over to Maxine, he said, "Hey, boo," and quickly moved on before her mouth caught up with her wanting-to-destroy-him attitude.

The décor was on the mark. Wild magnolias were his favorite, and they were beautifully arranged throughout the room. If only he could lay Kimberly across the dessert table between the peach cobbler and chocolate mousse, he'd be satisfied for the moment.

"Hi, Dad." Darius hugged Wellington.

Wellington tapped Darius on the shoulder and whispered, "Son, that Johnson of yours is going to get you in bigger trouble. I'm sleeping in the guest quarters tonight, so stop by and see me after you take Maxine home." Wellington patted again.

There was his aunt, Jazzmyne. Funny how a woman could be married to a man, give birth to two children, and neither one was by her husband. Wellington had told him the story about how Jazzmyne's father died not knowing she wasn't his daughter. But at least Granddaddy Keith, who was Wellington and Jazzmyne's real father, knew he had at least two. Even Darius's children would have to take a paternity test. And thank God—from what Wellington had told him—Melanie and her twin, Stephanie, were not related to them.

"What's up, Shelly? Brandon?" Those were Auntie Jazzmyne's kids. Thank heavens Shelly was his cousin. Darius had standards and didn't knowingly do family, no matter how far removed.

His mother's best friend, Candice, was standing next to her husband, Terrell. Since acting worked out so well, Terrell had finally married Candice, and he retired from modeling. Said he was tired of being on the road all the time and was ready to have a few kids.

Then there was his stepfather, Lawrence. "Happy birthday, son."

"Thanks, Dad."

If things got too hectic, he could disappear out the back door and jog to his place. The remaining unwanted guests—Ginger, Zen, Miranda, and Heather—he evaded. Heather and Zen were cool, but it was going to take some serious explaining to Ginger and Miranda to convince them it wasn't his fault. Latino women were far more dominating than sistahs. And the lie he'd have to tell Maxine, huge. Damn, what was his problem? He didn't owe anyone an explanation, especially his fiancée.

That reminded Darius of the time Maxine had shown up at his condominium unannounced. It was her first time stepping out on the wild side, trying to be freaky. When he opened the door, there she stood flashing him. A black G-string was all she wore. She was hot. He was heated and tempted, but all Darius remembered saying before closing the door was, "I'm busy." No one was there, but someone was on the way. If he allowed her to get away with that shit, she'd do it again. And that wasn't happening. He wanted his future wife the way he'd met her, conservative. Darius could get a freak anytime he wanted. Maxine's house was less than a block from his place and closer than that to his mother's.

Jada gave him a big hug and whispered, "This is the last surprise party your mother will give you, darling. Darius, how could you?"

Darius held on to his mother and replied, "You should have told me. Look, Kimberly isn't wearing any clothes under her coat." Kimberly was now at the dessert table, talking with Maxine and swaying her ass to the classical music playing in the background.

"I'll take care of her, Darius. You need to greet the rest of your guests."

That was what he was afraid of. "Thanks, Mom," Darius said as he kissed his mother on the cheek.

Jada graciously escorted Kimberly out of the room. Knowing he'd have another chance to taste that chocolate cream pie tonight, maybe he'd leave his party early and spend the night at Kimberly's place. Darius bounced his head and did the Harlem Shake to P. Diddy's "We Ain't Goin' No Where," when what he really wanted was for everybody, except his family, to get the fuck out. His shoulders bounced up and down; first the left, then the right. His body joined the movement.

My Dear landed a huge kiss on his jaw. "How's my favorite grandson?" Then My Dear did her version of the dance in slow motion, so Darius moved faster.

Laughing, Darius said, "I'm your only grandson."

Darius missed his grandpa, Robert. He'd died three years ago of heart complications caused by his diabetes. The doctor had said if My Dear hadn't changed Robert's diet, he would have died a lot sooner. But all the years of unhealthy eating had caused irreversible damage to Robert's heart and kidneys. My Dear had faithfully taken him for dialysis treatment. First once a week, then twice a week, and eventually the doctor had prescribed a home machine because Grandpa needed his treatment every day.

Never opening a single present, Darius briefly thanked his guests for coming. All of his women had left with the exception of Maxine. Two or three family members relocated to the pool.

"Darius, can I speak to you out front?" Maxine politely grinned with a fake smile because My Dear hadn't left yet. Her tone indicated she was blazing mad. Just like his mom. The softer she spoke, the madder she was.

"Sure. Give me a minute, boo."

Darius kissed My Dear good night and looked at his watch. Ten o'clock. He reflected on how much he appreciated Grandma's protection, not only tonight, but all the time. It reminded Darius of his childhood when he knew his mother wanted to punish him for doing something he had no business doing, but whenever My Dear was near, Darius would run as fast as he could and lay his head in her lap. My Dear never failed him. Jada would say, "Just wait until we get back to L.A." or "Wait until *your* My Dear leaves."

Jada was kind, but when Darius pushed too far, she'd fiercely lash back. The verbal beating was worse than any whipping he could imagine. Each word would break him down until it was impossible to hold back his tears. Darius hated when his mother made him cry. Dealing with Maxine was a piece a cake. She'd never see him cry. Fortunately, his mother didn't harbor bad feelings, because a day or so later she'd always apologize. Then she'd sit down with him and have a heart-to-heart talk. She actually helped him to become more understanding of women's impulsive behaviors. But heaven help him if he screwed up and My Dear wasn't around. That was his ass for sure.

Interrupting his thoughts, Maxine said, "Darius, who was that—"

"A friend. I was giving her a ride home and needed to stop here to pick up, um—"

"Darius, stop lying! I'm sick of your lies. You were planning on having sex with her and then with me in the same night!" Maxine was so courteous she wouldn't curse him out like she should have.

"No, I wasn't going to fuck you. No, I mean her. Look, Maxine. Do you." Darius shrugged his shoulders and tilted his head.

"Do yourself." Maxine took off her engagement ring and put it in her purse. "The wedding is off."

Darius nodded. "Yeah, but you're no fool. I see you tucked away the five Cs of ice. It's yours. I'm not going to ask for it back." That was unless she was serious.

"You would if you knew I started seeing Rodney again. And yes, we did make love. On your birthday because I knew something like this was going to happen *again*." Maxine stood there with one hand on her hip and the other on her purse.

If his fathers hadn't taught him never to hit a lady, her ass would be kissing the concrete right now. Darius was speechless. Pissed! Furious! How could she say that fucking shit to him? He knew she was lying, but the shit still hurt.

Maxine spoke softly. "Darius, I've stood by and watched you screw all these other women, yet you claim you love me."

"I do." Darius gently held Maxine's hand.

Jerking away, Maxine said, "No, you don't. You may want to, but I'm convinced you don't know how. And I can't take any more. I can't change you. If that's the life you want to live, then our engagement is off."

"Okay. Then, give me back the ring." Hopefully, she wouldn't. This was the first time she'd crushed his ego.

The first time he'd spotted Maxine had been on the beach. She wore a banana-colored lace dress down to her ankles. The bottom of her dress was covered with sand. His mother used to wear lengthy dresses, but hers had splits. Not Maxine's. He liked her sense of purity. As he moved closer, he noticed the teddy bear toe ring was cute. The red, black, and green wristband didn't match. "Why are you ruining such a beautiful dress?" She replied, "Beauty comes from within here,

here, and here," touching his head, heart, and hands. She always strolled alone, so eventually he started joining her. As he got to know her, he learned she was a virgin. That was ninth grade. He wanted to be Maxine's first, but his promiscuity pushed her into Rodney's arms.

"Just like that, Darius. I don't think so," Maxine said now, ennunciating each word. "I've earned this ring, and I'm keeping it."

Yes! "You think so, huh." Darius paused and rubbed his mouth. "Damn, boo, you look good. Stop being so ugly. It's ruining my birthday." Darius pulled Maxine into him. Rodney was a chump. Square. Boring. That was why he took Maxine away from him. Surely she wouldn't creep back to that loser. "Stay the night here with me. We're having a family brunch on the patio in the morning. My Dear is cooking, so you know we're going to chow down," Darius said, chewing like a robot. Maxine laughed, so he held her tighter. "I like your new style, boo."

Lifting Maxine's chin, he tilted her head back. His lips softly pressed against hers. For a split second he thought about Kimberly. Kimberly would wait. Maxine would, too, but she was with him at the moment. Like the flavor of kettle popcorn, their sweet tongues tasted Maxine's salty tears.

He didn't like hurting her. It wasn't the first time and definitely wouldn't be his last. Sex with more than one woman was something he had to have. Why? Darius didn't understand. Maybe he'd gotten his insatiable hunger from his mother. When he lived at home, he heard them having sex almost every night. The more he tried to deny it, avoid it, suppress it, the more ferocious his appetite became. Darius craved women. Black. German. Latino. Tall. Short. Gorgeous. Average-looking. Fine. Healthy. It didn't matter. The main requirement was that they were hygienically in touch. But leaving Maxine was out of the question. The only other women he trusted were all related to him.

"Let's go to my room." Hunger lusted in his eyes. He needed to hold her and to sex her like never before.

"I'm not staying the night. I don't have a change of clothes," Maxine said.

Ignoring Maxine, he carried her to his bedroom and then handed her a bath towel and washcloth. "Shower without me. I'll be right back." Darius roamed through the house. No one was in sight. He went to the kitchen, opened the freezer, retrieved a bag of frozen mixed fruit and put the package in the microwave for fifteen seconds to remove the frost. Then he emptied the bag into a bowl and scurried to his room. He'd talk with his dad tomorrow.

"Make yourself comfortable." Darius tossed the universal remote on his bed as Maxine used his towel as a wraparound. He placed the bowl on top of a magazine that was lying on his polished nightstand. Darius showered, allowing the hot, steamy water to pulsate against his muscles. Lathering his cloth each time, he thoroughly cleaned his penis and the crack of his ass three times, stepped out of the shower, and tiptoed into the bedroom.

Sucking Maxine's butt cheek hard enough to leave a mark, with a click of a few buttons on the remote he switched to his musical mix for making love: Maxwell, Joe, Luther, and Kenny G. "So, you forgive me?" Before she could answer, Darius covered her mouth with his. His tongue journeyed down to her collarbone and traced the outline, leaving a necklace of moisture. Picking up a slice of frozen peach with his teeth, he followed the wetness. Slipping three blueberries into his mouth, he juggled the coolness about her nipple. Gently alternating between biting her nipple and the fruit, syrupy juices escaped.

Reaching for the raspberries, Darius place three under his

tongue and one inside Maxine's navel, which he'd retrieve later.

"Um, ooh, ah," Maxine groaned and moaned, occasionally squirming.

He rotated her other erect nipple under his tongue until the raspberry seeds popped out; then he massaged the grittiness into her breast. Bypassing her belly button, he selected a strawberry from the dish, moistened it with saliva so it wouldn't stick, then spread Maxine's legs. Tracing the outer vaginal lips, first with the fruit, then with his tongue, he continued to her inner lips, surrounding her hymen. Chewing the strawberry, he released the liquid stream as it rolled over her clit, and down between her cheeks. Darius teased her rectum, slowly circling the entry and flicking his tongue above and below her opening. Retrieving the chilled banana, Darius put the tip in her vagina while flipping the man in the boat on his head until Maxine gasped for air.

"Just let it flow, boo. How ya' feeling?" Darius said.

"Weird. Like I'm going to go into convulsions," Maxine said. The sheet was crinkled between her fingers.

Darius paused, placed his hand on her heart, and said, "Relax. Take a deep breath and release the sheets." Once Maxine was tension free, he continued.

Replacing the banana with the real thing, Darius moved like a worm, slowly working himself in and out of Maxine until he exploded with the force of a car backfiring. Maxine's scream startled him. Quickly, he muffled her with a pillow. Her body trembled uncontrollably.

"Something's wrong with me," Maxine cried.

"You're fine, boo. You just experienced your first major orgasm. Freaked me out, too, the first time. But the wet side of the bed is yours tonight. You earned it." Partly satisfied, Darius slurped the smashed raspberry from Maxine's navel. Finally, Maxine had the big one. Now he knew she was hooked for life.

"No, it's not my side. Take me home."

"Now? You've got to be kidding. Woman, lie next to me. Wait until the morning." Darius lay on top of the comforter and tucked the pillow behind his head. With Maxine's head on his chest, his limp penis rested on his stomach as he fell asleep in his favorite position, on his back.

Chapter 18

Without opening her eyes, Jada eased her foot over to Lawrence's side of the bed. The farther she stretched, her leg remained sandwiched between the silk sheets. Realizing she heard running water in his bathroom, she dashed to hers. Brushed her teeth. Washed thoroughly. Put a streak of perfume in between her cleavage and slipped back under the covers. If he hurried, Jada could make love to her husband before helping her mother prepare brunch.

Lawrence walked in wearing an animal print towel that covered what she wanted to see most. "Come here for a minute, honey." Jada tossed the sheet back and spread open her arms and legs. As handsome as the day they married, Lawrence smiled and flashed her, opening his towel, then dropping it to the floor. His penis swung like a pendulum. Jada rocked on her knees as if she were horseback riding. Patting his side of the bed, she said, "Lie down." As soon as Lawrence assumed the position, she mounted him.

"You know you want it, so take it," Lawrence said, grabbing her breasts.

The rougher he got, the faster she rode. Lawrence slapped her cheeks together. While she galloped, he bucked, spanking her ass. Almost throwing her out of the saddle, he held her hips, but didn't lessen the pace.

"You the man. Bring it on. Keep up with me now. Ah, yeah." Jada laughed. Grabbing his hand with her superpowers turned on, she locked his fingers so tight his knuckles cracked. Then she stuffed her mouth with a pillow to silence her screaming. The big one was right around the corner.

Bam! Bam! Bam! Bam! Bam!

"What the shit?" Jada said as Lawrence sat up.

"Mom! Come quick! Something's wrong with My Dear! She's not breathing!" *Bam! Bam!* "Mama! Open the door!" Darius yelled.

Jada jumped off Lawrence, raced to her closet, and snatched her robe. The hanger fell to the floor. *God, please let Mama be well.* When she unlocked the knob, Darius was pacing back and forth, holding his head.

"Lawrence, take care of Darius!" Jada sprinted down the hallway past the four rooms that separated her from her mother. She heard footsteps on her heels, but didn't turn around.

Racing in, Jada felt for a pulse. She checked repeatedly.

"Oh, my God! Mama! Wake up!" Jada frantically shook her mother. "Please, Mama, wake up! Lord, this can't be happening. Please! Mama! Please!" Jada screamed as the tears poured down her chocolate cheeks.

"Where's Wellington! He knows CPR. Darius, go get your father!"

"I already called him." Stepping out of the room, Darius said, "He's coming right now. Dad! Hurry!"

Wellington entered the room ahead of Jazzmyne and said, "What's wrong?"

"Mama's not breathing! Help her!" Jada pleaded.

Wellington placed his ear next to Mama's nose. He pressed his fingers behind her ear. He began performing CPR while Jazzmyne picked up the phone.

Repeating Wellington's comments, Jazzmyne said, "No. She's not breathing, and she doesn't have a pulse."

Jada shouted, "Stop asking so many questions and just send the god damn ambulance!"

"They're on their way," Jazzmyne calmly responded.

Mama was lying with her eyes wide open, but not responding. Wellington alternated between mouth-to-mouth resuscitation and hand compressions to Mama's chest.

"I can't watch My Dear like this." Darius stormed out of the room, crying.

Reaching for the sheet, Wellington covered Mama's face. Then he embraced Jada and said, "The angels have taken her home. I don't think this was by accident. I think your mother was ready."

Pulling away, Jada said, "Try to save her! Keep trying!" Her fists pounded on Wellington's chest so hard his robe came untied. "Don't stop! You saved Cynthia! And she deserved to die! Save my mother! Please! Lord! Please! Don't take my mama." Jada slid out of Wellington's arms and slumped into the corner.

Kneeling before her, Lawrence said, "Baby, I'm here for you."

"Please. Just leave me alone," Jada whispered, pushing Lawrence away. Why now? Why Mama? She was supposed to live to see at least one hundred.

Wellington eased to the floor and rocked Jada in his arms. She struggled to free herself, but he wouldn't let go. "Everything must change," Wellington said softly. "We are *all* born to die. It's inevitable. Jada, your mother lived a wonderful life. She loves you the same as she always has. Unconditionally."

Jada wanted to confess to Wellington how she still loved

him unconditionally. Instead of speaking the words, Jada decided it was time for her to show her soul mate that even though twenty years had passed, she still felt the same. Wellington continued holding her in his arms, and she let him.

"I'll go outside and wait for the ambulance," Lawrence said as he quietly exited the room.

"I'll go with you," Jazzmyne said.

Shortly afterward, the paramedics moved in quickly. Jazzmyne and Lawrence came with them, but not Darius.

"I'm sorry," the heavy white man said.

"Try again!" Jada shouted.

"We're sorry, ma'am," the tall, skinny black man said. "We've done all we can." He proceeded to help his assistant.

When the white sheet went over Mama's head a second time, Jada screamed. Turning her back, she couldn't watch those strange men take Mama away. Darius stood in the doorway with tears pouring down his face. His eyes were beet red. Heavy heaves and sighs frequently escaped his shivering lips. Darius tugged aimlessly on his dreadlocks.

"I'll always be here for both of you," Wellington assured Jada with a tight embrace and gestured for Darius to come to him. "We will make it through this. I'm here for you." He kissed Jada on the forehead. "And you." Wellington kissed his son's forehead, too. He hugged Jada and Darius and prayed. "Heavenly Father—"

Jada jumped up from the floor. "I have to go with my mother to the hospital. The ambulance is leaving!" She ran as fast as she could and darted outside. Jazzmyne was standing in the driveway with Lawrence.

"Where's the ambulance! Where's my mother! Where'd they take her? She's gone, isn't she? Noooooo!" Jada screamed and cried.

Jazzmyne comforted her, and Jada's thoughts shifted from her mother's death and plunged into the depths of her soul. Suddenly, she felt alone. Frightened. Lonely. Maybe when

Darius and Maxine married they would bless her with lots of grandbabies, at least three, and she'd protect them just like her mother had guarded Darius.

Jada's hands became clammy. Was this the green light she'd prayed for? All these years she'd helped hundreds of thousands of people better themselves and their communities. What about herself? Her son? The time had come for Darius to know his real father.

Chapter 19

Less than twenty-four hours had elapsed since her mother's death. Ruby Denise Tanner was pronounced dead at 10:10 Saturday morning. Insomnia invaded Jada's body, since the paramedics left their house. Short naps and lots of liquids fueled minimal energy. There wasn't much Lawrence could do to console her, so the few moments he was home, he slept or watched television. He mentioned something about not dealing with the pressure, because if his mother went before him, he couldn't handle the pain. Jada knew the truth was he resented Wellington.

Wellington stayed all day Saturday and into Sunday morning. His presence upset Lawrence so much, Lawrence finally said, "If you don't ask him to leave right now, I'll tell him, and trust me, neither of you will like my approach."

Understandably, Jada told Wellington, "I really appreciate your compassion. I need to get some rest, so if you don't mind, please leave and I'll call you later."

Lawrence's mild-mannered personality was one of the things Jada admired most. Easy going. He didn't believe in arguing off the job, and clearly, Wellington's presence had tested his limits. In Lawrence's opinion, every situation had a logical solution. Easy for him, both of his parents were alive. Lawrence had two older brothers and two younger sisters. Why was it that the middle child always seemed well balanced when an only child appeared the opposite?

Wellington assured her, "I'm just a phone call away."

"Thanks." Jada stood in the doorway.

As Wellington drove off, daybreak had arrived. Knowing she'd toss and turn if she crawled into bed, Jada showered, slipped into her sweats, and drove aimlessly. Not caring about her destination, she accelerated to twenty-five miles per hour as if driving through a school zone. Sitting at corners where there weren't any stop signs, and driving through intersections when the red octagon symbol was clearly displayed, she crept along.

Honking his horn, an irate driver shouted, "If you can't drive it, park it, lady!"

What was his malfunction? Parking her car near Colorado Avenue, she somberly moseyed across the Santa Monica pedestrian bridge. The dawn atmosphere was serene. Bypassing the Ferris wheel, she watched as a few fishermen were baiting poles while other lines already tossed in the water waited for something to bite. The cop shop was quiet. The restaurant was closed, and no one was lingering at the end of the pier. Mama was her best friend. Her sister. Her brother. Her father after Daddy died. Jada had a million things to do, but every single one would wait.

Jada dusted off her yellow hooded jogging suit. Her head throbbed, so she removed her L.A. Lakers cap. As she kneaded her temples, she heard, "Let me do that for you."

There was no need to turn around as she had on her wedding day. Wellington knew the pier was where she cleared her mind. Jada fast-forwarded the video in her head of the night they met. She must have played it a thousand times. Particularly when the floral delivery person showed up at her office like clockwork every Friday with sixteen red roses and one yellow. Initially, the arrangements were sent to her home, but after she married, Wellington had them delivered to her job.

As Wellington took her cap and softly stroked her hair, Jada imagined, "That's not the only thing you can do for me." Her mother's death didn't seem real. Jada closed her eyes. Maybe the feelings of her wanting Wellington weren't real either. Who was she fooling? As ideal as her life had been, it still wasn't complete. If she confessed she'd lived a lie, that would be closer to the truth. She had a wonderful husband and the world's greatest son. Jada slowly turned toward Wellington. Taking her cap, she folded the brim until the sides overlapped; then she pierced her gaze into Wellington's eyes. Noticing his bared the same emptiness as hers, Jada clenched her hands which had become clammy.

"What's it all about?" Jada asked.

"What?" Wellington replied, as he gave her his undivided attention.

"Life. What's life all about? Why are we really here? What's our purpose? Where's my mother? My father?" She didn't care if he answered.

"You know, sometimes I wonder the exact same thing." Wellington took Jada's hat, placed it on his bald head, and gazed out over the water. The waves gently splashed against the posts.

The smell of the ocean reminded Jada of their first date in Carmel when Wellington chased her along the beach. "Death has a way of making you reevaluate your life," Jada said. "It's a reality you never experience until someone you love checks out. Now that my mother is gone, I feel alone. My mother and father loved me unconditionally, and that kept me strong. I have that same love for Darius, but what about me? Who's gonna love me for me?" Jada sighed. Tears began to fall. She turned away from Wellington, placed her elbows on the rail, and nervously squeezed her wet hands as though she'd applied too much lotion.

Wellington repositioned himself directly behind her. He placed his left leg next to hers. Propped his right leg upon the bottom plank. "See, that's where you're wrong. I've always loved you unconditionally, and I always will. If you hadn't left me, we'd still be together." Wellington eased Jada's hands into his and rubbed passionately.

Thinking he would comment regarding the sweat, she waited. After he didn't, Jada said, "There's so many things I have to do to make my life right before I die." She inhaled deeply and blew it out through her mouth as if smoking a cigarette. Jada watched the fog disperse into the coolness of the air. November this year seemed colder than any other.

"Speaking of Darius, I've decided to let him run the office by himself for the next two days. Until we leave for the funeral."

"We weren't talking about Darius," Wellington said. "But since you brought up his name. What in the world were you thinking about promoting that boy to CEO and VP? Darius is not ready to handle the responsibility."

"Please, not now. Darius will do well. I'm training him, and I'm going to send him to management classes." The truth: Jada would have done anything to keep Darius from completing another semester at Georgetown with Darryl. So she'd offered Darius a salary no one else would pay him, and promised if he did well, one day he'd become CEO. This was not the time for a declaration of guilt. She felt depressed and nauseated. But there was one confession she could make to change the subject.

"Wellington, I'm still in love with you." When Jada looked down into the water, she saw a blinding glaze. A mirage of her best friend Candice's face appeared with a frown. Jada could hear Candice protest. "Don't do it, girlfriend. After all these years you haven't learned." Losing her mother taught Jada that there was no lesson for loving someone unconditionally. Would she leave this earth never reuniting with her soul mate? Damn, he was standing right upon her ass, and married or not, it felt natural.

"Diamond." Wellington lifted her hair, and held it against his face.

"Yes," Jada replied.

"Do you know what two things worry me the most when it comes to women?"

Jada remained silent. She opened Wellington's left hand and began to trace his lifeline.

"One is letting down my guard and falling completely for someone who'll abandon me. The other is dying alone, and I don't mean lonely. It doesn't matter if the relationship isn't perfect. I'm not getting any younger, and I don't want to die a single man. I mean, what if no one knows I'm dead in my house for days? Or if I get killed in an accident, they find my driver's license and have to search for my next of kin? Even worse, what if I take ill or need surgery?" Wellington squeezed Jada's hands. "It hurt me so bad when you moved away. But I had to let you go. And every day I prayed you'd come back. And guess what. Now that I'm almost fifty-five, I'm still hoping. I know you're married and Lawrence is a wonderful guy, but I can't help the way I feel about you. I felt so *stupid* that I fell into Melanie's trap. After Melanie and I divorced, I thought if I didn't marry you, I wouldn't marry anyone. Then Simone taught me how to love again. I love her with all my heart."

Jada's fingers contracted. Her eyes narrowed. She felt the hairs on her nape rise. After all these years, she cringed whenever she heard anyone speak of Melanie. Jada hadn't seen Melanie in almost fifteen years. Their sex triangle was Jada's first and her last. Daddy used to say, "If a baby put his hand in the fire and gets burned, that's okay, because the baby has to learn the fire is hot. But if the baby put his hand in the fire a second time, something is wrong with that baby."

Wellington turned her around, pulled her in close, licked his lips, and passionately kissed her. She didn't resist. Then he looked into her eyes and said, "Diamond. You are the only woman I have ever totally loved with my mind, heart, and soul."

Suddenly Jada leaned over the rail and regurgitated air several times. Then she gasped for oxygen. Her thoughts reverted to her mother. The temporary escape from reality helped because as soon as her thoughts shifted, her chest became tight like something had squeezed out the blood. She felt her stomach balled up in knots so strong Wellington had to break her fall.

Chapter 20

Darius stepped into his mother's office as the sole operator. He kicked his feet up on the desk, leaned backward, and clamped his hands behind his head. This week he was the boss. Trapped inside, his feelings stirred like a shaken soda. Keeping the top on, he covered up his emotions because he had to be strong for his mother. Wellington volunteered to assist him in the office, but Darius reassured his pops he could handle it.

Since each of his executives had met or at least seen his fiancée last Friday, Darius took Maxine's photo out of his drawer and placed the picture on the credenza behind his desk. Her place was to support him, not to overshadow him. Up until Friday night Maxine had done great. Under his name his new title read CEO/VP. Damn, twenty years old and living larger than life. He was the shit.

Picking up the phone, he said, "Shannon, cancel the group meeting and set up individual meetings for me. I want to see Miranda in my office at nine o'clock." Miranda was definitely a morning person. "Zen at eleven. Heather at one o'clock, and Ginger at three." He'd saved the best for last.

"Is there anything else, Mr. Jones?"

"Yes, tell each of them to come prepared to workout the details of their proposals for the conference and tell them *not* to bring their assistants."

Fifteen minutes before Miranda would be announced, Darius entered his private restroom, freshened his breath, washed his face and hands, and put a splash of cologne at the base of his hairline above his collar. By the time he sat at his desk, he had five minutes to spare, so he waited.

Shannon buzzed again and said, "Mr. Jones, Miranda is here."

"Send her in." Darius sat up straight.

Miranda walked in wearing a red wraparound dress that stopped above her knees. "Well, hello and congratulations."

Darius changed places to the sofa and patted the cushion beside him. Miranda joined him. Her perfume and candy apple lipstick turned him on. "Thanks. I presume you mean my new positions."

Smiling, Miranda answered, "Yes, that and your fiancée."

On that note, Darius gave Miranda one foot of space as he scooted over. "So, how many sponsors do you have?" Darius asked. Maxine was not on their agenda.

Rubbing his knee, Miranda asked, "How are you doing? I didn't expect you to be at work today, considering your grandmother passed only two days ago. I know how close you were to her."

Moving a little closer, Darius said, "Well, my mother is in no condition to return. One of us had to be here, so that left me. It's hard at times, but I'll get through it. Thanks for asking." His feelings were genuine, but playing the sympathy card didn't hurt. Darius noticed Miranda staring at Maxine's photo.

"I can help take your mind off of things for a moment. That is if you'd like." Miranda extended the V in her blouse.

Unsnapped the front of her bra and exposed her breasts. Darius watched Miranda's nipples harden.

Darius gently grabbed Miranda's hair. He loved the way her silky curls wrapped around his fingers. Then he pulled her lips close to his, and said, "No Thanks." His erection objected, but he overruled because Miranda needed weaning. Red lipstick was too risqué and difficult to remove, so he fantasized about fondling Miranda's breasts: *One at a time. He stood, and Miranda assumed the position. She leaned over the couch. Darius loosened his belt and let his pants fall to his knees. He wobbled over to his coat rack and retrieved a platinum-wrapped condom from his inside coat pocket. Darius put the rubber on the head of his penis and stuffed the foil back where he'd gotten it.*

As he shuffled over to Miranda, he unrolled the condom to the base of his shaft. Darius spat on his hand and smeared it on the latex. Penetrating Miranda, he released what he'd held on to from his session with Kimberly yesterday. Darius came, placed the condom inside his handkerchief, and tossed the contents into a plastic bag.

"May I use your restroom," Miranda asked.

When Miranda returned, Darius noticed her lipstick had been refreshed, so he made a mental note to check for remainders. Women were always trying to leave clues. Hairs. Tissues. Fragrances. Even the little twist caps from the douche bottles. A brother had to minor in forensic science just to stay ahead of the game.

Resuming her seat, Miranda said, "So you're sure you won't take me up on my offer. You zoned out there for a moment. You do have a lot on your mind." Miranda reached for his tie.

Darius blocked her hand and put it on her lap. "So how many sponsors do you have?" Maxine was right. She deserved better, and since he didn't want to lose her, he'd try.

But it was hard as hell because he really wanted to explode inside Miranda instead of fantasizing about her.

"Six," Miranda said, moving to the seat in front of Darius's desk.

Following her lead, Darius sat in front of his credenza, obscuring Miranda's view of Maxine. "Six? How much are they collectively contributing?"

"One point five million." Miranda gathered the opening in her blouse.

"You're one million dollars short. We need ten million dollars in sponsorship funds to have a successful conference. How do you plan to come up with your fourth of the funds?"

"Well, before you came, we were able to do the conference with less."

"True, but the attendees were bored. That was the past. And that's why I'm CEO. You know everyone is going to love my entertainment lineup for the conference. Not to mention my location. Next year it's Trinidad!"

"And it's not a fourth; it's a fifth. So I only need five hundred thousand. How much do you have?" Miranda positioned her pen as if she were preparing to take dictation.

"I'm in charge! What I say goes, and if you don't give me some respect, you'll be out of here before the conference." How dare that bitch question his authority.

"But if you don't mind me saying—"

"Actually, I do. You have until Thursday to come up with one million dollars in sponsorships." Darius stood. "End of meeting."

"What changed you overnight. Damn."

"Life is short. My grandmother lived to see me turn twenty. I believe that's why she held on. She died at eighty-four. If I'm so blessed, I only have sixty-four years left. And I plan to squeeze in as much as I can every single day." Darius zoomed in on Miranda's breasts and said, "Somehow, I don't think I'll make it that far."

Miranda stood. "You won't if you start pushing me around." She unlocked the door and stormed out.

Darius returned to his restroom. He had just enough time to freshen up and inspect before Zen arrived.

Just as he was entering his lavatory, his intercom buzzed. He raced back and answered.

"Mr. Jones, Zen is here," Shannon politely said.

Why wasn't he surprised Zen was fifteen minutes early. "Send her in."

High heels and a short silk printed skirt made her appear taller and slimmer. Zen sat in front of Darius's desk and crossed her legs.

"So how was your weekend?" Darius asked.

"It could have been better." Zen focused on Maxine's photo.

"Yeah, I suppose mine, too. So how are your sponsorships coming along?"

"Three million and counting." Zen responded with confidence. She was definitely his competitor. If he weren't his mother's child, Zen would undoubtedly be sitting in his chair, and they both knew it. Unfortunately for Zen, legacy ruled.

Zen walked behind his chair and massaged his shoulders. Darius moved his neck from side to side. "Ah, that feels great. I'm so stressed." Zen eased her hand down his chest. Stopping her at his nipples, Darius said, "Not today." He gestured toward her seat. "Please. Sit."

Zen sat, then crossed and uncrossed her legs.

Resisting indulgence, Darius said, "After I return from my grandmother's funeral in Oakland, I'd like to take you on a trip. That is if you're interested."

"You're not embarrassed to be seen with a fifty-year-old woman?"

"Maybe. But not one that looks younger than me." Darius knew how to get next to Zen. "And one more thing. I need to take two of your clients and handle them personally."

Zen sprang from her seat. "I won't give them to you. But why are you asking?"

"Don't question authority. I'll give you the details later." It was time for Darius to shift the power where it belonged. His mother's company was overdue for male dominance. Women hated to admit it, but they loved to see men running things, including them.

"Authority my ass. Just wait until Jada returns." Zen paced in front of his desk.

Mixing business with pleasure had started to rear its ugly head. Attitude. Language. Things were definitely going to improve. "Don't bother to sit. Meeting adjourned. And choose your words carefully if you want to remain my employee."

"I did!" Zen shouted as she slammed the door behind her.

Darius took a deep breath, then grabbed his jacket and walked out. "Shannon, I'm going to lunch. I'll be back at one."

"Enjoy." Shannon smiled.

When Darius returned from lunch, Heather was waiting in his office. "You're early. Wait outside for a moment. I'll be ready for you in a minute."

"Wait outside?" Heather frowned.

Darius returned a look that required no further comment. Women. You definitely couldn't give them an inch. They would certainly take it all. He didn't need Heather to step out. It was the principle. Heather was smart, but also underhanded. He thought about Ginger for a minute. She was an absolute sweetheart. If Darius weren't engaged to Maxine, he might have considered Ginger. He was man enough to handle the fifteen-year age difference.

Darius picked up his phone and buzzed Shannon. "Please send in Heather."

"Certainly, Mr. Jones."

"Shannon," Darius said.

"Yes, Mr. Jones."

"Don't ever let anyone in my office without my permission." One more policy change in effect. Eventually, he'd have all of them trained.

"I asked her to wait in the receptionist area, but she insisted," Shannon explained.

"Shannon, you handle your responsibilities so I won't have to. If I do, then one of us isn't needed." Darius hung up the phone and motioned for Heather to take a seat.

"How was lunch? Did you save room for dessert?" Heather asked as she sat in the chair.

She'd messed up already. She should have asked, "How are you doing?" Darius knew Heather was trying to gain control, so he baited his response. "Always." Heather did give the best head. It didn't matter that she didn't have rhythm like Ginger. Maybe the offbeat was a plus. Or perhaps it was the chocolate she craved. At any rate, she ranked at the top of his list in oral copulation. Why couldn't Maxine's pussy feel like Miranda's? Her hands, stroke like Zen's? Give head like Heather? And have a butt that tasted like gingerbread? Darius had loved gingerbread since he was a kid.

Heather attempted to dive right in, but Darius stopped her. Fidelity was beginning to make him feel like a junkie going through detoxification. Since this was his first attempt to abstain outside of his relationship, Darius realized he was a sex addict.

"Please. Not now. We have to discuss business. Sponsors. How many do you have?" Darius questioned.

Heather sat and stared. "Enough. But I'm still working hard. I have a few leads."

"I say how many is enough. I want specifics." Darius impatiently waited for her answer.

"Two. But they're both contributing a half a million each."

"Two! You don't even need to be in my office. Get out and

don't come back until you have your two point five million dollars in sponsorships."

"Screw you, Darius. Your positions went to the wrong head." Heather exited, but surprisingly didn't slam his door.

He chilled until it was time for Ginger. Ginger was happy hour. Bright. Bubbly. Beautiful. She was his greatest challenge because she demanded royal treatment. Even for a nooner he had to take her to a five star hotel. Now that she knew he had a fiancée, Ginger would start pressuring him to call off his engagement and marry her like he'd promised. Thanks to his mother, Ginger had earned her Ph.D. from Harvard while working part-time from home. That was years ago. The one thing Ginger wore well was confidence. No matter how gorgeous a woman was, without self-assurance her attractiveness diminished significantly.

Shannon's buzz interrupted his thoughts. "Mr. Jones, Ginger is here."

Rubbing his palms together and bracing the phone between his ear and shoulder, Darius said, "Send her in."

Ginger was five feet, two inches and barley one hundred pounds; the oldest and shortest of her three sisters. Ginger always wore three-inch heels and had a commanding presence whenever she entered any room.

"Good afternoon, boss. How are you doing? Nice tie," Ginger said as she sat on the couch.

Darius loved the way Ginger always complimented him. Slowly Darius stepped from behind his desk and sat next to Ginger. The fragrance she wore smelled as rich as she looked.

He sniffed her nape. "Thanks. Nice dress."

"Darius, why didn't you tell me you had a fiancée? Why did I have to find out at your party?" Ginger walked over to Maxine's photo and picked it up.

"Ginger. It's not serious. It just looks good in my position." Darius knew sistahs weren't rational when it came to matters of the heart. If he didn't get Maxine's photo away from Ginger, there was no telling what she'd do.

"Well, how about this position?" Ginger dropped Maxine's picture in the trash and brushed her hands together. Then she resumed her seat next to him.

"Let's discuss your sponsors. How many and how much?" Darius walked over and retrieved Maxine's photo. Thankfully, the frame wasn't broken. He wiped it off with his handkerchief and returned it to its place.

"Ten and two," Ginger replied.

"Not bad. You only need another half million." Darius nodded. "You know I've had a lot of pressure on me since my grandmother's death. I promise when the time is right, I'll break off my engagement to Maxine. But until then, I have to play the roll, and we have to keep our relationship private. My mother would never approve of me marrying someone who works for our company, and you know that. So you'll have to quit this job eventually and find another one."

"Whatever, Darius Jones," Ginger said.

Darius smiled. "How about dinner tonight after work?"

"Only if you pick me up and spend the night." Ginger straightened his collar.

"I'll see you at seven." Darius escorted Ginger to the door. He knew he wasn't spending the night. He'd have just enough time to hit it and leave.

Chapter 21

Jada walked into the bedroom with Lawrence trailing behind. "Lawrence, I don't have to explain my actions."

"But, honey, do you have to find solace in Wellington?"

Jada sat on the edge of their king-size bed and untied her jogging shoes. Sweat was still streaming from her forehead from her early morning jog. "You know you've been at the office. And that's okay. I'm not complaining. But I don't need any added pressure. Darius is doing a great job at my company. So Wellington is just helping me out. That's all." The white jogging tennis shoes with blue and yellow stripes around the base dropped by the foot of the bed one at a time.

Lawrence stood in the middle of the floor and said, "The Madison trial should be over by Friday. I can take off next week."

Time with Lawrence wasn't what Jada wanted or needed. No one understood how she felt. Not even Wellington. At least he had Jazzmyne for a sister. Jada had no one. No aunts. Uncles. Generations of only children were destined for extinction. The heaviness inside her chest weighed like cement. "I don't know how much longer I can hold on. I'm losing my grip. I'm trying to stay strong while falling apart. It's driving me insane." Jada stared at Lawrence. Why was he so damn reasonable about everything? "We leave for Oakland in the morning. I'll see you when you get there." If her husband would give her some space, she could think clearer.

Lawrence sat on the bed beside Jada and held her hand. Hugging her, he said, "I'll be on the first plane as soon as we wrap up the details. Honey, I wish I could bear all of your pain and hurt."

No, he didn't. Those were only words that supposedly made her feel better. Jada stood and removed her T-shirt. Sports bra. Jogging tights. Underwear. They all lay alongside her tennis shoes. "You can come with Darius. I'm leaving with Jazzmyne and Wellington."

"Maybe I should wait here until you return. I don't want to make you upset. But I cannot stand by and watch another man confiscate my wife. I'm probably not explaining myself clearly but—" Lawrence hesitated. "Baby, it just doesn't seem like I'm needed. The night your mother died, you turned to him right in front of my face like I wasn't there."

"Morning. My mother died Saturday morning. Lawrence, don't be ridiculous. Of course I need you." Jada walked over to Lawrence and wrapped her arms around him. "I love you." Why was she baby-sitting a grown man?

"I'm sorry for acting so immature. Where are you staying?"

"At my mother's, of course. Jazzmyne and Candice may stay with me. After the funeral, I'll be at my mother's house until I feel like coming home, and I've decided not to sell the house. I can't." Jada walked toward the bathroom. "I'm going to take a shower and lie down for a while."

"I'll be in my study if you need me." Lawrence turned and walked away. Jada felt even worse. How could something so wrong feel so right, and how could something so right—like her marriage—be so right, but yet feel the opposite.

Lawrence had done nothing wrong. The only mistake he'd made was falling in love with a woman who was undeniably in love with someone else. She'd played it safe for the past ten very good years. Fifteen years if she counted from the day they met. Jada decided it was time for her to begin living her life on her terms. She'd lied to Darius. She'd lied to Wellington. He wasn't the father, and she'd known from the day Darius was born. Jada even lied to herself. She wanted Wellington in the worst way. Her heart said yes, but her head protested defiantly.

Jada turned the hot water up as much as she could stand the heat. Tears streamed from her eyes uncontrollably. She couldn't run far enough to forget her mother was really gone. She couldn't cry hard enough to eliminate the pain. She'd hoped her mother would live forever, but her mother had to die. And one day she would, too. There went her head trying to rationalize life and death. The water had started to turn warm. Her fingers had begun to wrinkle. How many more years for her? She certainly didn't want the grim reaper coming for her. If the Lord didn't hear her prayer twenty years ago, surely her next plea for forgiveness would fall upon deaf ears if she didn't do her part.

Wellington had stood by her side through the toughest times. Would telling the truth destroy their friendship? What friendship was based on lies anyway? How did she get to this point in her life? Miss Perfect was a pretender. Fake. Phony. Imposter. And no one knew. Why rock the boat now? God might forgive her. But would anyone else?

Jada reflected on the day when Darius was born. Wellington spent every night in her hospital room at Alta Bates. He took them home. Waited on them hand and foot. At first she couldn't trust him; now she was the one in question. Jada had decided that after the funeral, she would tell Darius, Wellington, and Darryl the truth. Jada hadn't seen Darryl since Darius's AAU game, but she knew exactly how to get in touch with him, through Terrell.

Cold water now flowed from the showerhead. Jada turned off the water and stepped out of the shower. She wrapped the oversized burgundy towel around her body, then picked up the strawberry-scented shea butter. Jada slumped at the edge of the bed.

"Oh, shit! You scared the hell out of me!" Jada hadn't noticed Lawrence was under the covers. "What time is it? How long was I in the shower?"

"Let's just say you won't have to shower in the morning." Lawrence removed the shea butter from Jada's hands. "Lie down." He massaged her feet, legs, and back. "Honey, why am I getting bad vibes?"

"Like what?" She couldn't believe she'd been in the shower for over an hour. Numbness overwhelmed her wrinkled flesh. Her torso became heavy as Lawrence's fingers traveled up her spine repeatedly. As Jada dozed off, she mumbled, "I'm so sorry, honey. I didn't mean to lie."

Chapter 22

Darius shut his office door and called Ashlee. "Hey, girl. What's up?"

"What's up with you? Still getting your bread buttered on both sides in the same place?" Ashlee remarked.

"Look, I'm about to shake things up big time," Darius bragged. "I'm going to make Zen, Miranda, Heather, and Ginger reapply for their jobs. Then I'm going to fire two of them right after the conference."

"Darius! Jada worked too damn hard to build *her* company. What the hell are you doing?"

"They've gotten too comfortable. They're lazy. They're not hungry for new acquisitions." Darius curled his fingers tight. "It's eleven weeks before the conference, and we haven't even met our goal. We should have exceeded it by now."

"You know why your mother's been successful all these years?"

"What's your take?" Darius turned his nameplate around and smiled.

"Because she's not greedy. Nor is she a control freak. Darius, she's entrusted a lot of power in you. Don't abuse it."

"You see, that's just it. I'm not. I'm using it to make *our* company better. We need to set the pace for this millennium. I've got a meeting in five minutes. I'll update you after the funeral. Later." Darius hung up the phone. Ashlee would share his vision once he gave her all the details.

The problem with women was they couldn't separate business from pleasure. Each one of his directors had come on to him first. He was pretty damn irresistible, so he couldn't blame them. Smooth just like his old man. The time had arrived for young, good-looking brothers to launch Black Diamonds into the future.

Picking up the phone, Darius answered, "Yes, Shannon."

"Mr. Jones, Maxine is on the phone."

"Tell her I'll call her back after my meeting."

"She—"

The phone banged against the receiver. He walked out of his office and entered the boardroom, where all of his honeys were looking fine. Darius pranced around the table, looking over their shoulders as he passed.

"Okay. Since each of you already know the budget is short, we'll start with accommodations. The Asian community has requested more visibility. Special street banners with the dates and times of their events, so I want everyone else to follow suit. The Latino partners requested an outdoor salsa dance contest with four guest speakers. Their speakers will educate the attendees on national programs during the competition. So, Miranda, you need to contact your project manager and make that happen."

"When is Jada returning?" Ginger inquired.

"Let's not worry about that. My mother is still recuperating. Just know that I'll be back on Monday morning, but I want e-mails Thursday and Friday from everyone."

"I'm not sending a report until after I've spoken with Jada," Heather commented.

"That brings us to the next agenda item." Scanning their

faces, he knew two of them had to go. Which two was the question? "Black Diamonds is hiring two new executive directors."

"It's about time," Ginger commented. Her brown pantsuit matched her lipstick.

Leaning in his direction, Zen asked, "So what are the new division titles?"

"Oh, there are no new division titles." Darius smiled.

"Then, what are you saying?" Miranda asked, moving in closer.

"We'll discuss the details after the festival. I suggest you ladies do your best. Meeting is adjourned." Darius stood. Although he didn't have his mother's approval on this move, Darius proceeded anyway. Why be in charge if he couldn't make decisions?

"We need to discuss this now," Heather emphatically stated.

Annoyed with Heather, Darius responded, "Right after I suggested you do your best, I said, 'Meeting is adjourned.' " Imitating Ann on the game show *The Weakest Link,* Darius placed his hands behind his back and said, "Goodbye."

Ginger didn't look so happy, but he had them right where he wanted. She'd showed him a great time the other night. Hopefully, she wasn't having regrets. She could save that until after the conference. Surely, they would all be at his mercy.

By the time Darius made it to his office, each of them was penciled on his calendar. The pressure from Ginger was suffocating and causing him major discomfort. Marriage was all she hinted about. But every time he saw her, he had to concentrate too damn hard for his big head to control the little one. Pressing the intercom button, Darius said, "Shannon, cancel all four appointments."

He couldn't wait to tell Ashlee, so he hit redial. "Hey, guess what? I did it!"

"Did what?" Ashlee asked.

"By the time I got back to my office, every one of them wanted me." Darius clicked his shoes on the wheels of his chair.

Sarcastically, Ashlee said, "How?"

Darius whispered, "In the worst way. Let's just say if women had balls, that's how I'd have them. Damn, I'm good!" Shannon interrupted him again. "Hold on, Sis, I'll be back in a sec."

"Mr. Jones, Maxine is on the phone."

"I told her I'd call her back."

"She—"

Darius switched over to Ashlee. "Where were we?"

"You're good, remember," Ashlee said.

"That's right. Thanks. I can hook my male friends up with high-paying jobs. What you think?"

Ashlee sounded annoyed. "I'll tell you exactly what's on my mind as soon as I see you. I'll talk to you later. I've heard enough."

"Cool. Later." Darius hung up the phone and "Crip Walked" to his restroom.

He could use a nice blowjob, but that probably wasn't a smart idea, considering how upset he'd made everyone. What did Maxine want? She knew he was running things, and yet she kept on calling. If she didn't watch her steps, she was going to get fired, too.

Chapter 23

"God, why do you keep blessing me when I know I don't deserve it?" Sitting in the front pew between Darius and Lawrence, Jada felt Wellington's presence in the row directly behind her. The Lord could have taken Darius away from her when he was gravely ill and only two years old. He could have left her distraught when she lost Wellington to Melanie. The dark flesh that wrapped around her body could have ruined her self-esteem. Not once did God fail her. She clearly saw that Darius was God's gift to her.

Losing a loved one resurrected new life. Since life came in many forms, delivery of a child was one way. Convinced her mother's death resuscitated the spirit she'd abandoned for twenty-one years, Jada refused to let her soul mate dissipate into the ever after.

"You know the Lord is blessing you right now." Pastor Tellings still spat into the microphone whenever he preached. "No one, uh huh, was more blessed—you don't hear me now—than Sister Ruby Denise Tanner. This day is truly a time to *celebrate* her transition. No sir-ree, we are not mourning a loss. There's no need to shed tears for a saint. Save your tears for the sinners. Sister Tanner was a woman who was never too busy for the Lord. Huh. Friends. Huh. Family. All right now, huh. *Strangers*. It didn't matter. Heaven is no longer missing this angel."

If Pastor Tellings shouted any louder, she was going to have to move or get soaked. Somebody in the choir needed to hand Reverend a handkerchief, spit catcher, or something. Jada turned around and watched the congregation. Everyone's head bobbed up and down. Doing a double take, she couldn't believe her eyes. Cynthia was seated next to Wellington. And who invited Darryl? He was seated in the pew with Ginger, Zen, Miranda, Heather, Ashlee, and Maxine. Who was running her business?

Why did the good ones have to die so soon? If anyone deserved to meet the Maker, it was Cynthia. Maybe her list of deceit was so long she would have created a backlog at the gates of hell, so Satan left her on earth to wreak havoc on innocent souls. She was the one who had invited Melanie from D.C., then had her stay at Wellington's. Of course Cynthia was conveniently out of town that week, so Melanie couldn't have lounged at her white house high up in the Sausalito Hills by her lonesome.

Clearing his throat, Pastor Tellings said, "Brother Darius Jones and Sister Jazzmyne Jones-Dupree are going to sing 'I Won't Complain.' Lord knows Sister Ruby never did."

Jada had a bigger problem than Cynthia: Darryl. How had he found out about the funeral? Forget that question. Jada already knew the answer. Terrell.

When Darius stood beside Jazzmyne, his face became flushed. Then his tall frame collapsed to the floor. Before Jada could move, Wellington, Lawrence, and Darryl rushed behind the altar. *This is not happening. Why today?* Wellington attempted to hoist Darius into the firemen's carrying position, but Darius's body fell back to the floor. Darryl placed his hand on Wellington's shoulder and said, "I'll help you."

"Lord, not now, please. I'm not ready." Jada thought she might be laid out next to her mama any minute.

Almost everyone gasped or mumbled. The noisy ones trailed Cynthia, making their way to the rear of the church. Darryl grabbed Darius's legs and helped Wellington carry Darius into the pastor's study. The room was more like a small home office: a bookcase, a desk, a full-length standing mirror that stood in everyone's way, a couch, and two wooden folding chairs.

"Would everyone please be seated," Pastor Tellings said. "Ushers, do not allow anyone else beyond those doors, and escort every one who is not family back out of here. Darius will be fine. Men grieve differently from women, and anyone who knows Darius, knows his My Dear meant the world to him."

The ushers moved each rubbernecker out. Jada bit her bottom lip. Jazzmyne, Wellington, Darryl, Maxine, Ginger, and Cynthia, who ignored the plea, stood packed like sardines. Lawrence left because the room was so overcrowded he couldn't get in the door.

Jazzmyne stared at Ginger and said, "Ginger. Out. Now. This is not business." Then she grabbed Cynthia by the arm and shoved her toward the usher. "Please help Mrs. Jones back to her seat."

Whew! Saved by Mrs. P.R. Great interference, but the real dilemma still existed. The choir started singing "I Won't Complain."

Pastor Tellings walked into his study and placed his hand on Jada's shoulder. Jada grabbed Darryl by the arm. *Don't look at Wellington.* Her eyes tried to sneak a peep, hoping Wellington wasn't watching her, but he was. Damn it! Jada hesitantly looked away.

"Smelling salt. Where's my purse?" Jazzmyne ran out and returned with a small bottle. She removed the cap and passed it under Darius's nose several times.

Darius shook his head and whacked the container from Jazzmyne's hand. "Whoa. What happened?"

"It's okay, son," Wellington said.

"Yes, it's okay, son," Darryl repeated.

Shaking his head, Pastor Tellings said, "I'm going back to the congregation."

Darius looked at Darryl and frowned. "Why are you here?"

"I'm—"

Jazzmyne cut Darryl off. "Let's not forget why we're here. Darius will be fine. The rest of you can go back out front."

Darius looked at the small bottle. "What's this, Auntie?"

"If you went to church more often, you'd know," Jazzmyne laughed. "It's smelling salt." Jazzmyne gave Darius another whiff.

"Are you feeling okay, baby?" Jada asked Darius as she felt his forehead. "What happened to you?"

Blocking the yellow solution, Darius coughed. "That's enough, Auntie. I don't know, Ma. I just saw all those people and realized they were here because My Dear wasn't."

Seeing tears roll down her child's face, Jada cried and hugged Darius. The last time she'd seen him that emotional was when the basketball scouts had lost interest in him.

Darius looked up at Darryl and said, "Hey, Coach. You realized you needed me. Thanks for coming. Seeing you here means a lot to me."

"It's all good. I should have been around a lot sooner," Darryl commented.

Jada hoped Darius wouldn't respond. She wanted to rotate her eyeballs three hundred and sixty degrees at Darryl. The nerve of him all of a sudden just showing up, and of all places at her mother's funeral. "Let's get your grandmother buried. My mother is probably turning over in her casket. Let's go. Now." Jada resumed her seat between Lawrence and Darius.

"Is everything all right?" Lawrence asked.

"Yes," Jada whispered.

"Next we're going to have words from Jada Tanner," Pastor Tellings continued as if nothing had happened.

When Jada approached the podium, she wanted to pass out, too. Jada cleared her throat and stepped back, not wanting to get too close to Reverend's soiled microphone. "I wrote this poem for my mother, and I want to share it with everyone today, entitled 'Unconditional.'

Mama, if I had one wish
it would truly be
to love someone other than my child
Unconditionally

I watched you, Mama,
day after day
caring for the family

I saw you, Mother,
time and time again
sacrificing your needs
But not just for us
for strangers, too
and people you barely knew

Mama, if I had one wish
it would truly be
to love someone other than myself
Unconditionally . . .

Heaven is no longer
missing its angel
but, Mama, I'm missing you
tell Daddy I said hello
and one day I'll see you two

Often I've said
if I had to do it all over again
I'd do it all over again
and I wouldn't change a thing

But now that you're gone
I can clearly see
If—
No, When
I learn to love others unconditionally

Only then will I be free

Oh, Mama, if I had just one wish
it would truly be
to love someone other
another and another
my sister and my brother
my husband and my friend
and my soul mate

Unconditionally

Darryl hopped in the limousine with Jada, Wellington, and Darius. Just because he was accustomed to royal treatment didn't give him the right to ride with family, but to get his arrogant ass out would definately cause a scene. Darius and Darryl rambled on about the stats for different players, including themselves. The congested traffic made the ride to Rolling Hills Cemetery longer.

"Man, sounds like with the proper coaching, you would have been a star, too. But your head was too big for my team." Darryl gestured, as though he'd hit a three pointer.

"I know I could have started in the NBA. I was the next

Kobe Bryant, only better." Darius squatted and stretched out his arm like he was playing defense.

"Good for you your mother provided a solid educational foundation. So what are doing now?"

Nodding in Wellington's direction, Darius said, "My old man gets his props, too." Darius stuck out his chest. "I'm CEO and VP at my mom's company. But you never mentioned how you know my mom." Darius shifted his look from Darryl to Jada and back to Darryl.

Jada curled up in the afghan Miranda had hand made and sent to her the day before. Then she quickly shut her eyelids and pretended she was dozing off, regretting she hadn't accepted Lawrence's offer and ridden with him.

"Your mom and I were friends in high school. I proposed to her about twenty years ago."

Darius tugged at her blanket. "Mom, is that true?"

Jada opened her eyes and gave Darius a long, cold stare. "Yes, sweetie, it's true." Then she tensely redirected the same look at Darryl.

Darius and Darryl looked at each other and simultaneously said, "Back to stats."

Jada closed her eyes, leaned her head on Wellington's shoulder, and dreamt she and Wellington stood before the altar getting married. Darius gave her away again. Pastor Tellings asked, "If anyone gathered here today knows why this man and woman—" Cynthia's voice drowned out Pastor Tellings's, "If the truth be told, Christopher, that's one daughter-in-law I can live without."

Wellington stroked her cheek. "Ba, we're here."

As Darius and Wellington balanced her, Jada sat in the center seat directly in front her mother's coffin, gazing at the bleeding hearts. There weren't enough chairs for everyone or sufficient standing room for people to be sheltered under the tent out of the sun. Pastor Tellings kept his words brief as Mama requested. Friends and church members picked roses and carnations from the arrangements. Everyone was dismissed and asked to depart so Mama could be lowered into the ground. When Darius and Wellington reached for her arms, Jada firmly squeezed their hands and said, "Let me be alone, please."

After they left, Jada said her goodbyes. "Mama, thank you for all you've done. Please don't abandon me. I need you now more than ever before." Jada stood, picked up a single red rose and one white rose and a red-and-white carnation. Then she reached into her black purse, pulled out Darius's original birth certificate, laid it atop the coffin, and walked away.

Chapter 24

Mama's burial was everything except peaceful. Jada paced back and forth in her mother's living room. A steady breeze blew through opened windows in the three-bedroom home. Curtains flapped in the wind. The chilled orange juice cooled her throat, but not her body. Sweat poured from her fingers. *Ding. Dong.* A familiar but dreadful sound sparked the moment of truth. Jada peeked in the brass-trimmed mirror hanging above the fireplace and whispered, "Mirror, mirror on the wall, who's the bravest of them all." A gust of wind shook the blinds, rattling her reflection. Jada inhaled deeply as she opened the door.

"Hi, Ma." Darius kissed her cheek.

"Hi, baby. Give Mama a hug." She held on longer than Darius.

"Lawrence left already, huh. When are you going home?" Darius stooped to her level, looked at her quizzically, and asked, "Ma, are you feeling okay? What's wrong?"

The flow of air felt hotter than the catastrophic heat waves in Texas. "Darius, I need to have a heart-to-heart talk with you." The dreadful tone resonated throughout the house again. "I'll get that." Jada held the knob, inhaled, and then quietly opened the door. Wellington stepped inside.

"Hi, ba. How are you feeling?" Wellington hugged, then kissed her.

"I saw that," Darius yelled from the next room.

"I got here as fast as I could. What's so urgent?" Gazing at the eleven-by-fourteen frame, Wellington smiled. "I see your mother still has our picture hanging on the wall."

Before Jada could answer, a third tune chimed, and her stomach twisted into knots like a soaked dishrag being wrung dry. Jada took another deep breath, released it, and then opened the door. There stood Darryl with two young men and a little girl. "Come on in," Jada sighed. "Have a seat here in the living room. I'll get Darius."

Jada made a detour to the bathroom. Bending over the toilet, she regurgitated her breakfast: juice, croissant, and fruit. She splashed cold water on her face, removed her lipstick, and rinsed her mouth with blue Listerine.

She made her way to the kitchen where Darius was peeping in the refrigerator, uncovering the leftover dishes Mama's church family had delivered yesterday. Most of them were untouched because Jada hadn't encouraged the visitors to linger. Cynthia and Melanie had been the first dismissed. Melanie, that slut, had some nerve stepping foot into her mother's house dressed in black from head to toe: purse, shoes, hat, veil, gloves.

"Jada, I'm so sorry you've lost someone close to you again. My condolences," Melanie had said.

Jada had reached back. This bitch must have forgotten whom she was playing with. Maybe the first time she'd knocked Melanie across the room hadn't been enough. Yesterday Jazzmyne had held her back.

"Tell Wellington his wife said hello. If you need anything, just let us know." Melanie waved bye as though she'd won the Miss Universe contest. "Ciao."

"Melanie. Leave. Now. You, too, Cynthia." Jazzmyne had said, wrestling Jada to the next room.

Jada had enough on her mind now not to worry about Melanie or Cynthia. "Darius, honey. Please join us in the front."

"Sure, Mom." Darius stuffed a whole slice of sweet potato pie in his mouth and followed her.

Darryl was scanning their prom picture above the fireplace. She'd been so preoccupied she hadn't noticed that against her wishes Mama had put the brown-and-gold foil paper-framed snapshot back on the shelf.

Tensely, Jada said, "Everyone please have a seat."

"What's going on? Hey, B-ball six-nine is becoming a regular part of the family." Darius smiled. He tapped Darryl on top of his fist, and Darryl reciprocated. Everyone knew Darryl's nickname.

"Darius. Please have a seat, be quiet, and listen for a minute. There's no easy way to say this. I've prayed about how to handle this all your life, sweetheart. Darius. I guess it took Mama dying for me to realize that I had to tell you the truth before it was too late. So with that having been said, Darryl Williams is your biological father, not Wellington."

"Aahhh heck no!" Darius jumped up and bounced around the open space in the middle of the floor. "You're kidding. Right?" He paused in front of Darryl. "Is that why you came to my game five years ago and gave me a scholarship to GT?"

"I wish I could say no, but, son, I honestly wasn't sure if you were mine until I saw you at your AAU game." Darryl remained seated.

"Baby, I wish this weren't true." Jada froze. Wellington scooted as far back as he could in Daddy's old recliner—the one Robert used to sit in—folded his arms, and rested his chin between his thumb and pointing finger.

"So you mean all this time—" Darius stopped talking. He

sat on the love seat next to a little girl who hadn't been introduced. Then he stood. Sat. Paced. But didn't say a word.

"Look, son, I'm sorry," Darryl said.

"You've got that right," Wellington responded as he looked over at Darryl.

"Look, don't be talkin' 'bout my daddy," the girl said. Her head swayed side to side as she stared Wellington down.

"Why?" Darius whispered. "Mama, why did you do this to me? You can't begin to imagine how angry I am with you."

Praying her confession would alleviate some of his pain, Jada recapped the day she'd told both Wellington and Darryl. Reaching for the Kleenex box on the coffee table for a tissue to soak up her tears, Jada said, "I feel so bad about ruining everyone's life. I know no apology can give back twenty years, but I am truly sorry."

Darius tapped Wellington's shoulder. "And why aren't you upset? You knew about this, too?"

Wellington stood toe to toe with Darius, embraced him, and stepped back. Looking into Darius's eyes, he said, "No. I didn't. But let me explain something to you, son. You *are* my son. A very brave man stepped up to the plate and raised me as his own." Wellington shared his adoption history with Darius. "I don't wish this type of devastation on any person. Honestly, I'm disappointed in your mother. But God wants us to learn the importance of forgiveness. You have every right to be mad. Just don't let your anger destroy you." Wellington looked at Darryl. "Any man can make a baby, but a real man accepts responsibility. Darius. Look at me, son. I have no regrets. I love you no matter what."

Darius turned to Darryl. "And where were you? Why weren't you there for me? How do I know you're my father for sure?" He kept pacing.

"Like Jada said, she called me once, I said the baby wasn't mine, and since I hadn't heard from her again, I figured I'd leave well enough alone. I guess the truth was I didn't want to know. Then one day Terrell called and insisted I needed to see you play. So I showed up at your game. But seeing how bad your attitude is, for what it's worth, I'd say you're definitely my son," Darryl said, looking at Wellington. "I'm ready to get to know you. We hit it off pretty well yesterday and while you were at GT. That is until you started trying to impress the females, and they became more important to you than practice."

"Naw. Forget that bullshit." Darius crisscrossed his hands several times. "And stop looking at Wellington. Look at me. I demand a blood test. And even if it shows you are my father, Wellington is my daddy. I don't even know you, man!"

Jada could see Darius was on the verge of crying. "Look, I created this mess, and I accept full responsibility. Be mad at me. Not Darryl. I'm trying to make things right between us."

"You can't take the blame for his ignorance. He treated you like shit! That's his fault." Darius pointed at Darryl and said, "You are to blame! It is your fault! I hate you, man!"

The young girl jumped up in front of Darius and said, "Don't you point your finger at my daddy."

Darius looked down at her. "Who are you? Sit down and be quiet. This doesn't concern you."

"That's your sister," Darryl said. "And these are your brothers, Kevin and Darryl. They came to meet you."

Neither of the guys said a word.

"This isn't something you spring on me all of a sudden and expect me to be happy." Darius opened the front door. "Mom, since you started this, you can arrange for the paternity test. I'm outta here. Peace. I'll see y'all in L.A." Darius slammed the door so hard the walls and floor vibrated throughout the house like a 5.0 earthquake.

"Darius, wait." Jada fell to her knees and crawled to the doorknob.

Wellington firmly said, "Let him go. He needs to be alone right now. A man has to think things through for himself. When he's ready, he'll come to you. Forcing him to come back will only make the situation worse."

Jada eased her way up from the floor and leaned against the wall.

"Well, I guess you can call me with the arrangements." Darryl stood. "If he wants to see me again, he'll have to come to me." Looking at each of his kids, he said, "Let's go."

The little girl extended her iridescent-colored nails to shake Jada's hand. "You're pretty. Just like my mommy. It was nice seeing you Mrs.—"

"Tanner," Jada said as she gently shook her hand.

"Mrs. Tanner. My name is Diamond."

Jada squinted in Darryl's direction as he hunched. "Nice to have met you, Diamond."

"Hi and bye, Mrs. Tanner. I'm Kevin." Kevin extended a firm handshake.

"And I'm Darryl." Darryl hung his head, but gave a firmer shake.

"Give my brother this." Kevin handed Jada his business card. "If he ever comes to New York, tell him to give me a holla."

Darryl walked out after them. "You have my number. I'll wait for your call."

Wellington stepped in front of Jada, held open the door, and closed it behind Darryl. "That's the same guy who confronted me the night we met." Wellington shook his head. "Ba, you should have told me the truth."

"Yeah. I know." Jada plopped down on the sofa.

"He was pitiful then, and he's pathetic now. 'Call me next week if we're still on for Friday night. *Baby*.' " Wellington laughed.

"You remember what he said?" Jada laughed a little, too.

"I remember everything about the night we met, our first

date, our first kiss and I don't mean the hand kiss. The first time we made love. I remember everything about you, woman. Everything." Wellington paused. "Changing the subject, I hate to admit that Simone and Melanie were right. They both told me Darius wasn't mine, but I'm guilty, too, because deep inside, I wanted you to have my child. A part of me didn't want to know the truth. The other part is glad I do. But Simone and Melanie are wrong. Darius is my son, and one day you'll be my wife."

Chapter 25

Monday morning Darius proceeded with the usually scheduled executive meeting. His life was fucked up. The man he thought all his life to be his father, wasn't. A basketball legend was his real dad. That just went to prove money didn't make the man. Darryl could have helped his career into the pros instead of benching him, but his mother never said a word. Why now? Her lies were why she hadn't come to any of his GT games. Darius balled up his fist. "This doesn't make any sense." The pound against the desk left an imprint in the black leather pad.

Marrying Maxine, all of sudden, *was* what he needed more than ever. No one had spared his feelings, and if he didn't straighten up, eventually she'd turn on him, too. His mother would be out of the office for another week. That was enough time for him to annihilate her little conference. Vengeance was his. Darius arrived in the conference room fifteen minutes before his ten o'clock scheduled meeting.

The burgundy leather high-back chair where his mother usually sat was all his today. He stared at the tapestry on the wall until it became distorted. The colors resembled his past.

Patches of blue for how he had suffered yesterday. Red. Anger. That was how he felt right now. Yellow. Sunshine. He'd had the best childhood. Green. Financially, he was set for life. Kudos. Wellington and his mother had done something right.

Ginger cleared her throat. "Darius, did you hear me? I said good morning."

"Oh, yeah. Good morning," Darius responded. His eyes were glazed and heavy with sadness. His heart was aching, but how could a Scorpio man express any outward signs of weakness. That was against DL. "Excuse me for a moment. I'll be right back."

Inside his restroom, he splashed cold water on his face, placed an Altoid underneath his tongue, and slapped on after-shave. "Aaahhhh. That's more like it." The cynical smile in the mirror awakened the personality he knew best. Darius briskly moved down the corridor to the conference room.

"Good morning, ladies. We really appreciated your support this past weekend. It meant a lot to the family. Thanks for the cards, flowers, expressions of sympathy, and for coming."

"You're more than welcome," Ginger replied.

Everyone's eyes followed his to Ginger. Then Darius picked up his Mont Blanc pen and jotted down, *That bitch will be the first to go!* The pressure applied at the exclamation point left a dent. "Ginger, Zen, Miranda, and Heather in that order, you know what to do."

"Do we have to go over this again?" Heather protested. "What about the shortage of hotel rooms?"

"Yeah, and inadequate conference space," Miranda followed with support.

"Ginger, I'm waiting." Darius wrote, *Move Heather and Miranda ahead of Ginger.* Then he drew the head of a hangman. Naturally, the ones who didn't have their shit together would be the first to object. By the time each of them gave an update, the hangman was dangling from the post.

"Zen, I want you to accompany me to New York tomorrow. We're doing site visits for your locations." Before Darius could finish, Ginger chimed in.

"Don't you think *all* of us need to go?" Ginger questioned.

"Ginger, make that your last time interrupting me," Darius continued.

"Miranda, you'll meet me on Wednesday. Heather. Thursday. Ginger. Friday. Bring your project managers with you. Shannon will make your arrangements. Meeting adjourned." Darius stood and walked out of the room. Again he'd saved the best for last. Ginger could stay the weekend in Manhattan with him if she wanted. He'd dehumanize them one at a time in more ways than one.

Bouncing back to his office, Darius decided Ginger couldn't stay. She'd talk marriage the entire time, and he planned on never making a commitment. Not with her anyway. Ashlee could come instead. He needed someone who'd listen to his problems. Soon as he walked into his office, Shannon buzzed.

"Yes," Darius answered.

"Maxine is on the phone," Shannon replied.

"Okay." After Maxine had left the morning after his birthday party, Darius had ignored her calls all weekend because he'd spent his time with Kimberly. Not responding to Maxine's voicemail messages the following week hadn't helped, either. Then he'd virtually ignored her at his grandmother's funeral. "Hi, boo. How are you?"

"Terrible. I'm worried about our relationship. Darius, we need to talk."

She shouldn't have been surprised; he seldom returned her calls. That was how he'd treated her when they first started dating. Things hadn't and weren't going to change. Deal with it or leave. Whenever he required time to think, he didn't want to listen to some female chattering in his ear. "I have a lot of shit on my mind. That's all. Let me make it up to my boo next week."

"Next week? I have to wait an entire week just to speak with you face-to-face?" Maxine's annoying whine reminded him why he hadn't returned any of her calls.

"Look, you know I have to run the company. I'm leaving for New York tonight. I'll be back Sunday evening. I'll take you to dinner. You make the reservations." Dinner was out of the question. Darius would be too tired, but at least it would minimize their discussion today.

"Well, in case you were planning a rendezvous, I thought I should let you know." Maxine began to sob continuously. Suddenly she was gasping for air.

"Let me know what?" Darius whispered.

Maxine wasn't that sensitive. What did he do?

"I really need to see you, Darius," Maxine pleaded.

Good try, but not today. "I'll call you when I get back. We can talk then." Darius hung up the phone and keyed his new schedule into his palm pilot.

Shannon buzzed again. "Ginger would like to see you."

"Uuuuhhhh. Send her in." Darius powered off his palm pilot.

Ginger's perfume arrived before she did. Ginger sat. One leg overlapped the other as she swiveled in the chair. Her nails tapped on his desk. "So why separate dates?"

"You can excuse yourself. Close the door on your way out." Darius stood and loosely folded his arms as he moved over to her and peered down.

"Okay. I apologize. Don't be so touchy. Can I see you tonight?" Now Ginger was close enough for him to feel her breasts touching his wrists as she stood and slowly brushed up against him.

Damn. His dick said, "Yes." But the words, "I don't have time," came out.

"So do you have time now?" Ginger's tongue traced her full lips which were covered with a clear gloss outlined in bronze.

"New lipstick color. Looks good." He lowered his left eyebrow. Darius hesitated as Ginger walked over and locked his door. Then she moved over to him and wrapped her arms around his waist. As she brushed her face against his white shirt, Darius made a mental note to change it. Like his mother, he faithfully kept a change of clothes in his office.

The unzipping of his pants made his penis expand. His head stuck out the top of his white silk boxers. Ginger maneuvered to get the goodies. Her pink tongue circled around the tip several times. Then she slipped it into her warm mouth. Darius looked down. He couldn't believe his eyes because Ginger had never sexed him in the office. Maybe Ginger was trying to secure her position. His cellular phone rang. Ginger didn't stop. She looked up at him. He hated that. "Don't watch me watch you," he wanted to say. Instead, he cupped his hands on Ginger's head and redirected her focus. It was probably Maxine calling back. The sex felt so good Darius refused to budge.

"Awk," Ginger gagged and pointed at her mouth as she headed to his restroom.

"Sorry," Darius said, moving out of her way.

Darius tucked in his Johnson and zipped up his pants. When Ginger stepped out, he walked in. "I'll be out in a second." Darius washed his privates and changed his suit. He opened the door, looked around, but Ginger was nowhere in sight. Good.

Glancing at his palm pilot, he turned it off. But hadn't he powered it off already? The red message light flashed on his cell phone. Darius hit the message button. Punched in his code.

"Darius, this is Maxine."

"Duh," Darius said as Maxine's trembling voice continued.

"I wanted to tell you face-to-face, but since you don't have time to see me . . ." Maxine sniffled. "I just received a call from Rodney, and he's HIV positive. And so am I."

Darius stared out of his corner office window. First Darryl. Now this. What was next? He slammed his phone to the floor so hard the battery pack popped out. Darius grabbed his keys.

"Shannon, I'll be back in about two hours."

"Okay, have a nice lunch," Shannon said.

All kinds of thoughts invaded his mind. Darius did ninety-five on the freeway whenever he could. Then he zigzagged between cars. Parking behind Maxine's PT Cruiser, he got out of his car, hit the lock button on his remote, and walked to the door. He rang the bell.

"Hi, Mrs. Moore. Is Maxine home?" Darius was too upset to fake a warm hug, so he stood erect.

"It's a pleasant surprise seeing you here. Come on in. Maxine is in her room. She's not feeling well. She won't tell me what's bothering her, but I'm sure seeing you will cheer her up."

"Thanks." Darius walked upstairs and knocked on Maxine's door.

"Come in."

When he walked in, she hurriedly hung up the phone. Darius closed the door. "Who was that? Rodney?"

"Darius, I didn't want you to find out that way." Maxine sat on the padded vanity stool and faced him.

Pacing back and forth, Darius stopped in front of her and said, "So you're serious about this HIV?"

"I wouldn't lie about something like this."

As his backhand descended toward Maxine's face, Darius halted. What if she was infected? He might contract the disease, too, if her blood mixed with his. "So you fucked Rodney? Is that what you're telling me!"

Scurrying to her bedroom door, Maxine opened it. "Yes, I did. I told you I had."

Thinking about the fruit salad and how he'd eaten Maxine inside out after his party, Darius threw up on her Persian rug.

"Give me back my ring, and I don't ever want to see you again." Was that the same way Darryl had treated his mom?

"But, Darius," Maxine pleaded.

"But Darius nothing! Give me my fucking ring, Maxine!" Darius retrieved his handkerchief and wiped his mouth.

"Fine!" Maxine removed the ring and hummed it at his head. "I'll report all of those Jezebels you work with, too, because I know you're sleeping with all of them! I hate you, Darius Jones!"

"Hate yourself." Catching his ring in midair, Darius walked over to the door. "I'm so angry right now, Maxine, I don't even need a reason to beat your ass or anybody else's. You've already given me two. One, you cheated on me. Two, you fucked a mutherfucker who's HIV positive. Strike three, Maxine, and I will lay your ass to rest." Darius rushed past Mrs. Moore on his way downstairs. "And bitches have the audacity to call us dogs."

Chapter 26

"Look, Simone, I've heard enough. Get your purse and let's go." If Simone didn't leave soon, Wellington would be late picking up Jada.

"I told you he wasn't your son. Just admit that I was right and you were wrong, and I'll leave." Simone followed Wellington into his bedroom.

"I have one better," Wellington said, putting on a splash of cologne. "Darius is my son. So are you prepared to let Jada meet Junior?"

"Hell, no! You'd better not bring Junior anywhere near her lying ass. My son is not related to her or Darius."

"Don't sit down on my bed. Let's go. And what do you mean your son?" Wellington had already decided Jada could meet Junior whenever she wanted because Junior was his son, too.

"Where're you going?" Simone sat back on the bed, looked at her watch, and said, "Why are you all dressed up and smelling good and it's not even eleven o'clock?"

"That's why I divorced you, remember? For the last time, Simone, let's go." Wellington left her sitting on the bed and went downstairs. The last time she played this game, he'd locked her in his house and gone to Los Angeles for five days. She'd unsuccessfully tried to break his advance security system by calling the police, but they wouldn't assist her. Instead, they had phoned him and he'd simply advised them Simone could leave whenever she was ready. If Simone hadn't been so upset the whole time, she actually knew him well enough to have figured out the code was Diamond.

Simone stumped down each step. Wellington escorted her to her car and drove off in his Bentley. Parking in front of Mrs. Ruby's house, Wellington lowered the volume on his radio and said, "Dial."

His automated female voice system responded, "Who?"

Wellington responded, "Darius."

The system replied, "One moment please."

"Hello," Darius answered.

"Hey. I thought I'd call and check on you. How're you doing, son?"

"As well as could be expected. I'm headed to New York tomorrow to manage a site visit for the conference."

"You know burying yourself in work is not going to take away the pain. Hey, maybe we should take a trip. Just the two of us." Perhaps if they were alone, Darius would confront and stop suppressing his true feelings, instead of staying mad at everyone. The last time they traveled together, Darius had been seventeen.

"Thanks, but no. I can handle this. Really."

"I know you're still upset, but think about seeing your brother while you're in New York." Having two older brothers could be good for Darius if he'd get to know them.

"I'll think about it."

"You the man." After Jada's confession, Wellington clearly understood why she'd prematurely promoted Darius. "I'll check on you tomorrow. Bye, son. I love you."

"Yeah, I know. I love you, too. I'll catch you later, old man." Darius paused, then said, "Hey."

"I'm listening," Wellington responded.

"Thanks."

"Don't mention it," Wellington said.

"Bye." Darius hung up the phone.

Going up to the house, Wellington rang the bell three times and waited about sixty seconds. When he released his phone from his waist holder, Jada opened the door.

"Come on in," she said, walking away.

Wellington followed her. "You ready?"

"If you are," Jada responded. "Let me get my purse."

"Whoa. You know I have to ask. What's up with all the gray?" Jada was dressed in all gray: boots, denims, and a waist-high sweater with no bra. "You hate that color, but, ba, it looks great on you," Wellington said.

"It's my mourning color. I didn't want to wear black, and since I hate that my mother's gone, this was the best color to coincide with my feelings."

Women made the simplest things complicated. "So have you eaten at Cioppino's?"

"No," Jada said, without exhibiting any curiosity.

Despite the fact that Melanie had introduced him to the place, Cioppino's had become one of Wellington's preferred Italian restaurants. Wellington drove to San Francisco and parked at the Mission and Fifth Street garage. Sunshine and crisp breezes greeted them.

"We can take the Powell and Hyde Streets trolley from Market Street. Hopefully, Saturday lunchtime isn't too busy. Besides, it's a beautiful day," Wellington said. By taking the trolley, he could avoid Pier 39, because they had shared too many memories there. Most of them good, but it was also the place where they had last dined prior to breaking up.

When they reached the San Francisco Maritime National Historic Park at Beach and Hyde, a tall black man dressed in a brown uniform announced, "Okay, folks this is the end of the line. Everyone must get off. My trolley, that is."

Wellington laughed, but most of the tourists didn't. They started snapping pictures of the driver as he pulled the cord sounding the bell. Jada had been quiet since they had left the house. Wellington glanced around. What were the odds they would run into Melanie? He jumped off the car and helped Jada.

Walking downhill toward Jefferson Street, Wellington asked, "How's Lawrence?"

"Huh. What? Oh, he's fine. Working, I guess," Jada said.

Okay, no more Lawrence questions. They crossed the street, turned right, and as they walked another block, Wellington put his arm around Jada's waist. "What do I have to do to perk you up?"

"Bring back my mother. Make up for the twenty years Darius didn't know Darryl. I really don't want to eat. My stomach hurts," Jada said, folding her arms under her sweater.

"But you need to eat something, so let's go inside."

"Why do you keep looking around? Are you expecting someone?" Jada asked.

"Of course not, ba." Damn, was he that obvious? He'd better stop being paranoid. Why had he brought her to Melanie's place anyway?

"Table for two?" the young Italian girl asked.

"Can we sit outside?" Jada asked.

Before Wellington could protest, the hostess grabbed two menus, a wine list, and said, "Sure."

Wellington pulled out the black wrought-iron chair and pushed it under Jada. "Wait here. I'll be right back." He dashed across the street and paid the artist to paint a portrait of them dining. Then he slipped into Cartoon World and purchased a small stuffed Tweetie Bird and raced back to their table.

As their waiter approached, Wellington placed the Looney Tunes bag on the yellow cement plant holder next to their table.

"May I take your drink orders?"

Looking at her nametag, Wellington asked, "Suzie, is Danté bartending?"

"As a matter of fact, he is." Suzie smiled.

"Then, we'll have two Danté specials." Jada needed to loosen up a bit. Danté's potent mix reminded Wellington of Pat O'Brien's hurricanes in the New Orleans French Quarters.

"Certainly. I'll be back to take your orders in a minute." Suzie checked on the table by the door, then went inside.

"Ba, stay another week. Darius can handle the office." One more week away from her office wouldn't hurt. Wellington wanted Jada to never leave, but seven extra days would be nice.

"I'll think about it. That's the only thing he'll talk to me about is business." The left side of Jada's mouth twitched. Her cellular phone rang. She flipped it open, looked at the ID, closed it, and put it back in her purse.

"I spoke with Darius a few moments ago. He'll be fine. He has to digest what's happening."

"Yeah, and then figure out how he's going to dominate the situation," Jada commented.

Toot. Toot.

Wellington hurriedly twisted his head, then grabbed his neck as he shifted in his chair. A car rolled up so close to the curb he could almost shake hands with the passenger without moving from his table.

"Hey! How are you guys doing?"

Whew! His chest rose and fell as he wiped his forehead. "Hey, Wendy. Where's Walter?" Wellington said, trying to play it cool. Walter was still his best friend, and Wendy was still happily married to that square brother.

"At work. Hi, Jada. You're looking good, girl. See you guys later." Wendy waved as they drove away.

"Are you sure you're not expecting someone?" Jada asked.

"Positive." So what if Melanie showed up. He no longer cared. Wellington took a deep breath and relaxed.

Danté walked outside carrying their drinks with a huge grin. "My man. What's up? Haven't seen you in a while. You look great as always. If you need a refill, let me know. And tell my girl Melanie I said hello."

Jada's eyes were focused on the silverware until Danté mentioned that name.

"Since you've bared your soul, how about I do the same? That way we can both either feel like shit or be relieved."

Jada's hazel eyes looked up at Wellington. "I'm listening."

"The reason you haven't met Junior is because Simone doesn't want him around you." Wellington weaved the white linen napkin between his fingers.

Jada sucked in air. "What! Why didn't you tell me this? Why not?"

"I just didn't think you'd understand." Wellington shook his head. "Plus, I was trying to establish my own position. But I've decided you can meet him whenever you'd like. I can bring him by before you leave."

Suzie walked up. "Ready to order?"

"We'll both have calamari salads on baby greens. The lady would like the grilled salmon filet. Are they really caught locally?" Wellington was making small talk to delay his confession.

"They sure are." Suzie smiled. "What else would you like?"

"I'll have the whole Dungeness crab with homemade pasta." Wellington motioned for Suzie to come closer and whispered in her ear. "I slipped Danté a small paper bag. Take the item, cover it in a pile of chocolate mousse, and bring it to us for dessert."

Suzie smiled and walked away, then soon returned with their salads.

"Is there anything else you didn't think I'd understand?" Jada asked.

"Yes, Melanie and I have managed to remain friends over the years. That's why I was looking around, because sometimes we eat here. And," he paused, "the triplets she was carrying weren't mine."

"I don't believe this." Jada picked at her calamari. "And what about your divorce?"

Hunching his shoulders, Wellington responded, "What about it?"

"Why does she refer to herself as your wife?" The fork poked in and out of her baby greens.

"Oh, don't pay any attention to Melanie. You know how she is."

"I don't believe you! How could you not tell me after all this time?" Jada said, pushing away from the table.

"How could I what? Lie for twenty years and expect everyone to pardon me?" Wellington stared at Jada. She couldn't seriously be mad at him.

"That's a cheap shot, but you're right." Jada reposition her chair. "I'm going back to L.A. next week. I have some unfinished business I need to take care of."

"That's a good idea." Go. He'd expected her to say that because she always ran away from her personal problems. Maybe she'd feel guilty and let him taste her tonight.

When Suzie brought their orders, Wellington fed Jada from his plate and ate off of hers.

Jada dipped Wellington's finger into the butter and sucked it off. The tightening of her jaws rushed familiar memories to both of his heads. Wellington shivered and noticed Jada's nipples were protruding. His penis responded in kind. "Damn, Lawrence is a lucky man." His heart rate quickened, remembering how The Ruler clamped perfectly between her breasts and measured the distance deep inside Jada's throat.

"I have a question I'll probably regret asking," Jada said.

"Then, don't ask." Wellington dipped Jada's finger in the sauce again and opened his mouth.

Jada spread the butter on his nose. "Did you and Melanie ever have—"

Wiping his face with his napkin, Wellington said, "A threesome with someone else?"

Jada nodded.

"You're right. You don't want to know." Wellington continued eating his crab.

"Do you think that's where we went wrong?" Jada asked.

"I thought about that for years. And my answer was consistently no. This is the best crab." Wellington took a lump of meat and fed Jada.

"Then"—Jada paused so she could chew—"what do you think?"

"To me there were a number of reasons: lack of trust, friendship, love. Those are the things we didn't have then, but we have them now, with the exception of trust."

"You don't trust me?" Jada frowned.

"I'll take the fifth. But I will say that's why you never came back to me. Your lack of trust and honesty made you insecure, and true love and friendship can't survive the test of time without honesty and trust."

"You're right. I do still love you," Jada said.

"But it's conditional." Wellington hunched his shoulders.

"It was, but it's not anymore. I realize tomorrow isn't promised. Hearing the news about Aaliyah convinced me I may not see the sun set. I want to die, with no regrets. Death has a way of clearing out the fog so you can see the road ahead. I might not make it to the horizon. That's about as far as I can see with my naked eye. But the third eye sees all. I'm trying to live my life through my third eye." Tears trickled down Jada's face.

"So what are you saying?" Wellington intensely stared at Jada.

"*We* shouldn't leave this world with any uncertainties. From now on, when I make a mistake, I want to make it based on love and honesty. I want to know in my heart I felt I was doing the right thing. Regardless of the outcome. I know what

I did to Darius and you was wrong, but I've tried to correct my mistake."

"Good point. A lie can only be repaired when you confess the truth, and we all make mistakes," Wellington said as he reached across the table and wiped away her tears.

"Can we start all over again?" Jada asked.

"No. Unfortunately, we can't," Wellington responded. "But we can move forward from this point in love, with honesty, trust, and friendship. I offer you all those things. Starting right here. Right now." Wellington signaled for Suzie to bring dessert.

Suzie walked up to the table, holding a covered silver platter.

"Jada Diamond Tanner—"

"Wellington, you are so crazy." Jada started to laugh and cry.

"I want to know—"

"Yes! The answer is yes!"

Wellington smiled hard as the waiter lifted the top. A lump a chocolate mousse sat before them. Wellington took the platter and drew circles in the cream with his tongue. He scooped the cherry off of the top. "Um." Then he dove full faced into the sweetness and retrieved a small bottle of chocolate-flavored cocoa butter lite oil with his teeth. He took Jada's hand and released the bottle in her palm. "Would you *please* give me another table shower massage?"

Jada roared with laughter, scooped the mousse from Wellington's lips, and ate it. Then she stuck her right hand into the dessert and smeared Wellington's face.

"Finally, I made you laugh." Wellington grinned as he sucked the remainder off her hand. Before he got to her ring finger, he positioned his tongue in a familiar crevice and French kissed her hand. Jada closed her eyes, and he moved on to the other fingers until he finished off the pinky.

"Everything happens for a reason. Don't ask, but this is

my fifth year. Something major always happens to me every five years since we've separated," Jada said.

"Do what's in your heart. I'm yours, if you want me," Wellington responded.

"For starters, I will stay another week," Jada said.

Wellington paid the tab and tipped Suzie and Danté. He handed Jada the yellow Tweetie Bird key chain, and they walked across the street. The painting of them dining at one of Cioppino's sidewalk tables was one he'd frame and store, knowing one day the picture would hang above the fireplace in their home.

Chapter 27

Sunday morning Jada exited the plane to find Jazzmyne waiting. Instead of staying an extra week in Oakland like Wellington wanted—and she'd promised—Jada returned home to her husband. Consciously, she'd freed herself of one lie. Jada's sense of urgency now lay ahead under her own roof.

"Hey, thanks for picking me up." Jada hugged Jazzmyne for almost two minutes.

"No problem. How're you feeling?" Jazzmyne stepped back and grasped Jada's hands.

"I don't know. Some moments are better than others. Girl, with the airport security madness, I checked all four of my bags."

"Girl, I'll get the car and meet you at United's curbside check-in. Passenger arrival was bumper to bumper when I came."

"Okay," Jada responded. She picked up a luggage cart in baggage claim, retrieved her bags, and rode the elevator to the upper level.

As Jada stepped outside the automatic doors, Jazzmyne waved. "I'm over here."

Jada rolled her cart to the skycap booth and asked one of the workers, "Is CR working today?"

"Yeah, he's at the next station. Hey! CR! Someone's looking for you!" the young guy shouted.

"Hey, baby. How you doing? I haven't seen you in a while. Where've you been?" CR said as he gave Jada a hug.

"My mom passed away. I just buried her." A lump formed in Jada's throat as she forced back her tears.

"Oh, Jada. I'm so sorry. If there's anything I can do, you know I'm here. Let me take your bags." CR rolled the cart.

"Thanks. Jazzmyne's parked over there." Jada pointed at the white new model Jaguar Jazzmyne was sporting.

"Girl, I thought I was going to have to come over there and get you," Jazzmyne said.

CR placed the last suitcase in the car, closed the trunk, and said, "Bye, and don't forget to call me if you need anything."

"Bye, CR." Jada blew a kiss.

"Yeah, bye, CR." Jazzmyne waved and drove off.

Pulling out her cell phone, Jada started to call Lawrence at work, then decided it would be better to surprise him when she got home. The last time she'd tried that was with Wellington, and she had been the one in for the surprise. Lawrence was different. Yes, he was a man, but he was respectful. That was exactly how Jada had to confront their situation.

As Jazzmyne drove by Sycamore Avenue, Yamashiro's restaurant popped into Jada's mind. The number was already programmed for speed dial. "Yes, I'd like to make reservations for two at six." Since she'd taken the two o'clock flight out of Oakland International, that would give her a full two hours to settle in and get dressed.

"Sorry. No availability for six. Let's see, can you come at seven?"

"Sure. I'd like a window table overlooking the gazebo. Last name is Anderson." Whenever Jada made accommodations for them, she used Lawrence's surname. The Sunday afternoon traffic along Pacific Coast Highway was slow. The gazebo had been closed off for years, but one hardly noticed because the sloping hillside and ocean view were breathtaking.

"Sorry. No window for seven. We have one for you at eight."

"Thanks. Eight is fine." A couple of extra hours wouldn't hurt. Although they would miss the sunset, eight was actually a better time for both of them.

"Are you going to work tomorrow?" Jazzmyne asked.

"No, I need another week." Actually, Jada was taking Wellington and Darius's advice. With so many events happening, she hadn't allowed herself to fully grieve. Another week off from work was necessary for more reasons than one.

"I dropped in his office a few times." Jazzmyne nodded. "Seems like Darius is doing a decent job."

Knowing Lawrence, he was probably working late, Jada thought. During their last conversation, he'd said the next time they spoke, she would have to call. The more Lawrence tried to console her, the farther she pushed him away.

When Jazzmyne pulled in front of their house, Jada noticed all the cars were parked in the driveway, including Darius's. They hadn't seen each other since he'd stormed out of her mother's house. She knew he was blowing off steam and he'd come back after he calmed down.

Jazzmyne placed Jada's luggage in the middle of the foyer. "You haven't heard a word I've said."

Jada looked at Jazzmyne. "What?"

"Nothing. I'll call you later." Jazzmyne got in her car, tooted her horn, and cruised out of the driveway.

Jada closed the front door and left her bags where they were. Peeping through the house, no one was in sight. The living room was empty. As she walked past her study, her computer was on, so she stepped inside and saw a shadow move.

"Darius? What are you doing in here?" Jada turned on the

light. Darius didn't respond. He minimized the screen and shut the computer down.

"Darius, I asked you a question," Jada repeated herself.

"Working." Darius continued to look at the seventeen-inch monitor displaying the words, "It's now safe to turn off your computer."

"Darius, get out of my office. That's why you have your own," Jada insisted.

Darius hit the power button and brushed past her. Jada grabbed him by the arm. Darius aggressively jerked away. "What is your problem?" Jada asked.

Looking down at her, he said, "You. Maxine. My Dear was the only real woman I knew." Darius stomped off. Later she heard a door slam.

Jada shook her head. "Children these days. I just don't know. I guess he's not over being angry."

In some ways Lawrence's upbringing had been fuller than hers because he had siblings. Family day, which was every fourth Sunday at the Andersons', was like a reunion. Lawrence's grandparents lived on a farm outside of Los Angeles. Pony rides. Dunking machines. Swimming pool. Jumping balloons. Swings. Cotton candy. Popcorn. Potato-sack races. There was always someone getting his or her hair braided or twisted. The youngsters gathered in a circle just before sunset and listened to the elders tell folktales. No wonder Lawrence made the perfect husband. But the Andersons and the Joneses could never combine events. Wellington's mother's nose was so far up in the air, she could sniff the clouds. Cynthia knew nothing about how to have fun, but she could raise hell all by herself.

Jada sat on her side of the bed. If she didn't get in touch with Lawrence, she'd be dining alone at the restaurant or at home. If his cars were home, then how was he getting around? She sent him a message on his two-way pager and plopped across her bed. The security light on the panel flashed. Jada rushed to her sliding patio door and stepped outside. Darius was putting a suitcase in the back of his car. She frowned and walked back inside. Better to just let him be. Kneeling beside her bed, she prayed, "Dear God, give me the strength to change the things I can. The courage to accept the things I cannot. And the wisdom to know the difference." Jada begged forgiveness for all her sins.

When she opened her eyes, Lawrence was standing next to her with a colorful bouquet of assorted fresh flowers. "Welcome home."

"Thanks." Jada stepped into Lawrence's open arms and embraced him. "How'd you get here so fast? I just e-mailed you."

"I was in transit. We have a big case in court tomorrow, so my dad picked me up and dropped me off. I'm happy you're back."

Jada hesitated, then said, "I'm not going to work tomorrow."

"That's probably not a good idea. In fact, you need to go," Lawrence insisted.

"What do you mean by that? My business is doing very well, thank you." Casually, she rolled her eyes upward.

"Exactly what I said. If you weren't so busy laying up in Oakland with Wellington, you'd know, too." The floral arrangement was now upside down in his hand.

"Okay." Jada sighed. "I see what this is about. I was going to put this off, but there's no need." Jada looked Lawrence directly in his eyes and callously said, "Lawrence, I'm filing for a divorce." After she'd said it, she felt like scum stuck to the bottom of a shoe.

"What! Divorce? Okay, you have every right to be upset. I've been lonely without you. I miss you. I just want my wife back. I admit I'm jealous, but there's no way I want a divorce."

Uneasily, Jada said, "There's really nothing to discuss. I hate to see our marriage end like this, but I cannot and will not continue to live a lie." The thumping in her throat quickened. She had to tell him eventually, and no time was the right time.

Lawrence bit his bottom lip and said, "Then, I guess it's fitting to let you know three of your four top executives have consulted with my father to sue Black Diamonds. And it's just a matter of time before the last one joins in."

"What in the hell are you talking about? Don't be ridiculous. I treat my staff exceptionally well. Lawrence, you don't have to use my company to get back at me." Jada sat on the red sleigh bench at the foot of their bed.

"I'm not." Lawrence loosened his tie and the first two buttons on his shirt.

"Well, what's the case about?" Jada figured she'd better learn as much as she could in case he was telling the truth.

"Sorry, confidentiality prevails. We naturally declined representation, but my grandfather gave them two referrals." Lawrence threw the flowers to the floor. His size fifteen squashed them into the carpet. "They're better off without you. So am I. I should have known I'd be next. Any woman who'd lie to her own flesh and blood surely wouldn't hesitate to pull a fast one on her husband."

Floral fragrances burst into the air. Sooner or later she had to tell Lawrence the truth. But Jada never imagined the conversation happening the way it just did. Damn. Fine. So be it.

Jada pressed the talk button on her cell phone twice to redial the restaurant. "Please cancel the Anderson reservation for eight o'clock." If Lawrence wouldn't tell her what was happening, she wasn't going to beg. There was another man who would. Theo.

Chapter 28

Darius was livid. After promising she would stay in Oakland another week, his mother had lied again by coming home early. Regardless, he was implementing his plan at her expense. Since New York had been a big hit, he'd invited Ginger, Zen, Heather, and Miranda to spend a different day of this week out of town with him again. His treat. Actually, at his company's expense. Darius had wanted to tell Kevin—while they hooked up in New York City—the shit Maxine had laid on him, but he wasn't sure if Kevin was blood or if he could be trusted.

Maxine couldn't have been serious. Her last name was definitely going to remain Moore, or at least it never would become Jones. As much as Darius lusted after sex, death was better than living with AIDS. Relocating to a new environment where no one would judge him or treat him differently was another option. New York was cool, but after the conference too many people in Manhattan may recognize him. Maybe he'd live in Canada, D.C., or Cannes.

Shit! Darius repeatedly slapped himself upside the forehead. He used a condom religiously, except when he was with Maxine. Was this God's way of punishing him for boning so many women? Or was Maxine trying to fuck with both of his heads?

Darius picked up his home phone and started dialing Maxine's number so he could curse her ass out: first for being unfaithful, then for backsliding to Rodney—because a man never wanted to be defeated by the same idiot twice—and ultimately for testing positive for HIV. Looking at his watch, it was only three o'clock in the morning. Before she answered, he hung up. What good would that do? Plus it would give Maxine the upper hand, and the only time he allowed a woman on top was during sex. His plane was leaving in a few hours, so Darius decided to use his cellular phone and call his best friend.

Ashlee answered in the middle of the second ring, "Hello."

"Hey, Ashlee. What's up?" he said as he left his house and got in his car.

"Just waking up." Ashlee yawned. "What time is it? Everything okay?"

"I'm on my way to meet Zen in Chicago," Darius replied as he cranked up his car.

Ashlee sleepily asked, "Business or pleasure?"

That's what happened when you confided in a woman. "You know me. But on the serious tip, I need your support on something."

"Sure."

Darius took a deep breath. "Maxine called and told me she tested positive for HIV."

"Darius, no! Not Maxine, she's such a nice person. Is she sure? But it's not like Maxine to say something like that unless she was sure." Ashlee lowered her voice and said, "And you?"

"I don't know. I haven't been tested yet. Ashlee, I'm scared. What if she's telling the truth and I have it, too? Then what?"

Ashlee coughed into the receiver. "Excuse me. *If* Maxine

contracted the virus within the past couple of months, *and* the two of you had unprotected intercourse during that time, that's not good. Once the virus enters the system, the viral load builds up heavily but tends to decrease after about eight weeks. I did say decrease not disappear."

Darius bit his bottom lip so hard he almost drew blood. "Now I'm really frightened, sis." He punched his steering wheel.

"Calm down. In addition to the level of infectiousness, you also have to be susceptible. It's a good thing you eat right and work out, and hopefully no blood was transmitted from Maxine to you. Oh, yeah, stress can also increase the probability of transmission because it adversely affects your immune system, so try not to drive yourself insane. I'm flying to L.A. I have two weeks vacation time. I'll go with you to get tested and stay until you get your results."

"I can handle this." Darius plunged his accelerator. "I just needed someone to listen. I recently took my paternity test, so I'll call my doctor today and ask him to have the lab run both tests at the same time."

"Then, it's all set. I'll be there, and we'll go for your results together," Ashlee insisted. "You're not planning on having sex with Zen, are you?"

"No. I'm not." He never planned to have sex with anyone. It just happened.

"I know you, Darius. Please refrain until after you get your results. Please, Darius," Ashlee begged.

There was no traffic at three-thirty, but he hated the new three hours prior to departure check-in regulation. He and Ashlee talked the whole way to the airport. Darius parked in the short-term lot and continued his conversation with Ashlee using his hands-free headset as he retrieved his bag from the backseat of his car. "Don't worry. I'm practicing safe sex."

"The only safe sex is no sex. It won't kill you to wait a few days, but you might kill someone else if you're infected," Ashlee scolded as if she were his mother.

The airport was crowded as usual. Darius strolled inside the terminal. His dreadlocks were bonded together with a black rubber band. The blue Fat Albert T-shirt had the whole gang on the front and was long enough to hide his new No Limit boxers with the platinum tanks on the waistband. His sagging blue jeans covered his untied Timberland's. Darius carried Ashlee's conversation along with his belongings to the security checkpoint. "I'll be cool. I gotta go. I'll call you tomorrow."

"I'll see you Thursday. You know I love you. You're the only brother I have."

"Bye, sis."

"Bye."

Darius placed his phone and earpiece inside his front pants pocket. Realizing he didn't know what gate to go to, he walked over to the monitor and scanned for his flight number. His seven o'clock flight was on time, surprisingly, because L.A. was notorious for delays. Darius continued his stride through security check. After waiting over an hour for the attendants to arrive at the gate, he walked up to the ticket counter with his confirmation in hand. Darius noticed her nametag and handed her the piece of paper.

"Chicago?" the flight attendant asked.

"Yes." Darius smiled. Tammy could have just read the information he handed her, but she was looking so fine it didn't matter.

Tammy keyed in the numbers and stared at her screen. Then she looked up at Darius and said, "I'm sorry. This reservation has been cancelled." She handed Darius back the piece of paper and asked, "Are you sure you have the right number?"

"I'm positive. Check again," Darius insisted as he searched

for his Executive membership traveler's card. "There must be some mistake." This time Darius flirtatiously smiled at Tammy.

Zen had taken an earlier flight, and his driver was instructed to meet her at her gate. Then they were to wait for his plane to arrive.

"I'm sorry, sir. The reservation is definitely cancelled."

Darius leaned over the counter. "I insist on getting on this plane." Darius spoke slowly and deliberately. "I did not cancel my reservation. If I had, I wouldn't be standing here. Do you realize how early I woke up for this flight?"

Tammy didn't respond. Instead, she made eye contact with the attendant standing next to her behind the counter.

"Well, let me purchase another ticket and I'll straighten this mess out when I have time." Darius pulled out his platinum American Express Business card and placed it on the counter next to his membership card.

"You'll have to go to the ticket machine, the purchasing counter, or customer service. I can't issue tickets at the gate." Tammy picked up Darius's cards, and looked at the credit card photo and then at Darius before handing them back. "You look much better in person. Sorry I couldn't be of more assistance." Tammy smiled.

Darius snatched up his cards. "Fuck!" Bumping into anyone in his way, Darius raced to customer service. The line was long, so he continued walking and skipped everyone else and stood in front of the next available representative.

The airline employee behind the counter said, "Sir, you're going to have to wait at the end of the line."

"I have a plane to catch, and they're boarding right now." Darius had seen other people get away with jumping the line all the time, so he ignored this Tammy's comment.

Opening her hand, she said, "Let me see your ticket."

"I have an e-ticket. Here's my confirmation number." Two women named Tammy in the same day. That was not a good sign. The first one was white. This one was black. And they both looked good enough to eat.

"You shouldn't have cancelled your reservation. This flight is overbooked. I can put you on standby for this flight, confirm you on the one o'clock flight, and you can fly standby for the next two flights leaving at nine and eleven, because they're overbooked, too."

"Never mind. Forget it." Darius picked up his carry-on bag and walked away. His cellular phone rang. The ID was blocked. Normally Darius would ignore unknown callers and let them leave a message. "Hello."

"Darius, this is Zen. I expected to get your voicemail. Where are you?"

"I can't make it to Chicago. Just have the driver escort you for the day and have him bill my account."

"There is no driver. Just me. What in the hell is going on?" Zen muffled her words to keep from shouting.

"I don't know. My flight was cancelled, and by the time I get there, it'll almost be time to leave."

"I'm catching the next plane back to L.A. Don't ever ask me to meet you anyplace ever again. I could have been at work." Zen hung up the phone.

Darius shook his head and returned to customer service to confirm his reservation for Tuesday's flight. Everything was solid. There must have been some kind of mix-up. Tomorrow's flight with Miranda would be better.

Darius paced the floor and looked at his watch. After yesterday's episode, he'd hired a driver to take him to the airport Tuesday morning. His driver was already thirty minutes late, and his flight was leaving in exactly two and a half hours. Perhaps his escort service screwed up his place of pick up. Ever since his mother had returned from Oakland, Darius had stayed at his condominium. How could she have lied to him for twenty years? Thirty-five minutes and still no driver, so Darius decided to call a taxi. After waiting fifteen minutes for the cab, Darius fired up his Escalade and tore out of the driveway. He parked, rushed inside, checked the monitor, and prayed he'd make it through security in time for his departure. Fortunately, he heard, "Boarding all rows for flight number two seventy-two to Vancouver." Darius confidently handed the attendant his confirmation. She keyed in his number twice.

"I'm sorry, sir. This reservation has been cancelled."

"Oh, hell no! Not again. Something must be wrong with your computers. My flight was cancelled yesterday and today!" Darius was raging mad.

"The flight isn't cancelled, sir. Your *reservation* is cancelled," Sophia responded.

"Somebody's going to get to the bottom of this. Let me speak with your manager."

Sophia picked up the intercom and announced, "Last call for boarding on flight number two seventy-two." Then she responded to Darius. "I can page her for you, but I'm not sure how long it'll take. If you'd like, you can go speak with her. She's downstairs in ticketing. Her name is Amanda."

Darius walked away shaking his head and decided it was best for him to go home before his mouth landed him in jail. When he arrived back at home, he cancelled and rescheduled his flights with Heather and Ginger to New Orleans and Las Vegas. Shit! He'd forgotten all about Miranda. Darius dialed her cell phone but couldn't get through. Miranda was going to be pissed, but he wouldn't see her until the following Monday because they had both scheduled Friday off for personal reasons. Hopefully, Miranda would take advantage of the luxury package he'd arranged for the two of them to enjoy in Canada.

Maxine probably thought her little stunts were funny. A scorned woman was a dangerous woman. Darius lay back in his recliner, turned on his TV, and placed his hands behind his head. The new black-and-red Jordan's he'd received in the mail over the weekend were kicked off his feet and landed on the hardwood floor. Who else would have a reason to be so vindictive?

Darius reached over, picked up his phone, and dialed Theo's number. Theo answered on the first ring.

"What's happening, my man?"

"How could you tell it was me?" Darius asked. "I have a blocked number."

"You know you can't play a playa'. Every number is displayed on my phone, including international numbers, my brother. Now, what can I do you for?" Theo asked.

"I need a favor, man." Darius rubbed his hand over his mouth and chin.

"Shoot."

Darius calmly said, "I need you to find out what's going on with my ex-fiancée."

"Maxine Moore?"

"That's the only one I've ever had," Darius remarked.

"Won't do it. I only do that kind of stuff for your mom. She's the boss."

"Well, I'm the man in charge now. Haven't you heard about my promotions?"

"Yeah, dawg. I heard. But I'm still not doing it. I gotta run. Peace, baby."

Damn! If Theo wouldn't do it, then Darius would hire his own private detective. He was definitely going to find out who was responsible for his cancellations and whether or not Maxine was lying about having HIV. And when he found out the truth, Maxine was going to wish she'd never met Darius Jones.

Chapter 29

Living with Lawrence was like having a roommate who also shared her bed. Spending most of the day behind closed eyelids, Jada slept through breakfast, lunch, and dinner. By six o'clock Lawrence had been dressed, and all she remembered seeing was the back of his suit as he walked out the bedroom door jingling his keys. No good mornings or goodbyes. Like watching *Ground Hog Day,* the next two days were exactly the same.

Obviously, Lawrence's real reason for begging her home had been to get her away from Wellington. Since she hadn't answered her cell phone and barely returned his calls, Lawrence claimed she'd spent most of her time in Oakland with Wellington. Making love to Wellington had come so close their lustful friction could have started a blaze greater than the Oakland Hills fire.

Lawrence's interest in her had fizzled. After she'd stunned him with the news, he left early for work, got home too late for dinner, and making love had been more like relieving stress. Lawrence came fast and dozed off even faster. His usual cuddles and discussions were conspicuously absent. She wanted to talk about their divorce, while he acted as if the separation wasn't going to happen. What did he think? One morning she'd wake up, come to her senses, and change her mind. Maybe, if her left brain shifted into gear.

Jada's situation confused her. Her heart said leave, and her head did, too; but guilt kept pressuring her to reevaluate matters over and over again. What if Wellington said he wanted her only because he thought she'd never leave Lawrence? Or what if she left an ideal relationship to chase a mirage? Even worse, what if Wellington and she were incompatible soul mates? Was there such a thing as soul mates destined to exist only in spirit? Jada simmered those thoughts on the back burner, took a long, hot shower, got dressed, and headed to her office.

Jada parked in her reserved space. The elevator was running slow, so she hiked up the stairs fifteen floors. As soon as she set foot in the door, Shannon scurried from behind her desk.

"Oh, Mrs. Tanner, you don't know how happy I am to see you." Shannon hugged her, then held her shoulders and stepped back as if to say, "Let me look at you." Then she wrapped her arms around Jada again.

"Okay, Shannon. That's enough. I missed you, too," Jada said.

"I'm sorry, Mrs. Tanner. I'm just so glad you're back. I'll let you get settled. If you need anything, I'll be right here." Shannon pointed at her desk.

Jada walked into her office and buzzed Shannon on the intercom. "Shannon, what time will Darius be in today?" Jada shifted through the pile of papers on her desk.

"He's out of the office until Monday," Shannon responded.

"Monday? Then, who's acting?" Jada placed the stack of papers back in her in-box.

"Zen, until he returns."

"Well, notify Zen I'm back. Better yet, set up a staff meeting at ten with all my directors and see if Jazzmyne can make it here by nine to meet with me first."

"Yes, Mrs. Tanner. Anything else?"

"No. That's all for now." Jada hung up the phone and went to Darius's office. The door was locked, so she used her master key. It didn't work. Jada frowned and went to Shannon's office.

"Did Darius have his lock changed?"

"Yes, Mrs. Tanner."

Reaching out her hand, Jada said, "Well, let me see your key."

Shannon shook her head. "I don't have one."

Jada stood silent for a moment. "Where's his mail?"

Shannon handed Jada a yellow nine-by-twelve envelope with Darius's name on the front.

"Thanks." Then Shannon handed her a letter from the Center for Disease Control addressed to Darius.

"What?" Jada whispered.

"It's probably a mass mailing," Shannon commented, handing Jada four more envelopes. "Zen, Miranda, Ginger, and Heather received a letter from them, too."

Jada's eyes focused on the letters. Without looking at Shannon, Jada mumbled, "Um, I see. Thanks." The quietness of Jada's office door glided and then clicked upon closing. "Center for Disease Control." Jada smoothed her fingers over the address and Darius's name. "Why would such a letter come here?" If she opened his, that would be an invasion of privacy and illegal. Jada placed the white envelopes in the center drawer and proceeded to sort through the rest of Darius's mail.

There was a check for two hundred thousand dollars from a Korean company, another for the same amount from a Japanese firm, and a third check for four hundred thousand from a business in China. Why was Darius receiving checks from Zen's clients? Jada made a note to address the issue in the meeting. Jada opened her middle drawer and peeped at the envelope with Darius's name. The short buzz on Jada's intercom startled her.

"Yes, Shannon."

"Jazzmyne is here to see you."

"Great. Send her in."

Jada greeted Jazzmyne at the door. "Hey, how are you?"

"How are you?" Jazzmyne asked as she wrapped her arms around Jada.

Jazzmyne's warm hug was comforting and spoke a million words. "Thanks," Jada said.

"You look good, Miss Lady," Jazzmyne complimented, and sat in the chair on the side of Jada's desk. "So what's so important?"

"I just need to get caught up on everything. I feel like so much has happened in such a short period of time."

"Well, hasn't Darius kept you abreast of the progress?"

"He hasn't really spoken to me since I told him about Darryl." She was to blame for lying to Darius.

"Girl, this is your business. Son or no son, if he's not keeping you in the loop, then you need to set the record straight. As your PR person, let me say, company first, family second, because love doesn't have anything to do with business."

"You're right," Jada responded. Jada thought about telling Jazzmyne about the letters but decided against it, knowing Jazzmyne would advise her not to open them. After the meeting, Jada could call Wellington for his opinion.

"Are you sure you should be back at work so soon?" Jazzmyne said.

"Yes, I'm positive. Sitting around the house was making me depressed and insane." Jada glanced at her watch. "We'd better get to the conference room."

When Jada walked into the room, two persons were absent. "Where's Heather?" Jada asked.

Ginger promptly responded, "Probably in New Orleans."

"Where's Darius?" Jada asked to see if anyone knew.

"Probably in New Orleans," Ginger responded again.

"Ginger, since you obviously know something the rest of us don't, would you please be more specific?" Jada stared at Ginger.

"I don't know for sure. I just overheard Heather and Darius talking in the lunch room," Ginger lied. The information in Darius's palm pilot had him scheduled to be in New Orleans on Wednesday. Ginger had been able to cancel Darius's reservations for Monday and Tuesday, so she knew Miranda and Zen were pissed on and off. However, Wednesday's plans had been cancelled before she could do it. But that was all right, because she was headed to New Orleans right after this meeting. Heather had confirmed his plans hadn't changed. After tonight, they would all have sufficient evidence to support their lawsuit. Darius had trampled over her for the last time. Starting today, she had the upper hand.

"Zen, did you change accounts with Darius?" Jada asked.

"No," Zen responded.

Interesting. Zen didn't elaborate. "Zen, why don't you start and give us your update for the conference?" Jada smiled.

Zen's report, indeed, reflected she was in control of each of her accounts. Upon request, Ginger and Miranda provided the status on their portfolios. Strangely enough, only Zen's clients had been redirected.

"Well, that concludes our meeting, ladies. Thanks—"

Jazzmyne interrupted, "Ginger, can you stay for a moment please?"

Ginger looked puzzled. "Of course."

As Zen and Miranda exited the conference room, Jazzmyne closed the door behind them. "I've done damage control for the firm for the past twenty years. I've worked with you for the same amount of time. I've sensed something between you and Darius, but after today's meeting, I'm positive. Now,

I want you to tell us"—Jazzmyne nodded in Jada's direction—"exactly what's going on between you and Darius?"

"Nothing." Ginger hunched her shoulders. "I don't know what you're insinuating."

"Okay, if you insist," Jazzmyne said.

"Ginger. Thanks for your support. You're excused," Jada said.

Jada stared at Ginger as she strolled out of the room as if she owned it. "What's going on?" Jada asked.

"I think you'd better call Theo and have him do an internal investigation," Jazzmyne replied. "I don't trust Ginger anymore."

Jada picked up her notepad. "Thanks. I'll call him soon, and I'll talk with you later."

Trying to show Darius she trusted him, Jada really didn't want to have her son investigated. If any of the allegations were true, she'd look like a fool for promoting him in the first place.

Jada returned to her office. She scribbled aimlessly on the paper. Slowly she opened her desk drawer, removed Darius's letter, and slid the gold metal opener under the flap. Numbness covered her entire body. She picked up a pencil and scratched her scalp to see if her nerve endings were functional. "Ouch!" Jada couldn't believe what she'd read. Without hesitation, Jada called Wellington at home.

"Hello," Simone answered.

"Hi, Simone. This is Jada. I need to speak with Wellington." Jada started rereading the letter.

"He's busy right now," Simone said as if Jada had disturbed them.

Jada could hear Wellington's voice in the background. "Who is it?"

"You said you weren't accepting calls. Either you are or you aren't." Simone seemed disgusted.

Jada could understand how that marriage had failed.

"Who is it?" Wellington repeated.

"Jada," Simone responded.

"Hey, what's up?" Wellington's voice was the next and only one Jada wanted to hear. Especially after listening to Simone suck her teeth.

"You have a minute?" Jada said seriously.

"Always, for you," Wellington said. "Simone, could you give me a moment of privacy, darling? Thank you." Wellington paused, then said, "What's wrong? I can hear the tremble in your voice."

Tears streamed down Jada's cheeks as she sobbed, trying not to let Shannon hear her. "I received this letter from the Center for Disease Control with Darius's name on it."

"So what you're saying is Darius received a letter from CDC?"

"Yes, and I know I shouldn't have opened it, but I did. Wellington, Darius might have been exposed to the HIV virus."

"What! You shouldn't have opened it, ba."

Jada had known he wouldn't agree; that was why she'd opened the letter before she called. "I know that."

"Okay, does it say who reported it?" Wellington asked.

"No. But that's not all. We also had a meeting this morning, and Jazzmyne suspects Darius and Ginger have been intimate." Jada sniffled.

"Listen to me. Don't tell anyone else about this. I'll be on the next plane out of here. I'll see you tonight. Make sure Darius is at home."

"He's out of town. He's scheduled back in the office on Monday. And Jazzmyne told me to call Theo and have him conduct an internal investigation."

"Don't tell anyone else about this until I get there. I'll see you in a few hours. You know I'm here for you." Wellington's kiss squeaked through the phone just before the dial tone.

Shannon buzzed Jada on the intercom.

Before she spoke, Jada said, "Hold all my calls, please."

"It's Theo, Mrs. Tanner."

"Okay, put him through."

Jada tried to sound upbeat. "Hi, Theo. How are you?"

"Ain't nothing stirring that we can't shake off like a cake mixer. You sitting down, baby doll?"

"Yes," Jada sighed. Maybe she should have stayed at home today.

"Word has it that a multimillion-dollar sexual harassment suit against Black Diamonds is brewing."

"Theo, I can't afford that! I'll lose my company! What the hell is going on?" Jada was tired of crying, so this time she didn't.

"I don't have all the details, but apparently your son has been playing Dick Executive Officer with each of your directors, and they all have proof."

Jada reflected on the CDC notices addressed to each of her staff members. "If that's true, I stand to lose everything I own."

"You stay cool. Act like you don't know anything, and tell Jazzmyne to do the same. I'll stay on top of this. By the time I finish digging up their dirt, there'll be enough to bury them twenty-four feet deep. Everybody's got skeletons. Trust me, doll. I got this. Don't worry your pretty little head. I'll be in touch. Peace."

What if they were all infected? Damn! Jada grabbed her purse and stormed out of her office. "Shannon, I'll be out the rest of the day. Call Jazzmyne and ask her to take over."

"What about Zen?" Shannon inquired.

Jada cut Shannon a sharp look and squinted her eyes, then said, "Jazzmyne." Reflecting on what Theo had just told her, Jada slowly walked away with all of the letters in her purse.

Chapter 30

Somebody's daughter was going to pay. Whenever a woman caused a man to suffer, another woman had to endure equal or greater pain. Emotionally. Physically. Sexually. Sometimes a female got slammed with all three, a triple dose. That wasn't part of DL. That was just the way some men were. Women shouldn't personalize unexplainable bullshit and beat downs as much as they should generalize the shit. The trickle-down effect struck most women at least once in their lifetime. And if she didn't have enough sense to leave after the first encounter, she'd better be on guard for the triple double because that kind of crap was like a bad penny.

Darius was grateful his Wednesday flight to New Orleans had been hassle free. Surprisingly, his driver had showed up at his condo on time, and when he'd handed the L.A. ticket agent his confirmation number, she'd handed him his first-class seat assignment.

When Darius exited the seven forty-seven at Louis Armstrong International, Heather was waiting with open arms. Unexpectedly, everything had gone according to plan, and their driver was there, too.

"How was your flight?" Heather asked after kissing Darius on the cheek.

"Fantastic." Darius played it off and walked side by side with Heather as if they were in town on business. He knew enough about the dirty South to avoid any racial confrontations. Forget the cops. The sistahs were the ones issuing the threatening looks.

The Big Easy had an eerie feeling in the air. Before Darius stepped outside of the automatic sliding glass doors that led to the garage, the morning humidity surrounded his body like an electric blanket set on high, sticking to his sweaty flesh. Massive pollution from cars and taxis of all colors—red, blue, black, white, green, purple—was trapped under the overpass that resembled a cave but with two openings, one at each end.

Nudging Heather, Darius said, "Notice how every cab is different." He pointed to his left, then to his right.

Heather's head followed suit. "Yeah, that's neat."

"Well, that neatness represents how divided this place is. Jews. Blacks. Whites. Creoles. Catholics. Baptists. Episcopals. And unlike Californians, they all speak their minds. Remember that." Darius appreciated the directness, because he never had to guess what a Nawlins' native was thinking.

A woman bearing four front gold teeth between the largest lips Darius had seen smiled, waved, and yelled, "My dear, I'm over here." The combustion invaded his lungs as he covered his face to hide his burning, watery eyes. He missed his My Dear more than he'd ever imagined.

With all the pressures riding on his shoulders, Darius would have sworn he'd died and gone to hell, because it was sinfully hot. The only thing that was missing was Satan sitting on his shoulder with a pitchfork yelling, "Burn in hell, Darius Jones, and bring as many victims with you as possible. Your My Dear can't save you now. Your soul is mine!" Laughter rang out as four little boys, each wearing shorts with no shirts, whisked by Darius and Heather. One day he would truly have to account for his sins.

"Are you okay?" Heather asked.

The feel of Heather's hand on his back made him more paranoid. Darius wanted to sacrifice his locks so his scalp could breathe, and if he did kiss his dreads goodbye, it would be a first. Suddenly, Darius realized he had never surrendered anything. He scratched his head and replied, "I'm fine. It's just too damn hot here. Didn't anybody tell them summer was over? I can't wait to get back home."

The limo escort, who had remained silent until now, chimed in, "Man, dat's why we move so slow. Look around. See anybody in a hurry? If ya do, they ain't no native for sho'."

"Aren't you sweating with that black suit on?" Heather asked the driver as he loaded the trunk with their bags.

"Baby girl, JT don' sweat. Don' drink enough wadah fo' dat. A sip here and a sip der'. Drink alcohol instead. In Nawlins that's the law, ya know. Everybody's gotta one-drink minimum, pe' day. And the chillins ain't no exception. Oooooouuu wee." JT bucked his eyes wide right in front of Heather's face. "JT got a li'l taste waitin' for ya wid some ice in the limo. Try it for ya self." JT opened the door. Darius motioned for Heather to get in. The ride in the limo to the Ritz Carlton downtown on Canal Street was about a half hour with traffic. Darius checked in and let the driver—who delivered to the doorman, who delivered to the bellman—deliver their luggage to the suite. Unlike Wellington, Darius was conservative with tipping. He handed each of them a ten-dollar bill.

When Darius unlocked the door, Heather walked in, glanced around, and said, "This is the type of room I want for the conference." Then she fell backward on the king-size bed and pretended to make a snow angel. "I'm starved. Let's get some crawfish and oysters on a half shell." Heather reached over, palmed Darius's ass, and laughed heartily. She had dyed her brunette hair blond for several years because it made her appear younger. The tapered style showed off her catlike eyes and girlish freckles.

Darius straddled Heather. He unbuttoned, then unzipped her black cotton slacks. The salt-and-pepper-colored hairs between her thighs didn't match the ones on Heather's head. Her pant legs were turned inside out as Darius dropped them to the floor. He unbuckled his baggy black jeans, kicked off his tennis shoes, the pair Miranda missed her chance to see, grabbed his penis, and started penetrating Heather as if this would be their last time together. That was the way he felt.

Heather's hands forcefully pressed against his chest. "Darius, wait. You forgot to put on a condom."

"I didn't forget." Darius leaned into Heather's hands as if he were doing calisthenics as he thrust harder. "You know you've wanted to feel this big dick inside you with no wrapping for a long time. Don't fight it, bitch. I bet it feels better than the one you have at home." Darius moved toward the bottom of the bed, carrying Heather with him until he was standing. Heather's back landed against the wall, and her legs dangled about his waist. Darius braced her with his hips as he clinched her breasts. He bit her nipples harder than the way Heather liked it. As Darius released himself inside Heather, he dug his fingers into her titties as though kneading a lump of dough to make a dessert.

"Darius! Not so rough. My husband will be furious if he sees any marks." Heather unsuccessfully tried pushing him away again.

"Welcome to the city that care forgot," Darius said as Heather's feet hit the floor.

"What's that supposed to mean?" Heather asked, slapping Darius upside his head.

Without flinching, Darius said, "Oh, if you stay in New Orleans long enough, you'll find out." He slapped her on the ass. "Let's shower and get dressed. You said you were starved."

* * *

Heather passed on dining out and ordered room service. That was fine by Darius because he needed to clear his head, so he had JT drop him off at the Riverwalk. Darius had replaced his T-shirt with a white muscle tank to adjust to the heat. As he stepped out of the limo, he experienced a Mardi Gras flashback. Darius pictured King Zulu and King Rex meeting up at the riverfront for Lundi Gras last year. That was his best stateside vacation ever.

Darius roamed down to the tall Jax building that used to be a beer factory but was now a huge mall. As he walked by, an air-conditioned breeze made its way through a crowd of shoppers entering the renovated brewery. Darius sat at the bank of the muddy Mississippi, watching the *Cotton Blossom* boat sail away. The contaminated water may have well been running through his veins, because he felt bad about how rugged he'd handled Heather. Surrounded by strangers, Darius held his head in his hands and allowed the tears for My Dear to flow freely. Then he picked at his nails. "Oh, fuck! I really did scratch Heather."

Drying his eyes, Darius keyed in the numbers to the hotel. "Darius Jones's room, please."

"Hello."

"Hey, Heather. Look, I'm sorry. I didn't realize I was really scratching you. Are you okay?"

"My back is a little sore, and my boobs look like sliced beets; but other than that, I'm fine."

"You want to meet me at The House of Blues? The show we were supposed see starts in an hour."

"Sure. That's why we came here, right? To have a good time." Heather's voice lacked excitement.

"I'll have JT pick you up. I'm already near Café Du Mondé, so I can just walk from here."

Darius made his way down Decatur Street and over to The House of Blues. The entrance was tucked away in a French

Quarter alley. There was no waiting, so he decided to sit on the restaurant side and order some red beans and rice to coat his stomach for the alcohol he'd consume later. When Darius lifted his head from the menu, he couldn't believe his eyes. Ginger was standing at the bar staring at him. Shit!

"You know what you want yet?" the waitress asked.

Darius shielded Ginger's view with the menu. "Yeah, an exit out the back door."

"Oh, your woman must be here. This happens every night. For fiddy dollars I can bail you out." The waitress opened her hand.

"How?" Darius didn't hesitate to pull out a fifty.

Stuffing the money in her bra, the waitress said, "Move over to the table in the corner."

When Darius stood, Ginger called out, "Darius? Is that you?" Her ass knew damn well who it was.

The waitress stopped Ginger in her tracks and said, "Excuse me, miss, Mr. Marley would like his pri-va-cy."

"Who? What? Who are you?" Ginger scanned the room as though looking for a manager.

"I know you want to say hello to him, but he's asked not to be disturbed. Don't have me get security on yo' ass."

"Certainly, just give him a note for me. Can you do that?" Ginger scribbled a message and handed it to the girl along with a five-dollar bill.

The waitress pointed at Ginger. "Okay. But no more notes." Then she walked over to Darius. "I don't know how long this is going to work. I think you'd better leave before your other woman gets here. You are expecting another woman, aren't you? Otherwise you wouldn't be hidin'."

"Yeah, and she's standing in the doorway." Darius slumped in his seat.

"Brother, if you mean that white woman? You are on ya own." The waitress took his menu, stuck Ginger's cash and note in her bra, and went into the kitchen.

"Oh, hey. There you are," Heather said as she slid in the booth with Darius. "Have you ordered yet?"

"No. Let's go." Darius tried to stand before Heather completely sat down.

Ginger walked over and sat in the same booth facing Darius and Heather. "Funny meeting you guys here." Ginger winked at Heather. "What's up?" Then Ginger stopped the waitress and said, "I'd like to have a menu and my five dollars back."

"Gladly." The waitress handed Ginger a menu and kept walking.

"Ginger, you look lighter. Did you get a facial today?" Heather returned the wink and attempted to spark a conversation.

Darius felt Ginger's heel pierce into his shin. "Ouch! Damn! Heather, excuse me. If you ladies don't mind, I'm going into the other room."

Heather stood so Darius could get up. "I'm tired. I think I'll go back to my hotel and rest." Heather stretched and yawned.

"Bye." Ginger waved to Heather and followed Darius.

Sitting on a bar stool next to Darius, Ginger said, "What's up with you and Heather?"

"In case you've forgotten, I'm the boss. We're on business." Darius motioned for the waitress. His stomach was fiercely growling.

Ginger sarcastically said, "You mean like our business trip tomorrow?"

Darius sighed heavily.

"Are you staying for the blues show?" Ginger positioned her leg between his.

"That's why I came to this side. Are you staying for the blues show?" Darius mimicked Ginger's tone.

"Only if you *want* me." Ginger kissed his neck.

"Suit yourself." If Ginger knew what was best for her, she'd stop coming on to him. His dick was getting hard watching her give head to a cherry stem she'd snagged from the bartender's stash while the dude wasn't looking. How did Ginger know he was in New Orleans? And what was up with the winks between Ginger and Heather? Was his game getting sloppy?

"I'll go." Ginger opened her purse and placed a room key in his hand. "I'm at the Intercontinental. Don't keep me waiting."

Darius slipped the key in his pocket. Ginger shook her ass all the way to the exit. "Um. Um. Um. Women. Did you see that?" Darius asked the bartender. "That's why men make better poker players. Women would rather lose the game, than fold. And being the gentlemen that I am, it's my duty—"

"To suck that head and pinch that tail." The bartender made a fist and stretched out his arm.

Darius did the same. As their knuckles connected, his male ego heightened. "Here's the money for the food. Tell the waitress I decided to be dinner instead." Darius squared his shoulders, stuck out his chest, and walked over to the Hotel Intercontinental.

Chapter 31

Can a woman ever understand the heart of her man? The functional purpose of the organ was far less complicated than the emotional aspect. Who was Wellington's woman? If he gave his heart and soul to one and his physical affection to another, and undoubtedly loved one more than the other, was love then the deciding factor?

Wellington's flight into L.A. was delayed due to weather conditions. It was a clear day in Oakland and even clearer when he arrived in Los Angeles, so the inclement weather had obviously been the airline's way of avoiding compensating the passengers. Jada had given Wellington so much to think about, the extra time was actually appreciated.

Simone wasn't Jada. But then, Jada wasn't Simone. Simone had never lied to him. She always supported him one hundred and ten percent. Even when he doubted the solidarity of their relationship and broke up with her, Simone didn't abandon him. Jada, on the other hand, lied to him and showed minimal excitement when he shared his dreams. Without saying, "Ba, this is all for you. For us." Wellington desperately wanted Jada to see that she was the vision behind all of his dreams.

The dagger that had plunged and scarred his heart had desertion engraved on the stainless steel blade. During their most challenging moment, Jada had dumped him.

His adoptive mother, Cynthia, would say, "Treat a man like a dog and he'll stay if you let him. Treat a man with dignity and respect and he'll walk right over you to get to the woman who treats him like shit. Shit doesn't just happen. Bullshit makes shit happen. And nice women finish right along with nice guys. Last. Too bad the good ones don't pair up before they become bitter."

Wellington had other issues to think about. Darius's behavior and his infection, if true, would tumble like falling dominos.

"Could you please open my window so I can get some fresh air?" Wellington asked the taxi driver.

"I can crack for you. Don't go all the way down," the driver replied.

"Thanks." The entire ride to his Inglewood condo was one long blur. When the driver pulled in front his building, Wellington pulled on the latch, but the door didn't unlock.

"I get that for you. That'll be twenty-one dollars and eighty cents."

After Wellington paid, the driver opened his door and retrieved his bags from the trunk.

Stepping into his condo, Wellington noticed his place looked almost the way he'd left it, except cleaner. The maids had done an immaculate job. He tossed his bags in the bedroom corner. Plopping down in the plush chair next to the window, he dialed Darius's number.

Answering right away, Darius said, "Hi, Dad. What's up?"

"Where are you, son?" After what Jada had told him, Wellington hoped Jazzmyne wasn't right.

"New Orleans. Why?"

Wellington shook his head. "What's your purpose?"

"You know me. Working to please."

"I need you to come home right away. There's an emergency," Wellington said.

Darius cleared his throat. "Is Mom all right?"

"Yeah, she's fine," Wellington responded as he picked up the remote.

"Then so. What's urgent?" Darius's voice trembled.

Wellington heard the old familiar broken speech pattern. Something was definitely wrong, and Darius knew exactly what it was. As a child, whenever Darius stuttered, juggled his words, or hesitated to speak, Darius knew his parents had discovered whatever he was trying to hide. "We can't discuss this over the phone. When will you be here?"

"I was headed to Vegas tomorrow; but I'm exhausted, so I'll come home instead. Plus, I have some unfinished business I need to tend to."

Unfinished, huh. "Anything your old man can assist you with?" Wellington said.

"Handle it I-I can," Darius said.

"Call me as soon as you get in, son."

"Bye, Dad. Sure."

"Bye." Wellington keyed in zero, zero, one, then hit the talk key. He fumbled the TV controller in his hand, but didn't turn on the television.

"Hello." Jada picked up in the middle of the first ring.

"How are you?" Wellington asked.

"I'm okay."

"All right. Listen. I'm at my condo. I'm going to shop for some food. Dinner will be ready by six. I'll get your favorite. Call me back when you can talk."

"All right, bye." Jada hung up the phone.

Instead of going out, Wellington logged on to the grocery Web site and e-mailed his shopping list. He took a shower. Put on his silk boxers. Lit some candles. Turned on Luther. Chilled a bottle of champagne, which had been delivered with the other groceries, while the TV watched him.

Startled by the doorbell, Wellington grabbed his robe, walked into the living room, then peeped through the hole. Jada looked wonderful.

Wellington smiled. "Hey, come in," he said as he opened the door.

When Wellington went to close the door, Lawrence stepped into view. "Hey, man. What's up?"

Wellington faked a quick smile and said, "Hi, Jada." Then he responded to Lawrence, "Hey, man. Have a seat in the front. I'll be right there."

"I'm not staying." Lawrence looked Wellington up and down. "But maybe I should."

"I told you that won't be necessary. Wellington and I need to discuss some personal matters concerning our son," Jada said.

"He's just as much my son as he is Wellington's," Lawrence responded.

"Don't go there, man. Jada will call you when we're done with our conversation. No disrespect." Wellington opened the door wider.

"I'll call you when I'm ready to be picked up," Jada said.

"Don't bother. Have Wellington drop you off." Lawrence's voice sounded deeper than usual.

"No problem. I can handle that," Wellington said as he closed the door behind Lawrence.

Looking at Jada, Wellington asked, "What was that all about? And why did he drop you off?"

"He thinks we're having an affair. Can you believe that? Anyway, I asked him to drop me off because we were in the area and I didn't feel like riding home just to get my car. After ten years of marriage, he actually believes I'm cheating on him. I've always been faithful to Lawrence." Jada went to Wellington's bedroom and lay atop the leopard body-length pillow.

"I should be so lucky. If he only knew," Wellington said

as he placed the other animal print body pillow between them and lay on his back. "So do you know any more than what we discussed earlier?"

"Not really. But Theo is investigating," Jada said.

"I—"

"I know. You asked me not to tell him; but time is of the essence, and Theo is loyal and trustworthy," Jada said.

"You're right." Wellington stared at the ceiling. "I talked with Darius a few minutes ago, and he'll be home tomorrow."

"What did he say?" Jada flipped onto her back and sandwiched the pillow between her legs.

"I didn't tell him over the phone." Wellington admired her out of the corner of his eye.

"Good. Where do we go from here?" Jada asked.

The last time Wellington had responded to that question, he remembered saying, "Judge Judy." That was when he'd divorced Melanie. Now he wished he could respond, "To the altar." But instead he said, "One day at a time."

"Do you remember when Darius was one and he pulled off that little girl's diaper at the mall?" Jada laughed.

"Yeah, we should have known then he'd be a lover."

"But do you think he'd jeopardize my company, knowing I've worked so damn hard?" Jada clamped her ankles around the pillow.

"Honestly, yes, I do. But he won't be the only one to blame even if he is having an affair with Ginger."

Jada looked over at Wellington. "What does that mean?"

"You gave him more responsibility than he could handle. And as for Ginger, she may have approached him. Even if she didn't, we may have to say she did." Why was he being considerate of her feelings by censoring his words?

"I will not compromise the integrity of my staff," Jada said.

"Too late for that. I hate to say I told you so—"

"So don't say it. I'd better call Lawrence; it's getting late," Jada said.

"So you're having another one of your little temper tantrums." Wellington laughed. "You've only been here a minute. You came over here so we could talk, and because you can't handle the truth, you're leaving. I'll get you the phone."

"No. Wait." Jada reached for his arm and said, "You're right. I just have a lot on my mind. I told Lawrence I'm filing for a divorce. But I feel guilty leaving a man who has done right by me for fifteen years."

"Then, don't do it. Look, Diamond, I don't want to be with you unless you're comfortable with your decision. I can't lie. I'd marry you today if I could. But not if you have doubts. There's no rush. Plus, two people's lives would be in shambles because I'd have to end my relationship with Simone."

"Yeah, right. Simone," Jada whispered. "I'm just being selfish."

"Selfish isn't a bad thing. I just want you to be sure." Wellington felt Jada's lips touch his. "Let me get the phone before we both end up regretting this moment. I'm thirsty. You want a glass of water, too?"

"Sure." Jada rolled onto her stomach.

Wellington went into the kitchen. By the time he returned, Jada was asleep. He covered her up, opened his sofa sleeper, and slept in the living room. If Lawrence couldn't trust Jada, that was Lawrence's problem, not his.

Chapter 32

Jada arrived home from Wellington's a few minutes after seven. Palm trees lined each side of the circular driveway leading to the front door. Looking at the digits on the fee meter, Jada reached into her purse and gave the driver exact fare plus a fifteen-percent tip. As she stepped out of the cab, the morning sunrise nestled behind the clouds. If she'd timed it right, Lawrence had already left for work. Entering their home through the large oak double doors, Jada went into the kitchen, tossed her purse on the counter, and poured a glass of cranberry cocktail. One, two, three steps down into the sunken living room, Jada relaxed on the sectional sofa's fluffy white pillows. The tartness invaded her palate and tingled the nerves inside her mouth.

Gazing at the sparkles reflecting off the chlorinated water in the pool out back, Jada stretched her arms high as she yawned and said, "Ah, I needed that."

"Needed what?" Lawrence asked as he stood adjacent to the freestanding ivory-marbled fireplace.

"Oh, shit!" Jada grabbed an oversized pillow with one

hand. "You scared the hell out of me. I thought you'd be at work by now."

"I would *if* my wife had come home last night." Lawrence approached Jada and sat on the sofa. He lifted her feet off the couch and placed them in his lap.

"I apologize. I was so exhausted, I fell asleep." Jada ran her fingers through her uncombed hair.

"Before or after?" Lawrence questioned as he massaged her toes.

With each stroke Lawrence pressed harder. Then he kneaded the arch in her foot with his knuckles. Jada placed her juice on the rectangular table behind the sofa. "Before or after what?" Jada stared at the pool and waited for his response.

"Stop playing games. You're an intelligent woman. Look me in my eyes and tell me you didn't have sexual intercourse with Wellington last night." Lawrence brutally pushed Jada's feet to the floor and scooted next to her.

He was so close a strand of thread couldn't slither between them. Jada's side was now wedged into the corner. The tension in their eyes met and locked. Like a pretzel, Jada twisted and braced her back against the side and calmly responded, "Lawrence, I'm divorcing you, so this conversation is a waste of our time. But just for the record, I've never cheated on you. Never." Forcing her way out of the cramped space, she picked up her glass and started walking away.

Lawrence snatched her arm so fast, all she could do was watch the crystal goblet beat the cranberry cocktail to the hardwood floor. Jada jumped back as the glass sliced into her flesh. "Let go of me! Are you crazy!" Jada frantically jerked her entire body.

"Why do you keep talking about divorcing me?" Lawrence shouted. "You're the one who's crazy!" He twisted and squeezed Jada's bicep harder.

"Ouch! You're hurting me!" Jada punched his arm as hard

as she could, but Lawrence didn't flinch. So she swung her arm three hundred and sixty degrees, inside of Lawrence's and broke his grip. Sprinting to the bedroom, she sat in the middle of the floor. When Lawrence entered right behind her, Jada noticed a red trail from the doorway to her feet.

"Honey, I'm sorry. I don't know what got into me. Please forgive me."

"Lawrence, it's best if you don't speak to me right now. You see this. Look at my leg." A thick stream of blood flowed from the white flesh hanging out. "Ouch! Damn! This hurts." Jada pressed above the cut, trying to alleviate some of the pain.

"Don't move," Lawrence said. Racing to his bathroom, he returned with dry and wet towels, gauze, tape, and peroxide.

"I'll do it myself." Jada snatched the wet towel.

"Why are you throwing away a wonderful marriage to chase a fantasy? Don't you care about me? Us? Jada, you're not twenty-three or thirty-three anymore. What about Simone? And Wellington's son?"

Jada picked up the peroxide. "I never said I was divorcing you to marry Wellington."

"Sure you did. 'Who you are speaks so loudly, I can't hear what you are saying.' "

"Yes, the famous quote of Emerson. I know. Save it for the courtroom." Lawrence was right, but that didn't make her wrong. "Maybe if you just let me be, I can sort things out in my mind."

"So now am I supposed to wait like a good little boy until you decide what's best for us. Forget you! You can pack your belongings and get the hell out of my house." Lawrence slammed the door so hard their wedding picture crashed to the floor. Before Jada could move, a large piece of glass lodged into her arm. "Fuck you, Lawrence!" she yelled as she pulled it out.

What goes around comes around. Jada hopped on her right leg into the bathroom and turned on the shower. She couldn't blame Lawrence for being upset, but that was the first and last time he'd put his hand on her. There was no easy way to leave. Talking about the divorce wasn't going to change her mind. Ever since Mama died in the house, an air of sadness floated throughout. Maybe that was why Darius hadn't slept there after the funeral. Maybe that was her justification to move out.

Jada showered, toweled off, and limped to her walk-in closet. Wearing a pantsuit wasn't an option; it was mandatory to cover the bandaged cut on her left leg and the Band-Aid on her arm. All her life she'd maintained perfect skin, even the chicken pox hadn't left any marks. Now she probably had to get stitches. Jada selected the watermelon colored outfit, hoping it would brighten her spirits.

Jada played "Lost Without You," one of her favorite gospel songs by BeBe and CeCe Winan, as she cruised along the freeway. Far from perfect best described her life, but without God it would be farther. Each brain cell was apparently preoccupied, because she almost totaled a car simultaneously merging into a competing lane from the opposite direction. "And Friday is still a day away," Jada said, shaking her head.

Darius's life was leaning like the Tower of Pisa, the walls of her marriage were caving in like a demolished building, and her business was following suit. Everything she'd worked and lived for could end up ruined at any moment. After parking in her assigned space, she exited her car and pressed the lock button on her auto remote. Peripherally, Jada monitored the faces of strangers on the elevator. Although some of them crossed paths at least once a week, good morning, good evening, and an occasional good night was the extent of their conversations.

Arriving at her office, Jada said, "Good morning, Shannon," and smiled.

"Good morning, Mrs. Tanner. You have a ten o'clock with Theo, Wellington, and Jazzmyne," Shannon said, handing Jada her schedule card for the day.

"Thanks." Jada extended her arm as far as she could without moving.

"Are you okay?" Shannon frowned.

"Yes, I'm fine." If Shannon noticed, surely everyone at the meeting would, too. Jada entered her office, sorted the papers she needed, and worked in the conference room. Otherwise, she'd have to hobble into the room as if one of her legs was shorter than the other.

Sitting at the head of the table, Jada drew a triangle and layered it with five tiers. Then she scribbled, "Comfort has a price." She thought about the poem *Tragedy* that Theo had insisted she memorize:

Major in the art of tragedy
Cataclysmic in nature's mastery
Essential for basic survival
Of all that is among the living

Eye for an eye cannot see
The desire for tragedy inside thee
Dormant deep within our souls
Not eternally awaiting an unmarked time

The conscious of how deep it lies
Will master the display of hate
The unconscious of its demise
Are the ones who repeatedly fall prey

Theo had emphasized, "The people you trust the most, you watch the most, and the individuals you trust the least, you watch even more. In a nutshell, don't ever get too comfortable with your surroundings." To believe her son, her flesh and blood, would jeopardize everything she'd worked for was devastating. Then again, to have Darius's life built on a foundation of deception was worse. Maybe Darryl would have been a great father if given the opportunity. It seemed as though his other children turned out all right. Like a masked thief in the night, she'd robbed both of them. Jada prayed, "Lord, let Thy will be done."

Shannon buzzed. "Mrs. Tanner, everyone is here."

"Thanks. Send them in."

Jazzmyne sauntered in wearing a red, black, and green scarf draped over the shoulders of a black suit. She looked more like Loretta Divine every day. Wellington entered behind Jazzmyne and sat near Jada. Jada wanted to relocate from the head seat to encourage a team atmosphere, so she said, "Wellington, would you mind moving to the next seat?"

"No problem."

Jada internalized her pain as she stepped on her healthy leg and sat adjacent to Wellington. Jada looked at Wellington and said, "You smell good."

Wellington smiled. Jazzmyne laughed, then said, "You two need to quit."

"What? I just gave him a compliment, that's all," Jada said.

Always the last one in and the first one out, Theo finally entered the room, wearing sunglasses so dark no one could see his eyes. "Okay, so we're ready to roll?" Theo sat beside Jazzmyne and across from Jada. His Wesley Snipes blue-black complexion blended with his suit.

"We sure are," Jada responded, admiring Theo's hairless, buttery-smooth face.

"Baby doll, I ain't gon' lie. You got some serious problems. Even Theo's gon' have ta work overtime to get ya out, and even then ya might not come out smellin' like a rose. Let's start with Darius since he's the root of what ails ya. The boy has no dick control. And he shouldn't be in top management."

Jada cut her eyes toward Wellington and said, "Don't you say a word."

"Baby doll, fire your son effective immediately. Have security change all his passwords and change the locks on his door. I need to go through everything in his office, and then you return only his personal items to him."

Tears formed in Jada's eyes.

"Don't get soft on me now. I've seen you bulldoze the best of 'em. When he comes here, treat him like an employee. Save being a mother for when ya at home."

Watching Theo scratch item number one from his list, Jada said, "Okay, but what about my staff?"

"I'm gettin' to 'em in a moment." Theo looked directly at Jada and said, "Darius's fiancée, Maxine Moore, is HIV positive."

Jada covered her eyes and leaned on Wellington's shoulder.

"Help her to stay with me." Theo continued, "Obviously, Darius has to get tested right away."

Jada watched Theo twirl his pen, because he never used a pencil, as he marked a line through number two.

"That brings us to item number three, your employees. Since your Dick Executive Officer has screwed all of your directors, they each have to get tested. But here's what's important. Look at me, baby doll. You have to fire 'em, too. Pronto!" Theo's palm slammed against the table as if he had the big six in dominos.

"But my conference is coming up soon. I can't. I won't." Anger and resentment percolated inside Jada like brewing coffee.

"Okay, you jumped to item four. Cancel the conference. Now back to three. If any of your executives test positive before you release 'em, you'll have eternal internal sabotage.

You'll never be able to fire 'em." Theo flipped his pen. "Five. Close your company."

"What!" Jada stood and stumbled, quickly grabbing her leg. Wellington caught her by the arm. "Ouch." Jada moved his grip from her wound.

"Okay, obviously Theo has more work to do. Let's hear it, baby doll. What's wrong with your arm and your leg?"

"It's nothing. Really. I just slipped in the shower this morning." Jada already had more on her plate than she could possibly handle.

"If you insist," Theo responded. "Six. Miranda, Heather, and Ginger have legally consulted with an attorney, but not at your husband's firm. They're suing for two million dollars each. Zen is undecided. Your son was in New Orleans yesterday with Ginger and Heather. They should be back today." Theo flipped his pen, stuck it in his pocket, stood and said, "Let's meet again next week. I'll call you. And get yourself to the doctor today, baby doll. Sees ya laduh."

Reaching across the table, Jazzmyne asked, "Jada, what happened to you?"

"Lawrence and I had a little disagreement." They would find out sooner or later.

"Oh, just so you know, I was listening intently to Theo," Jazzmyne said. "Don't fire anyone."

"But what about Darius?" Jada asked.

"Demote him. Take away his positions and all authority, but don't fire him. His ego will hand in his resignation. I'm going to devise an alternative plan that we can discuss Monday."

"Was this disagreement about last night?" Wellington asked.

"Kind of, but—"

Shannon buzzed. "Darius is on his way in."

Wellington jumped out of his seat. "Sis, take care of Jada and take her to the doctor. I'll call you later."

Wellington met Darius at the door. Wellington snatched Darius by his T-shirt and said, "Boy, I'm so furious with you I could beat you like Rodney King." Then he shoved Darius away. Wellington walked over to Jada, kissed her on the forehead, and grabbed his jacket from the coat rack.

Stomping his foot in rage, Darius said, "Why is everybody fucking with me?"

"You reap what you sow. Let's go." Wellington pushed Darius, causing Darius to stumble out of the conference room.

Chapter 33

Darius lived his entire life on the edge. No regrets. That was the requested inscription for his tombstone. As he headed into his general practitioner's office, he shook hands with the Grim Reaper, realizing his death might come sooner than expected. If the Lord blessed him with a negative test result, he vowed to cease his promiscuous ways. If he wasn't so fortunate, suicide was a forgivable sin and now option number one. To ensure he wouldn't change his mind, as soon as Wellington had left his apartment yesterday, Darius bolted a hook screw in the bedroom wall of his condo. The noose lay on his bed along with his goodbye note.

Dear Mom and Dads,

I'm sorry for the pain I've caused. I know you worked hard to make certain I had the finer things in life. Somewhere along the way, I detoured. I didn't mean to let you down. After today, you won't have to worry about me. I'll be in a better place, and you'll be better off, so in the end everyone's a winner.

Tell Maxine she's the only woman I've ever loved. I wish I were as strong as she. She deserves a man who will respect her. If I could turn back the hands of time, I would have treated her better. The one thing I've learned is that bad things do happen to good people like Maxine and Lawrence.

Lawrence, man, I'm sorry for kicking your ass last night. Especially since my Dad roughed you up before I did. You're a nice guy, and if I could take back the beating, I would because you never laid your hands on me. I lost it when I saw my mom's arm, but when I saw the stitches in her leg, I flipped out. Maybe in a way I was taking my frustrations out on you.

Wellington, you're the greatest dad a son could have. If the paternity test proves you're not my father, it'll only be on paper. You're number one in my book, man. Don't tell Junior how I died. Just let him know his big brother is watching over him.

Mom, if you hadn't lied to me all these years, maybe I wouldn't be writing this letter. You're selfish. You've always protected your heart but were too blind to see you were destroying everyone else's life, especially mine. I've added my final rule to DL. Don't cry for me. Cry for yourself.

Love don't love nobody,
R.I.P. Darius Henry Jones

Holding his hand, his guardian angel, Ashlee, sat next to Darius—as promised—in the waiting room.

"It's going to be okay," Ashlee whispered. She lifted his hand, gently pressed her lips against the back side, and held it there for a while.

Darius mumbled, "I guess I deserve this."

"Nonsense." Ashlee looked into his watery eyes. "Remember when you donated ten thousand dollars of your money to your elementary school to rebuild the children's playground. And when you missed a week from college to take care of My Dear. Although your mother told you to go back to school, you refused to leave your grandmother until she was well. And what about the time you volunteered to play Santa Claus for the kids at Children's Hospital. That's the Darius I know." Ashlee placed her hand over the left side of his chest and said, "Darius Jones, you have a generous heart."

"Yeah, but I also have a generous dick." One that would be buried six feet under before sunset if he received bad news.

"We'll get through this together." Ashlee patted his knee.

The doctor's assistant walked into the lobby. "Darius Jones."

Darius stood. "That's me." Ashlee gripped his hand.

"Come with me, please." The assistant turned to Ashlee and said, "I'm going to have to ask you to wait out here. This is confidential."

"It's okay. I want her to be with me," Darius said.

"Okay, then follow me. My name is Roxanne." The assistant held the door until everyone was inside her office. "Please, have a seat. Well, I have good news." Roxanne smiled.

"Whew!" Darius sighed as Ashlee gave him a hug.

Roxanne's smile disappeared. She raised her eyebrows and continued, "Bad news, and not so good news."

Darius's smile disappeared. Ashlee squeezed his hand.

"Which would you like first?" Roxanne asked.

"It doesn't matter. Just tell me." Darius stared at the floor.

"Sure." The assistant cleared her throat. "The good news is"—she handed Darius an eight-and-a-half-by-eleven sheet of paper—"your HIV antibodies test result is negative."

Darius leaped out of his seat, picked up Ashlee, and twirled her around in place like a ballerina. "Yes!" He wrapped his arms around Ashlee and wouldn't let go. "Thank you for being the best friend I've ever had. I don't know what I would've done without you."

Darius bowed on his knees and thanked the Lord. "I haven't forgotten about my promise to you. Thanks for giving me another chance."

Roxanne cleared her throat. "You need to hear the rest."

"Oh, yes." Darius smiled back.

"Wellington is *not* your biological father. Darryl Williams *is* your father."

Nodding his head, Darius said, "I can live with that, but Wellington will always be my father."

"Now for the bad news." Roxanne paused and looked at Darius. "You've contracted syphilis."

Darius's eyes widened.

"Not to worry. It's curable," Roxanne said.

Darius thought about Heather and Ginger because he'd had sex with both of them in New Orleans without using condoms. After Heather left The House of Blues, Darius spent the night with Ginger in her hotel room. But his test was taken before that. Maxine? Damn!

"Here's your prescription." Roxanne slid the white paper across the desk. "I need the names and addresses of your partners so we can advise them to get tested."

"Why do you assume there's more than one?" Darius asked.

Roxanne bit on the tip of her pencil. "Yeah, right."

Roxanne looked sexy with the eraser head in her mouth. Darius proceeded to jot down the information.

"Thanks for your cooperation." Roxanne picked up her chart and opened the door.

"Let's go to your place and celebrate," Ashlee said. "I'll cook you a wonderful dinner, and we can watch *Baby Boy.*"

Darius thought about the suicide setup and quickly responded, "Let's eat out. My treat." *Baby Boy* was actually a good movie selection because the lead actor Jody somewhat reminded Darius of himself. Had he been spared life number nine, or had God blessed him with nine more? Refusing to take any chances, from this day forward, Darius Henry Jones was a new man.

Chapter 34

When a man loved a woman but the woman no longer loved the man, how could she take her final bow with grace? How could someone love another for fifteen years and then suddenly find that person undesirable? Would Jada's feelings toward Lawrence be the same if Wellington weren't in the picture?

Rolling over to Lawrence's side of the bed, Jada stared at his bruises. Last night wasn't one she wanted to remember, but unfortunately she'd never forget. First Wellington and then Darius: if they hadn't all been family, she would have called the police herself.

Jada whispered, "Are you okay?"

Opening his right eye, Lawrence said, "I had hoped you'd be gone by now."

Although it wasn't her fault, Jada said, "I'm sorry. I never meant for this to happen." She honestly didn't. Barbaric was not an adjective she wanted describing her character.

Lawrence braced his back against the headboard. "That's the problem, you never do. Let you tell it, nothing is ever your fault."

Sitting up in the bed, Jada said, "What does that mean?"

Lawrence closed his eye. "You didn't mean to lie to Darius. You didn't mean to lie to Wellington. You didn't mean to hurt my feelings by asking for a divorce." Lawrence sighed, then said, "If you were standing before a judge, this would be an open and shut case. You're starting to sound like a broken record."

"Well, broke may be the operative word. I might lose everything I've worked for. Um. Do you mind if I ask you a question about consultation?" Jada hadn't involved her corporate attorney. Theo had advised her to wait because if she was sued, she'd need a lawyer who specialized in sexual harassment cases.

"Yes, I do. I don't believe you have the audacity to ask me for help. But then again, your selfish ass is always thinking of Jada, Jada, Jada. Besides, you know I won't tell you anything except you're right. Instead of being unfaithful with Wellington, you should have been paying closer attention to your child. But I guess like mother, like son. Now that you're in trouble, you expect me to bail you out." Cramming the pillow underneath his head, Lawrence turned his back.

"Lawrence, I've never asked you for one damn thing. Everything that happened to you yesterday you brought upon yourself. If you hadn't laid your hand on me, none of this would've happened. So if you want me feel sorry for you, I don't. I'm not going to accept the blame for your actions." Jada tugged the covers.

Pulling back, Lawrence said, "Are you still moving out of the house next weekend? My friend Howard Kees, the best real estate broker in California, has found a buyer."

Jada looked over at Lawrence and pushed the blanket to his side of the bed. "Doesn't he live in Oakland?"

"What's your point?" Lawrence asked.

"Fine. I'm not going to fight you on this one. I said I'd be out, and I will. Just call me when you have my half of the proceeds." Jada sighed heavily.

Lawrence calmly said "Oh, this house was a gift deed from my parents to me. I've always maintained it as separate property. So if you want me to feel sorry for you, I don't, because you'll get nothing from me."

Jada curled the king-size pillow into a tight ball. "Uh, I hate you." Moving to the edge of the bed, Jada slammed the pillow between them.

"I'm saddened to hear you say that, because I love you with all my heart." Lawrence stroked her hand.

"Don't touch me." Why were separations so ugly? Shit was snowballing downhill faster than the mudslides along Pacific Coast Highway. Maybe she should stay with Wellington or Darius until her belongings were moved out of this house. When the phone rang, Jada reached over to her nightstand and answered, "Hello."

"Hi, ba. How are you?"

"Fine." That way Wellington would know Lawrence was nearby. She started to say great just to irritate Lawrence. Just the fact that Wellington had called would upset Lawrence for sure.

"Look, put Lawrence on the phone for a minute," Wellington said.

Jada handed Lawrence the phone. "It's for you."

"Who is it?"

Jada didn't respond.

Taking the handset, Lawrence said, "Hello."

"Hey, man. This is Wellington. I want to apologize for what happened yesterday. Two wrongs don't make a right."

"Fuck you! This isn't over yet. Apologize to the lawsuit I'm about to slap on your fornicating ass!"

"Maybe in time Jada will forgive you, and you'll forgive me," Wellington said. "Let me speak with Jada."

Lawrence tossed the phone in Jada's direction and left the bedroom.

Jada exhaled and picked up the phone. "Yeah."

"Has Darius told you the news?"

Jada started pacing the floor. "No. What news?"

"He can tell us together. Can you meet me at his place? I'll call and let him know we're coming over."

"Okay, I'll see you in a few. Bye."

"Bye, my Nubian princess."

Jada tossed the phone on the bed. Limping to the bathroom today was more painful than the day before. If she knew the person who created the phrase "Shit Happens," she'd shake their hand.

Jada waited for Wellington to press Darius's buzzer. "Did you tell him I was coming with you?"

"Of course. And even if I hadn't, you're his mother." Wellington placed his arm around Jada's waist.

"Who is it?" Darius's voice blared from the intercom.

Wellington responded, "It's your parents, son, let us in."

Jada whispered to Wellington, "Has he told you already?"

Opening the door, Darius said, "No, I have not. Come on in. Y'all want anything to drink?"

"Y'all, Darius? Please stop speaking like that." Jada picked up the frame holding their family photo. "Water for me, please."

"I'll have the same," Wellington said.

Darius returned with three empty glasses and three bottles of water. He placed them on his Afrocentric coffee table and sat next to Wellington. "Well, I guess you guys want to know what I already know. Darryl is my biological father and my HIV test was negative."

Jada joined them on the sofa and sat next to Darius. She stretched her arms open and was happy when Darius leaned his head on her shoulder. Wellington wrapped his arms around both of them. For a while no one spoke.

Darius stood and said, "That's enough. Now everything is out in the open."

Jada asked, "How's Maxine?"

"I stopped by her place earlier. Physically, she looks fine. Emotionally, she's depressed. How's Lawrence?"

"I'm not so sure." Jada toyed with her watch.

"Why do you always have to mess up everybody's life?" Darius carried the empty bottles to the kitchen and returned.

Wellington calmly said, "Son, your mother didn't deserve that. Apologize."

"And you're no better. Why are you always protecting her?" Darius sat on the opposite side of the table.

Jada stood. "I think I'd better go."

"No, sit," Wellington said. "You can't keep running from the truth. We're a family, and we're going to speak our minds so we can heal our hearts."

Jada reluctantly sat down. Darius's words had chopped her into confetti. Her body went numb as she nodded and silently cried. Darius resented Darryl, and he didn't even know him. Her child was hurting much more than she'd imagined, so was Wellington. Jada thought about what Lawrence must have been going through as well. Her daddy's wisdom whispered softly in her ear, "Be true to yourself and the others will heal."

Chapter 35

Another moment of truth stared Jada directly in her eyes. As she glanced around her office, awards from presi-
ents of the United States, prime ministers of Great Britain,
onsulates of China, and a host of other government officials
overed her walls. Soon her plaques may sit in a box collect-
ng dust.

Theo had gone through everything in Darius's office. Jada
igured she'd humiliated her child enough. Fearing she'd dis-
over something else she didn't want to know, she asked
azzmyne to pack his belongings and lock them in his office.

Shannon buzzed Jada on the intercom and said, "Mrs.
'anner, Jazzmyne is here."

Regardless of how well Jada knew a person, everyone had
› be announced. "Send her in."

"Hi, Jazzmyne, I sure hope you have good news this morn-
ng," Jada said, limping to her desk.

"Hey, how's your leg?" Jazzmyne asked.

"Worse than I thought. The doctor suggested I take a few
ays off, but—"

"I understand. Listen, I came in before our meeting to discuss saving your company." Jazzmyne pulled out a chair and sat at the round table.

Jada moved slowly and joined her. "Wow. Knowing you, you spent all weekend thinking about this, and I'm anxious to hear your strategy."

Jazzmyne handed Jada a package of documents. "These are drafts for your review. I'll give you a fast overview since the others will be here shortly. Don't fire Darius. Demote him to his previous position. Promote Zen to vice president but not CEO. Give everyone, including Darius, a reasonable award. Bonuses are cheaper and smarter than paying attorney fees. Plus, you're not admitting any guilt. Now, before you say anything, we already know Darius is going to resign because of his fragile ego. Let him. He's the only sacrificial lamb that will save Black Diamonds. It's a blessing his HIV test came back negative, so even if anyone else gets positive results—and we pray they do not—they didn't contract the disease from Darius. And finally, the sexual harassment lawsuit is a wash because Darius explained how each of them came on to him. Truly, that was more detail than I needed, but clearly there's no case. He has photos with each of them at various venues having a good time. That's it."

"You really did spend time thinking about this. But how can I be sure my directors won't quit anyway."

"That's where the cash comes in." Jazzmyne rubbed her fingers together. "Highlight all the good they've done for their communities and project an individual five-year plan for future projects. They won't leave. Trust me. Ginger and Miranda may get rehired, but they'll have to prove themselves. Zen and Heather have to worry about new careers based on their ages."

Jada stood and hugged Jazzmyne. "Thank you so much. You'll be the first one rewarded."

Jazzmyne closed her folder. "Just doing my job. Besides, ou worked to damn hard to build this empire."

Shannon buzzed and said, "Mrs. Tanner, Wellington and heo are here."

"Send them in, and, Shannon, I need three copies of a packet my office." Jada smiled at Jazzmyne because she had made er day. Jada waved her hands in the air. She was so happy e felt like celebrating.

Theo walked in saying, "So, baby doll, you got those pink ips ready. It's time for smack down."

"Everyone, please, have a seat," Jada politely said, beaming.

"What's so wonderful?" Wellington asked.

"Jazzmyne developed an alternative strategy to keep my usiness intact."

Shannon handed everyone a copy and exited the room. hen Jada had Jazzmyne lay out her proposal in detail. veryone, including Theo, was impressed.

"Great job, sis," Wellington said.

Jazzmyne smiled softly. "Thanks, brother."

Shannon buzzed again. Jada hobbled over to her desk and ressed the intercom. "Yes, Shannon."

"Sorry to interrupt, but Darius is questioning why he n't get into his office."

"Tell Darius to wait for me in the conference room. And ll Zen, Ginger, Heather, and Miranda and have them re- ort there, too. Immediately."

"Certainly, Mrs. Tanner."

Jada sat behind her desk and said, "Well, that's a wrap. I'll are the news with my staff. Jazzmyne, I need you to join e at the meeting and to assist me all day tomorrow with nducting individual meetings."

"No problem," Jazzmyne responded.

"My work here is done, baby doll. I'll sees ya later." Theo ft Jazzmyne's packet on the table.

"Thanks, Theo." Jada sensed Theo felt his services weren't valued because Jazzmyne had outsmarted him. But Theo was important, and Jada would continue consulting with him as she always had on an as needed basis.

Wellington looked at Jada and asked, "You available for lunch?"

Grazing her hand over his shoulder and down his arm, Jada said, "Anytime for you."

"Great, call me when you're ready."

"Sure." There was nothing left to Jada's marriage except false pretenses.

As she and Jazzmyne entered the conference room, mumbling converted to silence. "Good morning." Jada sat at the head of the table. "I'm glad you're all here today. The last few weeks have been challenging for everyone. Thanks for your support. It was nice seeing each of you at my mother's services."

"Ma, why is my office locked?" Darius heaved himself up and leaned over the table.

"Darius, don't interrupt me again. I'm aware of the potential lawsuit and must candidly admit that I'm appalled."

"Ma, what lawsuit?" Darius asked, looking around the table at his counterparts.

"Darius, effective immediately, I'm demoting you to director." The expressions on her executive's faces spelled relief. "Zen, starting tomorrow you'll assume the well-deserved position of vice president. By the end of the week *each* of you will receive a six-figure bonus."

Darius stomped out of the room and slammed the door. Jazzmyne stood.

"Please, sit. He'll be just fine." Jada continued, "I'm not trying to buy your loyalty. No amount of money can buy the loyalty, commitment, and dedication each of you have displayed over the years. Anyone who wants to hand in ıeir resignation please feel free." Jada paused. "Should ou decide to stay, Jazzmyne and I will meet with each of ou privately tomorrow to discuss your future with Black iamonds. If not, the bonus is yours. You've earned it. Any omments?"

No one responded.

"Then, this meeting is adjourned."

Jada escorted Jazzmyne to the elevator, returned to her ffice, and phoned Wellington. "Now would be a good time pick me up."

"I'll be there in ten minutes," Wellington said.

As much as Jada could complain, she had more reasons be grateful. "Lord, thank you for not holding my imperections against me. For none of us can be You, but we can orever try. Thanks for saving my company and my son." Jada etrieved her purse from the lower desk drawer. Standing in er doorway, she turned back and looked at the awards, then losed the door.

"Shannon, have the interior decorator hang all of the plaques my office in the conference room by close of business. I'll e out the rest of the day. Here's the new chain of command."

"Certainly, Mrs. Tanner."

"One more thing. Thanks for your hard work." Jada handed hannon a bonus check. The rest of her staff could wait until ıe end of the week.

"Oh, thanks, Mrs. Tanner!" Shannon ran and hugged Jada.

"No. Thank *you*." Jada affectionately embraced Shannon nd headed toward the elevator.

Wellington was parked out front with his convertible top ropped back. He hurried to open her door. "Hi, ba." Lawrence ould have done the same.

"Can we go to your place instead? I'm not feeling so ell." Jada eased her way into the black sports car.

"Of course." Wellington cautiously drove to his place,

easing over the speed bumps and decreasing his speed gradually before coming to a complete stop.

Jada was tired of constantly worrying about Darius, Wellington, Lawrence, and life in general, so she cleared her mind, centered her spirit, enjoyed the view, and appreciated the moment.

Chapter 36

Arriving at her Malibu home with the movers, Jada unlocked the door. She could have instructed the three gentlemen to use the garage exit like Lawrence requested, but Jada was moving out the same way she moved in, through the front door.

"Every item with a gray tag stays, and everything with a blue label goes." Last week had been so horrific all she wanted to do now was to get her belongings and move ahead. Jada had outgrown her childish ways after she'd egged Wellington's house and cars so many years ago.

Lawrence accosted one of the movers and said, "Take everything through the garage. If you damage my floors, your insurer will pay substantially."

Jada walked up behind Lawrence. "I didn't expect to see you. Don't you have a big case coming up Monday?"

"You got a minute?" Lawrence asked. A kid who had just dropped his fresh ice cream cone couldn't have looked sadder.

"Sure." Moving the gray tag aside, Jada sat beside Lawrence on the sofa.

"I've been thinking about the ten years we've been married and the five before that. It's been as perfect as any relationship could have been. The only thing I've concluded is that you've always wanted Wellington, but never had the courage to be honest. So I came along, and you saw I could fill your void. You capitalized at my expense. Now you're trading me in like a used car. Why?"

"I don't know. But I can never decrease your value. Only you can do that." Jada hunched her shoulders. "My daddy used to say, 'You do what you believe is best at that time, and if you live long enough, you'll learn you should have done better.' I feel horrible about how our marriage is ending." Jada looked into Lawrence's eyes. "I love you." She paused. "I love Wellington. I've hurt my son, you, and Wellington. Hurting the people you love was supposed to be reserved for other people, not Jada Diamond Tanner. But I'm tired of playing tug-of-war with my fears, because no matter which end of the rope I pull, I slip and fall. I'm ready to face my fears head-on. You were right when you said you were better off without me."

When Lawrence went to hug Jada, she flinched. "You don't think I'm going to hurt you, do you?"

"Naw. I'm just overreacting." Jada inhaled deeply and slowly released the air from her lungs.

Holding her hands, Lawrence said, "I can't make you stay, but I'm not going to let my pride keep me from saying what's in my heart. I wish you wouldn't leave. I know we can save our marriage through counseling or whatever it takes. But if you go and things don't work out, you can always come back home."

Home had to be where the heart was because he'd already sold their paradise. Jada hugged Lawrence. Unlike when she'd parted from Wellington, this time she was sure. "I have to do this for me." Jada kissed Lawrence on the lips. On her way out the door, she instructed the movers to deliver her items to her new residence in The Valley.

Today truly would be the first day of the rest of her life. Being in her new environment brought fresh hopes as Jada blew the dust from her deferred dreams. Living alone didn't feel lonely; instead, it felt like a revelation, a new beginning, and an opportunity to set her life on the right course. Jada sat in the center of her living room and folded her legs. Resting her hands on her knees, she took three deep breaths, then closed her eyes, allowing only good thoughts to enter her mind. In the midst of silence, she heard her spirit say, "Thanks for reuniting with me."

Opening the gold envelope she'd retrieved from her security deposit box, Jada ripped the matching paper with the wedding vows she'd written for Wellington. With pen in hand, she wrote new declarations from her heart:

To My Soul Mate,

As I take your hand in marriage, I acknowledge our spiritual bond. No one has ever made me feel the way you have. From the day we met, I realized by your side was not only where I belonged, but also where I was wanted and needed. Everything happens for a reason. Each time I was spiritually and emotionally torn, I turned to you. Not to my mother. Not to my son. Not to my husband. I turned to you, and you were always there welcoming me with open arms.

While our relationship had its share of ups and downs, those challenges united us as one. I discovered, even after being in an ideal marriage, I was spiritually unstable. You could have humiliated, degraded, and scorned me for lying to you, but you chose tenderness, patience, love, and understanding. You've taught me mistakes are less important than confessions.

If I only have this day, this moment in time, as we stand spiritually naked baring our souls and confessing our love before God, my life is complete. Your forgiveness has made me stronger. Wellington Jones, I promise to love you unconditionally, today, hence, and forever more, until death do us part.

Diamond is forever yours

Jada was true to her words for better or for worse. Her eyes were dry, and her heart was peaceful like a feather floating in the wind. As she folded the new vows, she meditated again so her mind could join her heart in harmony.

Chapter 37

Love was the only game where every single player held a trump card. And one just never knew when their partner would reveal the Big Joker. The odds of hitting a multimillion-dollar lottery with a one-dollar ticket were easier than winning at the game of love.

Wellington cruised along the freeway and exited into Danville. Junior was visiting with Simone's mom, so this was a convenient time to break the news. He wanted to tell Simone in her own home for several reasons. If she became upset enough to break something, it would be her property. If she couldn't think straight, she wouldn't get into a car accident. And he could leave when he was ready, without worrying about having to put Simone out of his house.

Walking up to the door, Wellington rang Simone's doorbell three quick times so she'd know it was him.

Simone stood in the doorway wearing silver thigh-high satin shorts and a matching camisole. "Hey, baby. Come on in. This is a pleasant surprise. Junior is at my mom's." Simone flicked her tongue like she was teasing the sensitive spot on the head of his penis.

"So what are you up to?" Wellington walked in and sniffed twice.

Closing the door, Simone said, "You know me. Just cooking and cleaning."

Simone's place was always immaculate, and Wellington appreciated whenever she volunteered to tidy his. "Um. Smells good. What's cooking?"

"Seafood jambalaya. And I'm also going to steam some Dungeness crab legs. It'll be ready in a minute. I'll be right back," Simone said, dashing toward her bedroom.

Damn, he was going to miss Simone's meals. Sitting on the oversized couch, Wellington thumbed through the photo album. "Ha!" Junior's face looked as if he'd seen a giraffe after he backed into a goat at the petting zoo. Wellington laughed so hard that day; Junior ran to Simone crying.

Maxwell's song "Lifetime" started playing as Simone danced her way into the room. The scent of Angel perfume lured him into the mood. With each melody Simone moved a little closer. Turning around, she bent over, peeped at him between her thighs, and spread her cheeks. Facing him, Simone removed her satin shorts and held them under his nose. Wellington took the shorts from Simone and whiffed so hard the material suctioned into his nostrils. Then she removed her top and gently buffed his little head. All that remained were clear, high-heeled slip-ons with the fuzzy tops. Running her index finger inside her vagina, she slowly fed him.

This was not supposed to happen. Simone coaxed Wellington to her bedroom. The last time he'd tried to be macho and carry Simone, he'd ended up with a slipped disc.

"Wait, let me turn off the stove." Simone returned so quickly he was in the same position.

Laying her across the comforter, Wellington sucked her toes. Slowly his tongue traveled up her leg, her thigh, and gently teased her clit. Bringing Simone to the edge of orgasm, he slapped her on the ass. On her knees, Simone braced herself at the edge of the bed. Doggie-style, Wellington slowly penetrated her walls, gliding deeper and deeper while he alternated spanking Simone's ass.

"Yes, Daddy. That's how Mama likes it. I'm cumming with you, Daddy. Go ahead and knock that first one out the way so we can really get it on."

Knowing there would be no second round ever again, Wellington released everything he had to offer. Collapsing beside Simone, he said, "Damn. Woman, you are too much."

Simone went to the bathroom and returned with a smoking-hot wet towel. Cleaning him off, she asked, "Is everything okay? Why'd you stop?"

"Yeah, give me minute." Wellington rubbed his head.

"Just seems like you're tensed. Almost like you forced that orgasm out." Simone tried reviving The Ruler, but he only shriveled up more.

She knew him too well. He might as well tell the truth, because lying would truly complicate matters. "Diamond asked me to marry her."

The towel smacked against his privates like silly putty sticking to the wall.

"Ouch! Got damn, Simone. What did you do that for?" Wellington covered his dick just in case.

"How could you make love to me without telling me this first! And what did you tell her?"

Wellington inhaled oxygen as he spoke. "I said, yes."

Simone straddled Wellington and started punching him in the chest. "I hate you! I hate you!"

Grabbing her wrists, Wellington said, "I didn't mean to hurt you. I love you. You know this."

"Fuck you, Wellington Jones. And fuck that Hollywood whore! I hate her ass, too!" Simone jerked, but couldn't break Wellington's grip.

Wellington rolled Simone onto her side and held her close.

Simone started beating on his back. "Stop, Simone. Stop this shit right now!"

Simone rolled on her stomach, the tears flowing uncontrollably. Wellington couldn't express the hurt he felt because he truly loved Simone. But Simone wasn't Diamond. His chest ached, so he massaged it.

Simone whispered, "Get out," and it sounded like something straight out of *The Exorcist.*

She didn't have to tell him twice. Wellington half dressed, grabbed his keys, and headed to the front door, buttoning his shirt. Simone's sobs escorted him. He slapped himself upside the head, sat in his car, and stared at Simone's bedroom window. When Simone's mom pulled up behind him, Wellington drove off, pretending he hadn't seen or heard her toot the horn.

Wellington knew he shouldn't have been intimate with Simone; but his selfish manhood was weak, and he wanted to hold his woman one last time. There was no doubt in his mind that he preferred Jada. Jada hurt Lawrence. He failed Simone. All in the name of love so two bleeding hearts could run together.

Wellington cruised along the freeway. *Bam!* A car slammed into the rear of his Bentley. "What the fuck!" Looking in his mirror, he saw Simone, so he stepped on the pedal, weaving between eighteen-wheelers, school buses, and cars to lose her; but she stayed right on his tail. Finally, he exited before crossing the San Mateo Bridge because she'd probably knock his car into the water.

He hurried out of his car and raced to Simone's car door before she could get out. Simone shoved her door, knocking him down. Getting up in a continued motion like a professional ice skater, Wellington said, "Simone, you've got to stop this."

"Wellington, do you take me for a fool? Am I supposed to roll over and play dead? What about our son? This isn't some shit you just spring on me! Let me introduce you to my Virgo personality."

When Simone popped her trunk, Wellington jumped in his car, fired up the engine, hooked a U-turn, and made it across the bridge in five minutes tops, toll fee paid and all.

As Wellington entered his home, his phone rang. Before answering, he keyed in his security code. Checking the caller ID, he saw Jada's name. Trying to catch his breath, he said, "Hi. Ba."

"Are you okay? You were on my mind, so I called."

Panting, Wellington said, "I just told Simone about our plans." He massaged his chest.

"Why are you breathing so hard? How'd she take it?"

"You mean before or after she kicked my ass." Wellington walked onto his patio and sat by the pool. His doorbell rang repeatedly.

"How do you feel?" Jada asked.

"Awful. She didn't deserve that, and she intends to prove it." Wellington tapped his fingers on the glass table. "She's ringing my bell right now."

"I understand how she feels. I felt the same way when I found out about Melanie. Are you having second thoughts about us?"

"No, ba. Not at all. I just hate seeing Simone so upset. Look, let me call you later."

"I'm here if you want to talk," Jada said.

"Thanks." Wellington hung up the phone with an, "I love you," and walked to the door.

Simone was marching back and forth. He figured she'd tire eventually, and he didn't want to call the police on her because they would probably arrest him. Wellington went upstairs to his bedroom and watched rerun DVDs of *The Bernie Mack Show* so he could laugh the hurt away.

Chapter 38

The Fifteenth Annual Cultural Festival had arrived the week after finalizing her divorce. Not having Darius at the event created a void that even Wellington couldn't fill, but Jada was glad he'd accompanied her to New York. Jazzmyne had been right. After the demotion, Darius had quit and everyone else had stayed with her company.

Jada kneeled beside her hotel bed and gave thanks to God, not only for the conference, but also for Wellington. She prayed for Lawrence and Simone. A special prayer was sent up for Ginger, Miranda, Heather, Zen, and Maxine. Knowing that through Christ, all things are possible, Jada asked God to watch over Darius and keep him safe. No one knew her sweetie's whereabouts, nor had he called. Refusing to press the situation, Jada had declined Theo's assistance to locate her son.

Their headquartered hotel was packed with participants, as well as the other lodging establishments around the city, in New Jersey, and in neighboring boroughs. Jada dialed Zen's room extension. "Hi, meet me in the lobby in ten minutes."

Heather had left her room earlier to confirm the setup for

her clients in Greenwich Village. Ginger and Miranda were in Brooklyn and Queens doing the same. Jada stepped into a crowded elevator. More attendees knew her than she knew them, so whenever someone greeted her by name, Jada shook their hand, asked who they were, where they were from, and thanked them for participating.

During the limo ride with Zen over to Madison Square Garden, Jada smiled. "I almost forgot how much energy I feel when I'm in New York. I'm so excited I hope the majority of the people we see are heading to our conference or one of our events."

"As soon as this conference is over, I'll be taking a vacation. I might go away for ten days." Zen laughed.

When they approached Penn Station, lots of people were making their way over to the Garden. "We can get out here," Jada told the driver. "I'll call you on your cellular when I need you."

Making her way up the escalator, through the crowd, and up to the podium on stage, Jada began precisely at nine o'clock. "Good morning, and thanks for coming. I am simply the catalyst; make no mistake, this festival is successful because of your hard work and contributions. Your sponsorship dollars will enable Black Diamonds to help create fifty new small businesses in your communities. Your sponsorship dollars will help prevent over one hundred small businesses from closing in your communities. Your sponsorship dollars will create grants for new and viable programs for homeless shelters, boys and girls clubs, staff training for small businesses, childcare for working single parents, and so much more. This year Darius Henry Jones had landed a fifty-million-dollar collective commitment from the top commercial financial institutions. Under the Community Reinvestment Act these institutions by law must reinvest in their communities. We're happy to have their long-term support and commitments and I'm pleased to say each of the bank presidents have joined us today. Everyone in this room is a winner. I know you're anxious to hear the recipients for outstanding achievements and best practices, so without further ado, I present to you your mistress of ceremony and Black Diamonds' new vice president, Zen Chin.

The audience gave Zen a standing welcome. Jada exited backstage through the curtains and made certain everything was in place. Ginger, Miranda, and Heather had arrived and were already on top of things. Jazzmyne's publicity techniques brought more local residents than usual and plenty of local entrepreneurs.

The top award went to Ginger's client. Darius, Zen, Miranda, and Heather's clients placed in order second through fifth. Too bad Darius wasn't there to present his award. The day was long, and the week was longer; but everyone pulled together, and the Fifteenth Annual Cultural Festival surpassed the previous ones, largely in part to Darius's broader vision. Chris Tucker, Paul Rodriguez, and Margaret Cho kept folks laughing for days. At the closing banquet Friday night, Jada presented each of her staff with personalized plaques to show her appreciation for their contributions.

Before departing Manhattan, Jada visited Shandolon in Jersey, thanked her for the shea butter, and asked if she had something new. The tropical scents reminded her of Lawrence, and she didn't want to revert to her chocolate-flavored cocoa butter lite oil. Shandolon promised she'd create an exclusive shea butter fragrance—sweet with a hint of spice that no man would resist—and name it Forgiveness.

"Honey, not that you need amnesty, but when you wear this potion, he'll forgive you for the things you haven't even done yet." Shandolon raised her hand to a high five.

Wow! Jada never imagined having a scent produced with her in mind, but that was a fantastic idea.

Jada laughed as she browsed the store. "I've looked everywhere for *Promises to Keep* by Gloria Mallette and *She*

Touched My Soul by Naleighna Kai. Every bookstore I've been to can't keep them on the shelf."

"Well, your search is over because my reorders arrived right before you walked in." Shandolon disappeared into a back room and returned, placed the novels in a tote bag, and gave it to Jada. "Consider this an expression of my appreciation of your support."

Heading back to her hotel room, Jada realized she'd missed her appointment for a much needed massage. Like their first date in Carmel, Wellington decided to lodge in an adjacent room. They agreed that sexual intimacy would take place after their ceremony, but Jada packed her entertainment DVD movie in case Wellington changed his mind.

Chapter 39

Sitting in the pastor's study, Jada read the poem she'd written over twenty years ago after breaking up with Wellington—"Never Again Once More":

Never say Never
because you just never know

But I'll shout
Never!
before I go
down that road again
I must have been insane

My heart was trampled
my feet were numb
my soul was yearning
and my brain was . . .
dummy!

Stupid I'm not
nor am I crazy
but I've complicated matters
and added a baby

Now I'm dazed and confused
and to make matters worse
I'm still in love with you
it hurts
it hurts

Like hell!
so straight to hell
with this roller coaster thrill

Never Again
will I play the fool
or let a fool play me

Never Again
will I sell my soul
or auction my dignity

Never Again
will I become enslaved
or labor for a master of love

Now I've got two hands
two fists
and leather boxing gloves

But at some point
the final round will be over
and I realize . . .
I'm still in love with you

My heart is still aching
and I'm still faking
pretending I'm whole
without
my Soul
mate

Never say Never
because you just never know

what you may do
what you might say

I love you
I love you
I do

Tearing the paper in slow motion, then tossing the pieces into the trash, Jada decided she simply would say "never again, ever again." Yes, she'd played the fool, and she felt foolish for allowing her pride to stand in the way of her sharing her life with the man of her dreams for over twenty years. Eternally grateful for this day, Jada sat in front of the mirror and powdered her nose, realizing she had a second chance that many soul mates did not or would not experience.

Jada stood and glanced in the freestanding, old-fashioned mirror. She tilted it at an angle where she could see herself head to toe. Her veil had been replaced with a diamond tiara Wellington had bought in New York. Since she was his Nubian queen, he insisted a crown was what she deserved to wear. No Vera Wang this time, but a specially made tapered dress of Kenté cloth and, at her fiancé's request, two splits, one up each side.

Something old: Zahra and Eunice perfumes. Something

new: her crown. Something borrowed: her father's lucky Chinese coin. Something blue: one of her mother's brand-new G-strings.

Pastor Tellings tapped on the door. "You ready? Mr. Jones is patiently awaiting his bride."

Opening the door, Jada said, "Yes, I'm ready."

"Wow, you look absolutely beautiful. May I?" Pastor Tellings extended his arm.

Jada tucked her hand in the corner of his elbow and exited the rear of the church, circling around to the front. "Thank you, Pastor."

Pastor Tellings kissed Jada's cheek. "We'd better not keep your groom waiting any longer." Pastor returned the way they came. The pianist played and sang, "In this world of ordinary people, extraordinary people, I'm glad there is you. . . ."

This time Jada opened the doors herself and gracefully walked down an aisle of pews garnished with bird-of-paradise. The tropical flowers were their audience because they didn't invite anyone to the wedding. Their witnesses were God, the piano player, and Pastor Tellings.

Wellington looked captivating in his black tuxedo accented with the same cloth as her gown. The gleam in his eyes begged for a kiss, so Jada gave him a soft one on the lips. They had both agreed to throw tradition out the window, because this was their day, and that was how they would live each moment forward.

As they exchanged vows, Jada read hers first. Then Wellington cleared his throat and said, "I wrote this the night we met, because I wanted to capture the essence of what my heart was saying." He removed the paper from his pocket and read.

" 'A Day I'll Never Forget'
now i ain't one to be inspired by words,

expressing myself in such a way is absurd
who would ever thought of a notion
did i ever even consider having that emotion

emotion, naw, that word is for squares,
damn, then why was i so consumed right there?
why did my chest well up and refused to let go?
why did thoughts in my head just start to flow . . .
to my mouth oh, did i mention my breath
i tried to catch one but there was none left.

now, what am i doing even saying these types of things?
expressions my manhood said could not bring . . .
forward or backward or whatever place or origin,
i was being myself being cool and cordial when . . .

well they say that spirits exchange through a tight grip . . .
of the hand or the heart, however it may be taken
ahhhhhhhhhh! where am i, have i fallen, or am i rising,
limbo perhaps, but i like where i am,
those voices, muffle into silence, i hear only
my heart knocking, my gasping, i do not think i am lonely
on this path that leads into the inner depths, of your iris,
or isis if that is who you really are
an image of pure beauty and i speak of the spirit,
you searched through my being with your eyes and i could feel it
a piece of me you've taken with you it is yours indeed,
before flashing by your presence i had no need

your words to me were spoken, your lips remained silent
helplessly surprised i began to try to fight it
your charm, your strength of character, your mind
if i turn away now you'll respond in kind
but who is that, and why is he telling me to return,
just follow your instincts he said and you will learn
this, is not unrequited
my feeling of disbelief was soon quieted

but then, i became such a mess,
i did not know my knees would not come to rest . . .
as they knock and with the rest of my legs, pace
i actually think my lungs and heart are beginning a race!
pow! There goes the gun they have left my torso,
the intensity in my essence builds up even more so.
i was the charmer not who is the one charmed?
if i give her hand i hope she does not break my arm

now to you. i have gathered myself,
took everything I have off my shelf
well not under my own power,
you have brought spring eternal to this flower,
the hope of butterflies, encased,
in a glass jar the shape of a vase
they call it my main organ, but damn if i don't hear . . .
your tune playing my melody as if you have been here . . .
well, maybe we just playin' the same song . . .
seems as if you have been here all along."

Jada's eyes swelled with tears that matched Wellington's. He wrapped his arms around her as Pastor Tellings performed their ceremony. Before Reverend said, "You may kiss the bride," their lips were locked.

Looking at Wellington, Jada hiked her gown above her ankles and said, "I bet you can't beat Mama to the limo," and dashed off. Taking in the rear view, Wellington trailed for old-times' sake just as he'd done on their initial date.

Chapter 40

Darius lounged at Ashlee's house in Texas, mapping together the jigsaw parts of his life as they worked to complete a thousand-piece puzzle.

"Why don't you spend this time getting to know your real—excuse me—biological father?" Ashlee said, trying to match up a side.

"Forget that loser. He denied me before I was ever born. Now I'm supposed to step to him. He has my number. If he calls, I'll listen. If not, like I said, forget that fool." Darius felt cheated out of an opportunity of a lifetime. There was no way his mother could make up his lost time.

Trading her part for another, Ashlee responded, "Well, you can think about it. So what are you going to do now that you're not working for your mother?"

"I have options. I'm thinking about laying low in D.C. for a while. Check out how my peeps are running things." Darius laughed, tumbling the tiny cardboard between his fingers. "Maybe I'll get involved in politics. Who knows?"

"You think you'll get back with Maxine?" Ashlee snapped her piece in place.

"Hell, no. And you know that. I can't take the chance of contracting HIV every day."

"She took a chance on you." Ashlee matched up another jigsaw.

"True dat. But you know how I feel about my dick. That shit is scary. I wrap my piece up every single time now. Sometimes I wear two condoms." Darius turned up the volume on *Training Days* and sat on the floor. "Have you ever felt like your life was being fast-forwarded to the end? Like this." Darius mimicked the sounds of squeaking mice as he advanced the movie with the remote. When he got to the scene where Denzel Washington was executed, he switched to slow motion. Dazed by every move, Darius shared his suicide contemplation with Ashlee for the first time.

"Why didn't you tell me then? Oh, Darius. I had no idea it was that serious to you." Ashlee hugged Darius.

"That's the problem. No one ever thinks my situations are serious until something tragic happens." Darius stared at the blood pouring from Denzel's mouth.

"Let's make each other a promise. If either of us needs to talk or we're feeling depressed, we'll call the other right away without hesitation. Deal?" Ashlee held out her hand.

"Deal." Darius gave her a firm handshake.

Ashlee smiled. "Let's take a vacation and have some fun. Life is too serious right now. We need to lighten up."

"Where?" Darius stopped the video.

"You choose."

"Okay. France. Cannes."

"Sounds good to me," Ashlee said.

"When?" Looking at the puzzle, he asked, "So you saved the last piece for me?"

The French Riviera was the ideal place to escape reality.

"Of course. You da man. Let's go next week. But only if you call your mother first. I know she's worried to death about you."

"Now you're trying to set me up. I thought you were legit." Darius observed Ashlee out of the corners of his eyes.

"I am." Ashlee picked up the phone, dialed Jada's cellular phone, and handed the receiver to Darius.

Darius exhaled heavily.

"Hello, Ashlee," Jada answered.

"This isn't Ashlee; it's Darius."

"Darius! How are you, honey? I'm so glad you called. I miss you and I love you so much."

"I'm fine, Mom. Just needed to get away. I'm chillin' here in Texas with Ashlee. We're going to Cannes next week."

"That's where your father and I are going tomorrow. You know we were married yesterday. We could wait there for you guys to arrive."

That wouldn't work. "Put Dad on the phone." Darius was going so he could place a moratorium on negativity, not to be reminded of her lies and deceit.

"Hey, son. How are you?"

"Why didn't you marry Mom when I was little?"

"Just keep living." Wellington laughed. "You know we miss you. It's okay to take time and clear your head. Just let us know where you are in case something happens."

"Cool, I gotta run. Tell Mom I love her." There was no need for him to put a damper on their good mood.

"Tell her yourself," Wellington said.

Just in case today was his last, Darius wanted no regrets. "I love you, Mom. Bye." His heart was conflicted because he hated her, too.

"I love you, too, baby. Call me soon."

Staring at Ashlee, Darius hung up the phone.

"See, that was easy. Let's go get some ice cream. My treat." Ashlee hit Darius across the head with one of her stuffed Tasmanian devils.

Picking up the fluffy brown creature, Darius yelled, "Animal fight!" He straddled Ashlee and rubbed the Taz's giant teeth in her face, hair, and chest. When his penis started rising, Darius jumped up and said, “Time to go.”

Ashlee was the only true friend he had; she even forgave him for beating up Lawrence. Nothing would come between them, not even his chocolate dipstick.

Chapter 41

Jada puckered her lips to blow out the candle on the nightstand. Before she exhaled, Wellington's cellular phone rang. Jada watched him. Twisting his head, he contemplated. Hesitated. Quizzically, he answered, "Hello?" and braced himself up on his right elbow with his back still toward her.

"I hear congratulations are in order."

The tone was sharp and rather cynical. Hopefully, Wellington wouldn't lower the volume, because she could hear the person on the other end.

"You must have the wrong number," Wellington responded.

"Oh, I never have the wrong number when it comes to you."

Silence lingered; then Wellington said, "How did you get my new number? Look. Don't ever call me again. I'm *happily* married now." Wellington sat up on the edge of the bed and rubbed his head as his penis slumped over his balls. Wellington shook his head from side to side.

"Who is it?" Jada impatiently asked.

Wellington sighed heavily, stared directly at Jada, and frowned. Jada took the phone.

"Hello. Who is this?"

"Enjoy the honeymoon while you can, because I never signed the divorce papers. Ah, ha, ha, ha, ha, ha," Melanie roared.

"Nice try. My attorney confirmed everything," Jada replied.

"Well, I hope your attorney is a forensic scientist, because Wellington signed my name to those papers. Ask him." Melanie screamed with laughter again. "Cynthia insisted, so legally I've never changed my name either, so welcome to the family. You see, that cute little thirty-something-year-old that has the cute little Wellington Jones II, my husband thought he was married to her for six months." Melanie laughed even louder that time.

"I hope you burn in hell!" Jada screamed into the receiver.

"Only if it's God's will," Melanie replied. "But isn't that the pot calling the kettle black, black. Who's your baby's daddy?" Melanie laughed.

"You're one pathetic, miserable bitch. Maybe if you weren't preoccupied with trying to destroy other people's lives, you'd have one of your own. Now, I really don't care what you and Cynthia do, but I have a strong, fine, sexy-ass black man waiting for love and affection that only one woman can give him. And that woman is me." Imitating Melanie, Jada roared with laughter.

Wellington smiled.

Jada hung up the phone and dialed Theo's number.

"What's up, baby doll? Speak to me." It was ten past midnight.

"Theo, I need your help." Jada felt like steam was blowing from her nostrils.

"That's why I'm here. Shout."

Jada paced about their San Francisco hotel suite. "Melanie—"

"I was wondering how long it was going to take you to ask me to handle her," Theo replied. "I have enough dirt on that evil woman to bury her in her own cemetery, and if you want, it would give me great pleasure to give that miserable, conniving old broad Cynthia a dose of her own medicine. She shouldn't leave here without feeling the burn of her own fire."

"Handle it for me, sweetie. Let them know I mean business." Jada felt relieved.

"Consider it done."

"Thanks, Theo."

"No. Thank you. You just made my day. I've got to pack and catch the next plane smokin' to Oakland. Enjoy your honeymoon, baby doll."

"Bye, Theo. You know I love you." Jada hung up the phone and kissed Wellington. "Theo's going to handle everything, baby."

Wellington sat on the side of the bed, resting his head in his hands.

Maybe Jada had it backward. Maybe shit happened like love.

"Now I know the answer." Jada wedged her face between Wellington's fingers, kissed him, and looked deep into his eyes. "I love you, Wellington Jones, and I'm blessed to have married you."

"You know the answer to what?" Wellington asked, extending his tongue.

After their sweetness united, Jada swallowed and said, "What does love have to do with anything? I've always asked myself that question. God puts us here for a reason. Often our desire clouds our purpose. But if the heart and spirit are in the right place"—Jada placed her right hand over the left side of Wellington's chest—"someone other than yourself should be better off because of your judgment, not worse. From this day forward, I will live to make our lives better."

"What does love have to do with anything?" Wellington asked again.

Jada paused, and responded, "Everything. I'll be back in a sec." Dashing to the powder room, Jada broke the seal on Forgiveness, massaged the fragrance into each breast, and opened one of her new toys. She strutted in front of Wellington and shoved him onto the bed. His eyes widened, and he grinned like the Grinch.

Jada's sheer black nightwear slithered down her gorgeous ebony temple. "Lie on your back and spread 'em," Jada commanded. She snapped the tip of her black licorice whip, extinguishing the candle's flame, and said, "Mama's gonna make you cum nice and slow all night long."

Epilogue

Six months later, all's well didn't always end the same. Life for Simone and Junior changed drastically. Dating wasn't Simone's strength, and Wellington was now regretfully her weakness. In the beginning, Simone became so angry at Wellington she ceased every form of communication. After his attorney served her with a court order stating Wellington was suing for full custody, Simone reluctantly agreed to visitation.

Family gatherings for Lawrence resulted in introducing a new acquaintance. After their separation, he'd hoped Jada would return; but she never phoned after their divorce was finalized; so he reluctantly moved on with his life, vowing never again to marry any woman that was incompatible *or* still in love with someone else.

Melanie and Cynthia retreated. Once Theo exposed them, they were ostracized by several organizations. Cynthia's dance with the devil finally ended with her second heart attack. Melanie buried Cynthia and moved to D.C. to be near her mother, Susan, and twin sister, Stephanie.

Maxine continued living at home and became a national

spokesperson for the Center for Disease Control. The travel was tiresome but necessary. To every man, woman, boy, or girl she met, Maxine gave her two-minute AIDS awareness speech, always ending with, "Get tested. Know your status. The life you save may be your own."

Darius survived quite well. He relocated to Washington, D.C., started his own business, and settled down with a Virgo woman who equally enjoyed having sex every day. After persuading her to get tested, Darius faithfully used a condom. Darius thought about Maxine often and prayed the Lord kept her emotionally healthy. Realizing if he was to heal from his past, he had to forgive his mother and biological father, and get to know his brothers and sister, Darius established a good relationship with Kevin and hired Darryl, Jr., to work for his company.

Jada left Zen in charge of Black Diamonds and flew to D.C. with Wellington to help Darius launch his business. They stayed an extra week, then headed home to Los Angeles. Encompassing all the joys they had imagined, Jada and Wellington lived each day as if they were honeymooners.

Poetry Corner

A Woman's Got To Do

A woman's got to do
Two things
Die and live
For herself—not you

Life is about choices
And she has a voice
She can scream
Or give you a look
She can whisper
Or give you a left hook
Of silence that is

But you still don't get it
You're too busy
And you know it all
Your boys come first
Your other women are next
And you still expect her
To give you her very best

A woman's got to do
Two things
Because she lives in fear
Just like you
But a real woman knows
What she's going to do
She can pamper her man
And spoil her kids

Work nine-to-five
And when the day has come and gone
She can do it the next day too

But only if she wants to

Life is about choices
And she has a voice
But have you heard her out lately
Or dismissed her plea
When she's done all she can do
And she just can't be
The woman you want to clone
And somehow she still can't seem
To leave your ass alone
Don't fool yourself

A woman's only got to do
Two things

So she gives all she has
And for you that's still not enough
Life is about choices
And she has a voice
If you want to hear what she has to say

Listen to her silence

Listen to her silence
Instead of your words
Drowning out her essence
As she painfully sighs
You turn your back
And the tears roll down her face
As she cries

Can't you see you're overshadowing her space
Her place
Is where she wants to be
Not where you've staked your claim

But one day you'll wake up
And she'll be gone

Why

Because

A woman's got to do
Two things
Live and die
For herself—not you

Don't Hide My Face

Don't hide my face
Behind someone else's name
Because you've sinned and are ashamed
Of what you've done

Tell him
I'm not his son

Don't hide my face
Behind your soul
Your conniving thoughts
Pot of gold

Mind
Mine

My
Legacy is off track
I'm traveling a road
I was told
Was the right path
Boy don't you talk back
To me
Is crazy
Cruel
Who wrote the golden rule

Not you
The woman I admire
Love
Respect
What the heck
Whose daddy is that

I thought he was
My heavenly Father
I pray
Every day
Don't hide my face
In your trace
Of lies
Why
Why not
I do unto you
Damn!

Who's my real father

This time look me in my eyes
Tell me the
Truth

Please don't cry
You don't even have to say why
If you don't want
Me to die
An impostor
Then stop your lies
For God's sake
Don't forsake me
Quit hiding my face
Mama
This time
May be my last chance
The truth
And nothing but
Who is my biological father

Don't say you don't know
I know
My mother is
No whore so
Stop hiding my face

Behind yours

You Say You Love Your Man

You say you love your man
But you nag the hell out of him
All day long
Then you cry all night
When he doesn't come home

You say you love your man
But you refuse to cook him a meal

Then you get pissed when he eats out alone
And chooses to leave your ass at home

You don't wash his back
You won't clean his clothes
And when he wants to have sex
You turn up your nose
You neglect to stroke his ego
Rub his feet
Or suck his dick
But you're outraged and furious
When he fucks another chick

You say you love your man
But you'll never love him
More than he loves you
Considering the foundation that you've laid
That's damn easy to do

You talk behind his back
You won't hem his slacks
And when he does something nice for you
You throw it right smack
Dead in his face

Did you do the same thing for that bitch!

You say you love your man
Girlfriend you need to quit
Because if you truly loved your man
You wouldn't treat him like shit

The following is a sample chapter from Mary B. Morrison's eagerly anticipated novel,
SOMEBODY'S GOTTA BE ON TOP.

It will be available in August 2004 wherever hardcover books are sold.

ENJOY!

Monogamy wasn't natural. Monogamy was a learned behavior that Darius couldn't be taught. When would women realize sex wasn't a bed partner of love? Besides, who would teach him how to be faithful? Jesse Jackson? Bill Cosby? Willie Brown? Bill Clinton? His dad, the ménage à trois king? All the men he respected, all the men he knew, were men. Fornicators. Adulterers. Players. The distinction of a real man was a real man kept his family in the foreground and his females in the background. Like backup singers. Once the song was over, their job was done. Thanks for having made him cum. Now go. With Darius, not many of his lovers deserved an encore.

"Ha!" Darius laughed then said aloud to himself, "You a fool boy." His office was quiet all morning. No constant phone calls or interruptions by his secretary, Angel.

Any woman who wanted Darius Jones had to commit to him and only him. His woman had to have a job. Not any job. A high paying job. Preferably her own business. So what if he had enough money to take care of her. Her mama. And her grandmama. A woman without a steady income was venomous. A woman with too much idle time was lethal. No piece of ass was worth his millions of dollars. He was the only heir to his mother's empire and one day would split his father's fortune with one sibling who was barely four years old.

Those broke leeches in thongs, jiggling their asses on beaches or benches, at the bus stop, were the ones who were constantly plotting and planning—pregnancy, rape, battery—on how to become rich off of a man. For sex. For real. Any wealthy man would suffice. Mike. Kobe. Deon. Including him. Bullshit conniving tricks. They weren't privy to suck his dick.

Rich pussy like the Vivica A's, and Mary J's, Halles, and Janets of the world needed stroking too. But they also had reputations worth protecting. Lawsuits to them translated into bad publicity. Lost revenue. They'd end the relationship before bringing forth charges. That's the kind of woman Darius wanted. And if Darius ever caught his woman cheating, she didn't need to waste his time explaining. Or packing. Because he'd personally have all of her shit moved out of his house. Immediately!

With Darius, no one got a second chance to make a bad impression. Except his mother. Darius pressed sixty-nine on his speed dial. His lungs expanded. The warm air escaped his nostrils, grazing his smooth upper lip.

"Hey, you," she answered.

Her voice penetrated his soul. Chill bumps invaded his skin. The hairs on his arms stood tall. Darius wasn't cold. He swallowed the lump clogging his vocal cords and said, "So, you packed yet? I can hardly wait to see you tonight. Make sure you arrive two hours early at the airport." Darius deepened his voice then emphasized, "I don't want you to miss your flight this time."

Darius rolled his leather high-back chair until his abdomen pressed against the edge of his glass-top desk creating a crease in his wool jacket. Slowly he smoothed his finger over the photographic image of her naturally pink-colored lips. Thin and seemingly oh so very soft. She looked ravishing in the family picture they'd taken a month ago at Thanksgiving dinner with his parents.

"Are you still in the office?" she asked.

His hand traveled from her temple and traced the outline along her straight black hair, which cast a strikingly beautiful contrast against her nearly white complexion. His eyes fixated on hers.

Loving someone more than himself, more than life, more than making money, was absurd and not what Darius had planned. But this special woman—naw, she was more than a woman, she was a lady—had stolen his heart. First she'd become his platonic childhood playmate. Now she was his best friend. His only friend.

The honeysuckle scent of her hair, the subtle movement of her hips when she walked, the provocative melody of her voice each time she innocently laughed while calling his name, the gentleness of her touch whenever she groomed his dreadlocks, the taste of her words lingering on his palate as he gasped into the receiver consumed his thoughts. Nervous energy growled in the pit of his stomach reminding him he'd forgotten to eat lunch again today. Consciously he erased his boyish grin. She evoked feelings Darius swore he'd never harbor for any woman after having been betrayed by his ex-fiancée.

"Of course I'm still in the office. And my staff too. Just because it's Friday and New Year's Eve, doesn't mean they're entitled to leave early. I might let 'em go at three. Maybe. Now answer my question."

"Don't worry. I packed last night. And my dad is dropping me off in a few. I'll call you when my plane lands in Oakland." She paused then whispered, "I miss you, brother."

Darius remained silent. Damn. Although they spoke every day, three to five times each day, he'd practically forgotten about the incident with her dad. Darius hadn't seen her father since the day, over two years ago, when he'd beaten her father's ass for causing his mother to hurt her arm and leg. In retrospect, Darius understood Lawrence's frustrations with his mother because after that physical altercation Darius's mother gave him the shock of his life. Thereafter, his feelings for his mother numbed his compassion toward women even more. If his mother were a liar, then every other woman was too. Except his lady on the opposite end of the phone. But the feasibility existed, so he couldn't completely trust her either. What a fucked-up world to live in, Darius thought, when the only person he could trust one hundred percent of the time was himself.

Forgetting about her dad and his mom, Darius massaged his erection through his pleated slacks hoping she'd continue talking, but hopefully not about her dad. Her voice had him so turned on he wanted to make love. To her. For years. *Say something. Anything. Please.* His dick urged, repeating her tone in his mind. *I miss you.* He'd missed her too. But silence lingered in his ear.

New Year's Eve this year would be unforgettable. He wasn't going to propose, but he'd finally gathered the courage to logically express the depth of his love. His birth parents weren't hers so factually they weren't related. And since his mom was remarried to her soul mate, Wellington Jones, the man his mother should've married instead of Lawrence, Darius felt Ashlee and he were two consenting adults capable of making their own decisions.

Darius's flight from Los Angeles would arrive into Oakland International Airport one hour before Ashlee's plane from Dallas was scheduled to land. His luggage would remain at baggage claim because he wanted to surprise Ashlee by waiting at her gate with a dozen of her favorite long-stem white roses.

Breaking the silence she finally spoke, "Did you hear me?" Lightly she articulated, "I said, I miss you."

Ashlee's delayed response made Darius believe she was also thinking about him. The cordless phone slipped from between his ear and shoulder so he quickly activated the speaker. "Of course I heard you. I just wanted you to repeat it. That's all." He placed his fingers against his thick lips then laid the same two fingers atop the glass frame over her mouth.

She inhaled then softly said, "I miss you. I miss you. I miss you. I miss you. I miss you. How's that? Turn on your cam so I can see you."

No way, Darius thought as he unzipped his pants and

squeezed his head suppressing the cum vowing to escape his hard-on. He imagined what she looked like in the nude. Although they'd visited one another for more than ten years—he still had no idea if her nipples were lighter or darker than her breasts. If her pubic hairs were curly or straight. If her clitoris was small or large.

"Hey, lady. I've gotta run. I'll see you later." Darius stood. Securing his relaxed muscle into his black silk boxers he then watched the tiny metal clamps overlap until the last one reached the top.

His lungs suctioned in the much-needed oxygen for his brain when she exhaled an intoxicating, "Bye."

Darius waited until she hung up then removed his tan coat, tossing it onto his chair. He entered the private restroom connected to his office and vigorously rinsed his face with cold water. While staring at his reflection in the mirror, Darius wondered why his mother had lied to him about his biological father? Why she'd waited twenty years to reveal the truth? Why didn't his biological father, Darryl Williams, Sr., display the same love for him as he did for Darius's two half brothers?

Darryl was a former NBA all-star whom Darius had overtly idolized most of his childhood, including the four years Darius started on the varsity basketball team in high school. Darryl was his college basketball coach at Georgetown, which explained why his mother never came to any of his college games. His mother apparently had an epiphany when her mother died and decided it was time for a damn confession. A truth that mentally scarred him. Possibly for life.

Fuck Darryl Williams! Darius Jones didn't need anybody but Darius Jones. His beloved grandmother, MaDear, the only woman that never lied to him, would've said, "Don't waste time disliking people who don't like you when you can appreciate the many people that do love you." Darius knew MaDear was right, but after MaDear died disappointment and resentment befriended him.

Although sometimes Darius drowned in his waterless tears, real men, when their hearts ached with sadness and their souls suffocated from failure, didn't show signs of weakness. Darius remembered because MaDear's husband, Grandpa Robert, whom she'd joined in heaven, told Darius when Darius was four years old, "Boy, looks like you been crying. Crying is for girls and sissies. Remember that." Darius never forgot. Tears. Confessions. There was no way Darius would ever let Grandpa Robert down by displaying a wimpish attitude. Sensitivity belonged to losers like Rodney, the undercover bisexual brother who infected his ex-fiancée with HIV. Anger and outrage were more acceptable. Darius thought again, what a fucked-up a world to live in.

Buying his office building and loaning him a million dollars was just another one of his mother's ways to compensate for her guilt. And he had every intention of making her suffer for the next twenty years or at least until he felt she'd repaid her debt. Everyone was indebted to something or someone. But if his mother hadn't married Lawrence, Darius would've never met his number one lady. So perhaps he should've been grateful, but gratitude required expressing feelings.

Shifting his thoughts back to his lady, he smiled in the mirror, running his fingers over his locks. He gathered each shoulder-length strand in a ponytail then admired the sweet brown succulent flesh hundreds of women had enjoyed feasting upon. Her flight would arrive at ten o'clock tonight. What would she wear to his parents' ball tomorrow? Hell, it didn't matter. Possessing the same qualities as his mother, his stepsister always looked great. Just like his ex-fiancée, Maxine. Ladylike. Feminine.

Why was his childhood so innocent and his adult life so skeptical? As a child he could do no wrong. Women adored him. Fantasies of having his own family. A loving wife who'd only love him and he'd exclusively love her. At one time he believed that was true. Until those two fifth graders told him he could have both of them or his boring girlfriend. She wasn't boring. She was quiet. There was a difference. But two were definitely better than one. Darius once believed marriage was sacred. Until he witnessed his mother divorcing Lawrence for no good reason other than she wanted another man.

Why did grown-ups lie about simple shit? Santa? The Easter bunny? Who was this dude Cupid? Someone who was supposed to make him believe he was in love? Most people weren't. Most people were lonely or afraid of being alone so, good or bad, they clung to the familiar. Not Darius.

Darius walked out of his corner office, one flight down the back stairway, entered the exit door, stood over his new employee and folded his arms high across his cashmere shirt. Quickly she clicked on the minimize box at the top of her computer screen and the game vanished.

"Naw, put the screen back up," Darius insisted, staring over her shoulder. "I wanna see how good you are because obviously you're no good for my company." Darius waited. "You've got ten seconds. Ten. Nine. Eight . . ." he always counted backward so when he stopped, he was at number one because he was number one. The best at business, politics, economics, sports, and sex. Especially, sex. Darius's eyes focused on the digital clock at the bottom of the seventeen-inch flat screen monitor. Two hours remaining before his driver would take him to the airport.

When the screen came into view, Darius pointed toward the door and said, "Get your shit and get the fuck out of my office."

"But, it's the holidays and there isn't any work to do. I can ex—"

"Don't waste any more of my time or my money." He'd warned her in the orientation last month not to use his company's equipment or services for personal reasons. At the top of the items listed on the acknowledgment form by his Human Resources Director was the computer, followed by the telephone—both cellular and office—supplies, beverages, and so forth. "What's my mission statement?" Darius asked, watching the woman hesitantly remove his company's cell phone and credit card from her purse.

She mumbled, "If it doesn't make money, it doesn't make sense."

"So, what? You thought I was joking?"

"But, I can ex—"

"Explain what! Explain why I'm paying you thirty-five dollars an hour to waste my electricity!" The back of his hand slapped into his opposite palm repeatedly as he continued. "Occupy my space! Drink my coffee! Eat my bagels! And play games on my computer!" Darius threw his hands in the air then said, "That doesn't require an explanation. The only thing I want to know is how your playing a sorry-ass losing hand of three-card draw," his pointing finger landed next to her score, "solitaire made me money? Prove that and you can stay."

The twenty-two-year-old recent college graduate, who was the same age as Darius, silently stared at Darius, then said, "But everyone in the entertainment business is on vacation except us."

"That's right! And you should be studying the screenplay I gave you yesterday because I specifically told you I need to hand this to my inside contact at Parapictures and give a copy to Morris Chestnut first thing Monday morning. Am I supposed to pay you and someone else to do your job? Huh? Answer me!"

Calmly she replied with a frown, "Why are you so upset? You're the one who said your mother's best friend Candice Morgan wrote the screenplay, so obviously Candice will select you as her agent. What's the big deal?"

"I don't care who wrote the damn script! Unless I secure the best deal possible before anyone else—" Darius shook his head. "You just don't get it. You may have graduated cum laude but you sure as hell flunked basic comprehension." He grumbled, "Damn, it's hard to get good help." Darius paged security from his mobile phone and said, "Escort my new employee out of my building. Immediately," and went back upstairs into his office.

How in the hell was he going to maintain an advantage over the other nine companies that were also given a non-exclusive right to shop the hottest screenplay on the market? As much as he wanted to attend the ball, he had no choice. He had to stay home and work. Darius speed-dialed his mother's number.

Candice and his mother had lost favor when Candice produced an unauthorized biography of his parents' love life including all the graphic juicy details his mother had shared with her so-called best friend. That's what his mother deserved for telling all her business to her so-called trustworthy girlfriend. Women. They all spent too much time analyzing every damn thing, talking too damn much, and complaining all the time. Maybe women were the ones responsible for fucking up the world. First Eve. Then his ex-fiancée. And of all persons, his mother.

Sighing heavily Darius answered, "Hi, Mom."

"Hi, baby, I'm glad you called. I was just thinking about you." His mother whispered, "Stop, Wellington. I'm on the phone with Darius." Returning to a normal tone, she asked, "So what time is your flight getting in?"

"Hi, son!" Wellington's voice cheerfully resonated in the background.

Wellington Jones, although he wasn't Darius's biological father, was the only man man enough to raise Darius from birth until now. When Darius's mother revealed the truth, Wellington had said, "You are my son. A very brave man stepped up to the plate and raised me as his own." Darius recalled how Wellington had shared his adoption history. "I don't wish this type of devastation on any person. Honestly, I'm disappointed in your mother. But God wants us to learn the importance of forgiveness. You have every right to be mad. Just don't let your anger destroy you . . . I love you no matter what." Darius wondered how Wellington could be so compassionate without losing his masculinity.

"Sorry, Mom. I'm not going to make it. Gotta work. Something important just came up." Darius couldn't dare tell his mother her life was the greatest story roaming throughout the industry, because his mother was livid with Candice while Wellington thought how wonderful it would be if another black person could join the ranks of becoming a millionaire. His dad felt there was no direct harm to them. Wellington's only request was that Candice change the names.

"Darius, you work too hard. You just started in this business. Give it some time, honey. You'll get the next movie deal and I bet it'll be a more lucrative contract."

"Mom, you don't understand. There's no such thing as working too hard. If I get this deal, my reputation will soar internationally. Mark my words. Darius Jones will instantly become a household name because this is a script all nationalities can relate to. Mom, somebody's gotta be on top. There's those who do and those who don't. And those who don't never come out on top. Gotta go. Gotta work. Happy New Year, Mom, and tell Dad I said the same."

"Well, honey. If you insist. But before you go, how's your proposal coming along?"

"Not as well as I thought. I just fired the person assigned to put together my presentation. The meeting for selection of an agent is Tuesday morning. Every interested agency is going to pitch why they should represent Candice. I have a meeting with my inside contact person at Parapictures on Monday. And if I'm lucky, Morris will show up as promised to the meeting."

"Okay, baby. Now, I've got to go. Your dad is trying to—never mind. I'll call you tomorrow. I love you."

"Yeah, mom. I know. Bye."

Darius gazed at the family photo, dialed his travel agent, and arranged for Ashlee to take a flight into Los Angeles.

Somebody's Gotta Be On Top

Stop!
Somebody's Gotta Be On Top
How much are you willing to pay
To live another day

What are you afraid of. . . .

Money isn't keen
It's the realization of a dream
In the color green
Envy
Slime
Slipping
Tripping
Through time
Exchanging hands
Yours
Mine

What are you afraid of. . . .

Wishing
Wanting
Never daunting
Taunting
Your faith
Or taking a risk
Or waiting for break
To take a piss
Shit!
Piss on
Those who sing
Piss off
Those who scream

I'm living my dream!
Stop!
Somebody's Gotta Be On Top
How much are you willing to pay
To live another day

What are you afraid of. . . .

Success
Achieving your best
Willing to live with less
In order to attain more
Are you afraid to open the door
Before you knock
Or maybe you're content
Shoulda
Coulda
Woulda
Only if. . . .
You'd spent
Time Time Time
How much are you willing to pay
To live another day
Frivolous chatter
Doesn't matter
Settling
Meddling
Gabbing
Back-stabbing
Shattering hope
Slippery slope
Walking a tight rope

What are you waiting for. . . .

An invite
When the time is right

Not tonight
Tomorrow
Sorrow
Today
You'll borrow
Someone else's
Money
Honey
Hopes
Dreams
Anything
Sign an I.O.U.
Promise to repay
In dismay
That which you haven't earned today
Belongs to someone else
Isn't that funny
Yesterday is gone
You're sitting at home
On a diminishing throne
Of hopes
Dreams
Envy
Green
You scream
Money ain't a thing!
That's a lie
Can't miss what you never had
Lad
Your slice of the pie
Is on someone else's table
You're able
But. . . .
Unwilling

What are you afraid of. . . .

Stop!
Somebody's Gotta Be On Top
How much are you willing to pay
To live another day
No pain
No sweat
No blood
No tears
Just fears
Who cares
What's new
What are you really going to do
Successful people are the same as you
Living with fears too

What are you afraid of. . . .

How much are you willing to pay
Today
Or Not
Regardless
Somebody's Gotta Be On Top